A Fame Not Easily Forgotten

— an Autobiography of Eureka Springs —

by

JUNE WESTPHAL

and

CATHARINE OSTERHAGE

RIVER ROAD PRESS

ISBN 978-0-9786014-5-4

ISBN 978-0-9786014-4-7

Boian Books, LLC

www.boianbooks.com
Eureka Springs, Arkansas

Second Edition of *A Fame Not Easily Forgotten* reproduced in its entirety as originally published in 1970, with the addition of an Index.

Litho Printers & Bindery
Cassville, Mo

A FAME NOT EASILY FORGOTTEN

is not an autobiography in the truest sense of the word, for an autobiography is the story of a life written by the person whose adventures are being recounted. However, we believe that a community, a town, can be much like a person, and that Eureka Springs has kept an excellent diary of her life and times through volume after volume of laboriously hand-written notations to be found in the archives of her city government, the daily press, civic clubs and fraternal organizations, as well as in the private writings of her citizens.

It is in this spirit, then, that this book tells a part of her story—a tale of fifty years in the life of Eureka Springs.

. . . the Authors

To

David James Westphal

and a whole new generation

of the children of Eureka Springs . . . .

ACKNOWLEDGMENTS

We wish to thank Wayne Brashear for his patient and painstaking work in reproducing excellent copies of many old photographs of early Eureka Springs and her people as well as the loan of several pictures from his own collection.

Mr. Ron Morgan, whose deep interest in Eureka Springs has recently brought him to the city as a resident, has also contributed many pictures of early Eureka Springs from his ever-growing collection, and we are grateful for the use of them. A thank you also to Mrs. Jeannette Rosewater Bullock for the use of her father's papers from her collection, and Miss Marie Dobbins for the information she supplied concerning the history of the Catholic Church in Eureka Springs.

We especially wish to express appreciation to the many friends who have made known their continuing interest in the completion of this book . . . and to Al, June's husband, for his patience during the long hours spent on the preparation of the manuscript and his encouragement and faith that the result would be well worth the great amount of time and effort required.

Contents

FOREWORD

Once upon a time a small stream of water broke away from its source far underground and slowly made its way to light and air. It came out of the darkness at a spot on the mountainside where it slowly dropped down on to a big flat rock. Virgin oaks and walnuts gave shade and the sassafras and huckleberry bushes grew around it. Over the ages the trickle of water wore a small depression in the rock where birds came to drink and went away refreshed. Animals also came to drink and felt a sense of well being.

The little stream continued to bubble out of the dark and finally, after uncounted centuries, came beings called Men. Indians they were of forest and plain. They too discovered the little water-filled basin in the rock, and after drinking from it their maladies were healed. News of the healings traveled far from the Spring, for that is what they called it in their language, as the water sprang from the ground. The spot became known as "Indian Healing Spring."

Many more years passed and the men who came were no longer red but white. At last the White man had learned the secret of the water that had been bringing healing for centuries.

With the coming of the White man began these adventures caused by that small stream of water that found its way to light and air on the side of a wooded mountain.

PREFACE

Eureka Springs, Arkansas is a remarkable place – and utterly improbable. Why would anyone in the late 1800s, traveling on horseback or in wagons, traverse dirt paths through the steep Ozark Mountains to what must have seemed like the end of the earth? Why would they settle and build elaborate structures on sharp, rocky inclines?

The answer is, water. Pure, abundant spring water reported to have extraordinary curative properties – hope of healing was that powerful and that compelling. So, come they did. Build, they did. And while the water may not have reached expectations, the beauty and magic of the place captured the hearts of so many, they stayed, or kept returning. They still do.

This town that water built is the story of *A Fame Not Easily Forgotten*, first published in 1970. The compilation of this book was sparked by the curiosity of native-born academician, June Westphal, and librarian Catharine Osterhage. Their dedicated efforts brought together the rich history and incredible legends of the town's first eighty years.

Today, June Westphal still holds the crown of being the town's most esteemed and generous historian – one of the best friends any library or community could have. Her systematic study did not stop with this book, but continues daily.

Catharine Osterhage died suddenly in 1970, not living to see the bound First Edition. But her inquisitive mind, thorough research and kindness are reflected on every page.

Eureka Springs continues to prosper as a tourist, retirement, and desirable community for residents and visitors alike. It is a living reminder of what a Victorian town looked like. That is, compact with steep and harrowing streets, gingerbread woodwork, and tended springs throughout town. With the entire original area having been placed on the National Register of Historic Places, preservation is secure.

The Carnegie Public Library mirrors Eureka Springs' natural and appreciative quality of life. 2010 marks the 100th year anniversary of our library. As part of a yearlong tribute, it seemed fitting and appropriate that a Second Edition of this early history be printed.

Eureka Springs Carnegie Library Board

Mickey Smith, President
Alan Epley, Vice President
Lucilla Garrett, Secretary
Mark Minton, Treasurer
Sally Williams Gorrell
Fred Hopkins
Lamont Richie

PROLOGUE

Visitors coming to Eureka Springs today ask many questions concerning the history of this unique city — questions which are almost impossible to answer. One question concerns itself with what was happening in the rest of the United States to make such a "happening" possible at that time. For one thing the War between the States had been over long enough for tempers to settle down a bit as Reconstruction measures became modified and even the die-hards had to admit that life still goes on. In addition the country was showing signs of prosperity and money was daily growing more plentiful. Mines in California, Montana and Colorado had brought more gold into circulation than was ever dreamed of. By 1878 one Southern gentleman was generous enough to write ". . . broadcloth is often seen and ladies wear costly outfits." A strong taste for travel had revived, and mountain resorts, mineral springs, and other watering places were having large numbers of patrons. Indeed, the desire for travel was more widely spread than before the war.

The spiritual and mental side of life was also feeling new influences and movements never felt before, especially in the direction of healing. Medicine and surgery were only beginning to feel their way along the paths of universal acceptance they were later to achieve. After the war doctors were both old and tired, and the younger ones were not sufficiently experienced to meet with the success gained by years of practice. When John Alexander Dowie began promoting his faith cure in far off Australia he met with wide acclaim—acclaim which later brought him to Illinois and his Zion City just beyond Chicago. In the East several lesser-known healers were attracting followers to various "faith" cures. In Boston another idea was gaining adherents to the Christian Science movement. The textbook *"Science and Health with Key to the Scriptures"* had been published by Mary Baker Eddy in 1875 and large numbers of those sick in both body and soul flocked to her meetings and read her book. Over the sea in Europe hundreds made pilgrimages to the various spas where the curative properties of the water were recognized. Sulphur springs in the Eastern half of the United States were attracting patients to their bathing facilities. So it was a real miracle when it was realized that in one of the Midwestern states the pure spring water which came out of the ground in such abundance also healed. Thus it happened that Eureka Springs could not help but attract a favorable, even an overwhelming, response.

Another event which may have encouraged the rapid growth of the community was taking place in Memphis and up and down the low areas along the Mississippi River in the neighboring State of Tennessee. A yellow fever epidemic was claiming hundreds of lives in spite of the efforts to check it. Eventually the epidemic was checked by vigorous quarantine efforts so that it did not spread beyond the low-lying area on the east side of the river. Undoubtedly many of the people who came to Eureka Springs during the early 1880's were hunting a more healthful location, high and away from the swamp lands along the big river. Eureka Springs offered healing for specific diseases through the use of the water, and also a healthful location and climate.

One of the most interesting questions, and one often asked, concerns the healing properties of the water. "Were they ever genuine, and if so when did they begin to lose these properties?" — also, "If they were genuine, why are they not made use of today?" In answer to the first part, the following diseases are listed as having been healed by the time Cutter published his *"Directory of Eureka Springs,"* in 1884:

Asthma	Dropsy	Hemorrhoids
Bright's disease	Dyspepsia	Kidney complaint
Cancer	Epilepsy	Paralysis
Constipation	Female trouble	Rheumatism
Catarrh	Fever sores	Skin disease
Diabetes	General debility	Scrofula
Eye diseases	Hay fever	

Earlier, in 1881, in his history of Eureka Springs, the same list of diseases cured by the use of the spring water had been published by L. J. Kalklosch. His list also included bronchial infection and baldness. It is interesting also to note that the testimony of those healed had come from Illinois, Iowa, Missouri, Kansas, Tennessee, Texas and Nebraska with a goodly number, of course, from Arkansas. In his *Directory,* Cutter included these same states and adds Indiana, Kentucky, Montana, Colorado and Louisiana. However, a majority of visitors were from Missouri and Arkansas since the area of the springs was remote and difficult to reach. Travel was a great hardship so only the most desperate cases were apt to try such a trip. Kalklosch had experienced healing and was eager to tell about it, as were both men and women from all walks of life. They included storekeepers, judges, lawyers, even doctors and many women.

All testimonials told of the use of the water from various springs, and no special one was singled out as having particular qualities for a specific disease. Both internal and external use of the water seemed to be recommended in most cases and no specific quantities were mentioned. Cutter also tells of the "Invalids Association" made up of persons healed by the waters. This Association met weekly to give vocal thanks and to join with others in rejoicing for their healing. Such testimony gives answer to the first part of the question.

Perhaps the answer to the second part could be that while the water flowing from the springs in such abundance is exactly the same in chemical content as the water which came forth in 1879, the mental content of the people is completely changed.

Mental attitudes all over the United States were to change greatly soon after the springs were discovered. Education, particularly in the South, had never been greatly stressed before this era. The rich either sent their children to Europe to study, employed a governess or supported small private schools, while the poor were not educated. Even in the North it was not considered necessary to educate women, and for lack of mental employment they had always suffered from a great variety of ills. Now for the first time mandatory provisions for free education were being written in the constitutions of both Northern and Southern states and great changes were to come with this widening of mental horizons.

By the end of World War I the medical profession had a firm hold on the minds of the majority of people and newspapers and magazines encouraged thinking in that direction, so that medicine and surgery finally seemed the most legitimate means to alleviate pain and suffering.

As for the scene in Eureka Springs, the newspapers began to omit the many letters written by grateful people healed by the water from the springs, and in their place appeared what was considered more lucrative advertising. Nationally-advertised pills and nostrums were advocated over and over again until they gained a kind of universal acceptance. The water never changed but the acceptance of its therapeutic qualities almost completely died out.

Finally the query, "If the healing was all a mental thing, why can't the desire we have today for a change recreate the acceptance given the healing qualities of the water in 1879?" Rediscovery, advertising media, and modern methods of exploitation might be able to again attract attention to the water. Large sums of money would need to be spent with the doubt that it would be successfully returned in the form of income from sanitariums or hospitals. The medical profession and possibly certain laws supposed to protect the public against fraud might be called upon to take action against such an idea. Certainly the faith shown in the meetings of the Invalid's Association would be missing and also . . . the gratitude.

With the idea in mind of trying to answer these questions as well as other questions concerning the earliest days in Eureka Springs, the authors have prepared this book. They have no desire to detract either from the people who played their parts in the development of Eureka Springs from its infancy nor from those who as best they know have chronicled those days. Today the visitor is confronted with the long-established fact that the community was originally founded on water and like water has gone under many bridges before reaching its present level.

The first man to write about Eureka Springs was Professor L. J. Kalklosch, who published a small book in 1881. Cutter put out his *"Guide to the Eureka Springs of Arkansas"* in 1884. This little book was not intended to be historical, but today it is a dependable source for the happenings and places in early Eureka Springs. Published in 1940 and 1949, two little books written by Nellie Mills tell of the early school days. She started to school in 1880 and graduated in 1890, in the first class to graduate from the local school. Also in 1930 Cora P. Call, joined in the 1950's by Bonnie Lela Crump and Otto E. Rayburn, took up the tale of the Eureka Springs they knew and also repeated many of the pioneer tales, myths and legends surrounding the site. So far the establishment of Eureka Springs as a community has never been told as an historic fact. Myth and legend lend color and mystery, but soon a century will have passed and people will continue to come and ask "What really happened here?"

It is with this in mind that the authors have spent long hours reading such old newspapers as are available, old advertisements, the records of extinct organizations and other printed material. It was decided not to interview people, since memory is not always reliable and is often colored with the personal feelings of those who can, now, only repeat the stories told to them. Others have mined this field so we leave it to them and rely only on the written word, written when it happened. Omissions there are bound to be, as fire destroyed so many of the newspaper offices and their filed copies of early newspapers. Those papers now in the Carnegie Public Library were saved by happenstance rather than determined effort. Nevertheless, the papers available tell of men and events which were important to the formative years of the town. Had the history been different so would the printed record.

Believing that history is as interesting as myth, a great effort had been made to tell it as it happened: What it was like to come to Eureka Springs and live here during the first fifty years; also to try to answer those seemingly unanswerable questions concerning the "Water that Heals."

PART I

CHAPTER I

"IN THE BEGINNING . . . ."

It would be impossible to write a book which would tell in explicit detail the story of the early days in Eureka Springs. The city engendered legends and like Topsy both the city and the legends "just growed" and became a nine-days wonder for that time.

The stories which probably come nearest to telling what really happened will be briefly retold as this account is to be concerned with other aspects of the earliest days. The many legends concerning the springs credit the Indians with being the first to utilize the healing properties of this free flowing water. It is told how they came from near and far to avail themselves of this natural source of healing.

Early stories also agree that the first white man to discover and make use of the therapeutic qualities of the Basin Spring was Dr. Alvah Jackson who visited the area in 1856. It has been told that during the Civil War quite a few soldiers came to the locality for treatment of their war injuries. So many came that a sort of makeshift hospital was set up in a cave with Dr. Jackson as resident physician. When the soldiers no longer needed treatment the area of the springs returned to the peaceful solitude of earlier days.

One of the prominent citizens of the nearby town of Berryville was Judge L. B. Saunders. He had been suffering from a stubborn case of erysepalis which had not responded to treatment. He and Dr. Jackson were friends who had hunted together through the area of the springs and he also knew of the tales concerning the healing properties of their water. Now in 1879 he decided to try these properties for himself, and with an urging nudge from Dr. Jackson, he built a crude camp near the Big Spring, where he stayed to partake of the water. In a comparatively short time his erysepalis was cured. The Judge was well- and favorably-known throughout the state and word of his almost miraculous healing soon brought others to try the water cure for a variety of ailments.

By July 4, 1879, this word-of-mouth advertising had reached sufficient people to bring approximately four hundred of them to the site. In a few short weeks since Judge Saunders had been restored to health, a village of shacks and tents had been built up adjacent to the Big Spring, also called Basin Spring, as the flowing water had formed a natural basin in the rock. Near this spring the Judge had made his camp, a crude lean-to shack, and the new comers followed his example, trying to stay as close to the spring as possible.

All those present were in a holiday mood, and many had qualities of leadership, so a meeting was organized to give the place a name. Suggestions included Jackson Spring and Saunders Spring, but according to L. J. Kalklosch, who was present at the time, a Mr. McKay was among the group, and McKay no doubt had read of the discovery made by Archimedes, so he made the suggestion to call it "Eureka," meaning "I have found it." This met with general consent and the spot was christened Eureka Springs.

All through the rest of the long summer months people continued to come and put up more shacks and tents, until the region resembled a big camp meeting ground. Every one was desirous of benefiting from the waters and so were on friendly terms. Experiences were readily exchanged, and as ministers soon joined the group and began preaching from any convenient rock, the assembly began to take on more of the aspects of a camp meeting. Every one spoke to every one and no one took offense. Most were either ill or trying to care for

The Basin Spring — 1880

Eureka Street Business District, about 1882

Early Transportation to Eureka Springs, 1879

Eureka Springs, before the great fires, 1882

An early mode of transportation — the tallyho, about 1885

Depot, Missouri and North Arkansas Railroad, 1883

View of Eureka Springs, looking up toward Perry House — 1885

View up Mountain Street — 1885

Gathering of those seeking health at one of the springs — 1880

Crescent Spring health seekers —1886

A Baptism at Sweet Spring — 1882

Type of early home construction, about 1880

The Eureka Opera House, built 1883

A part of the Main Street Business District — 1890

A view of barren East Mountain — 1880

Crescent Spring —1882

those who were, and all were glad to exchange experiences concerning the beneficent effects of the water. A drinking cup shared with a stranger, or a bit of live coal to kindle a camp fire, were gestures of human kindness that were gratefully reciprocated.

People from all walks of life and in all conditions of health came with no idea of the living conditions available. The earliest and most pressing need was food and the first business established was a grocery store. A rough plank building was put up as close to the Basin Spring as possible and a $200.00 stock of groceries laid in. This grocery store helped to relieve the necessity of long drives to obtain food and seemed to have a stabilizing effect on the community. Even one store seemed to provide the impetus for other business ventures of a more permanent nature, and a small boarding house was followed by additional boarding houses and stores.

The fact that there were no suitable accomodations for invalids did not discourage the eager seekers for relief and they continued to increase every day. A bath house was built by the son of Dr. Jackson; young Jackson also put up a store building and brought in a stock of goods.

When the first campers began to build their crude shelters near the Basin Spring abundant stands of pine, oak, walnut and cedar covered the mountain sides. Since no one seemed aware of the beauty and beneficent influence of this virgin timber the hills were soon denuded to make room for the buildings of the rapidly growing community. It was fortunate that the first survey of land reserved the space around the springs for the use of all so that those trees were left standing. From the first shack built there had been an immediate demand for lumber. Fortunately, or unfortunately, a saw mill had been in operation near by so that the need was easily satisfied.

The need for food continued to increase with the increasing population. Quantities of food were necessary to satisfy the hunger of people leading an outdoor life. Not all were invalids and many were doing more active work than ever before. Soon farmers out where the land was level took advantage of this need for food, and wagons loaded with all kinds of farm produce made their way along the steep rough roads. Most of the farmers came from many miles away and their farm produce met a ready acceptance which rewarded their efforts with a welcome source of income.

In addition to the first grocery store other needs of the growing community were met with a tailor shop, a drug store, a hardware store, a meat market and a blacksmith shop. The usual characteristics of a frontier town were heightened when

> "a Mr. Jefferson, desirous of accommodating those not content with pure Eureka water, opened a saloon," the first of many.

The need for food continued to be of first importance, but the need for shelter grew as the summer advanced. At first many families came in their own wagons and other horse-drawn vehicles, but as the word of healing spread, hundreds came by twos and threes, and some kind of shelter where food could also be obtained seemed necessary. Several small boarding houses had been built and they were now followed by others which could provide a room with or without meals. While food was hard to obtain and harder to prepare the inconvenience did not stop people from coming and apparently no one went hungry.

A perfect frenzy of activity continued all through the summer of 1879 until the cooler mornings and chilly evenings began to foretell winter. The tents and shacks had been adequate for summer and early fall, but now they needed to be rebuilt to withstand the rigors of the winter climate. In December, 1879, the *Arkansas Gazette,* ever watchful of happenings in Eureka Springs, reported only 500 houses in suitable condition for winter. One of the early settlers told of his family sharing their already crowded house with those unfortunates who could not find shelter. On occasion they even gave up their beds if the need was dire.

Life was of necessity primitive. Since no one was sure of the duration of their stay, the comfortable house furnishings were left at home and only the bare necessities were hauled in. These were made to serve with additional home-made chairs, tables and other makeshifts for storage and sleeping. The spirit of hope and adventure was high, and while the lack of conveniences may have bothered some, the majority entered into the pioneer life with good grace and stayed on at the Springs.

The activity in the community now called Eureka Springs attracted a group of squatters to another spring to the north of the original settlement. When this spring had been discovered it was named Dairy Spring and a hotel and several houses were soon under construction there. The principal promoter was a Mr. Evans so the whole endeavor was called Evansville. Soon other springs were located over a wide area and all of the waters were found to be beneficial.

Early in February of 1880 a newspaper, *The Morning Echo,* made its appearance. A second newspaper, *The Herald,* also began publication. According to the editors one was to herald the glad tidings of the water that healed and the other was to echo them. Hundreds of these newspapers were soon sent all over the country to relatives and friends of those persons visiting the Springs. This publicity helped to bring more and more people even though travel to Eureka Springs was a real hardship. Some forty-five miles of stage or wagon travel had to be endured before the summit of a mountain was reached where all at once a "city of 10,000 to 12,000 souls seemed to spring out of the wilderness." The noise of building reached the ears before the eyes could appraise the scene. Only those Western towns built at gold or silver strikes had ever appeared so quickly or developed so rapidly and this town was being built on nothing more substantial than . . . water.

A few trails which had never been anything but trails for all the years were widened to take a team and wagon. A principal thoroughfare was hacked out of the undergrowth for about one half mile to the south of the Basin Spring. It was of course called Main Street and was soon extended at both ends. Being at the bottom of the gap between the mountains it could be made comparatively level. Spring Street took off from it at an angle, climbing by easy stages to the north up past the Basin Spring and on to the Harding Spring community. Mountain Street was a wagon track from north on Main Street almost straight up the mountain to a level road on top which turned south toward South Eureka.

From these main thoroughfares roads and foot paths branched off in every direction along the easiest grades where possible, and if not, then straight up the mountain. Spring Street was improved as rapidly as possible as it offered the easiest way up the mountain side.

The four communities, which later became the four Wards of the City, were Basin Spring Community, the first established; Harding Spring Community was next, followed farther north by Evansville which could be reached by a road running on top of the mountain, and the South Eureka Community a short distance along a road which branched off of Mountain Street towards the south. The distance between the southernmost point and that farthest north was about one and one-half miles. The entire community had developed on the west side of the deep gulch which separated it from East Mountain.

By the month of May, 1880, an estimated 2000 abodes had appeared like pasture mushrooms along the main thoroughfares, roads and paths. Wherever human beings could devise one, a shelter was built, hung or wedged. There was a complete disregard for order. In fact all up and down the hillsides hundreds of small houses were being put together for rental purposes. Rents soon reached astronomical heights and often these cheap houses paid for themselves in a few months. This unfortunate tendency to build haphazardly and without regard for streets and alleys resulted in both undue annoyance and later legal action.

Down in the town the streets and footpaths were alive with people of all ages. Among them were those who were lame, blind, short, fat, tall and lean. All carried some kind of container to hold water and all seemed in confident expectation of being "made whole" by the waters of the many springs. It was as if the healing flowed with the water, out of the ground. Dispatches sent to the *Arkansas Gazette* from a roving reporter who called himself Potomoc, verify the foregoing.

In the Harding Spring Community where the Clark and Hutchings grocery store was under construction, many new boarding houses were also being built. These additional accomodations were making it possible to provide adequate food and shelter for those coming to the Springs.

Human welfare, while not completely under control, was so improved that spiritual welfare became of importance, as ministering to the spirit was now thought to be of equal importance with ministering to the body. Many ministers of all denominations had come to the Springs on the heels of the earliest visitors. One of the first was a minister of the Christian Church who preached in the Basin Spring grove. His eloquence was such that other ministers came to hear him and few seemed to know or care his denomination. In November of 1879 the Annual Conference of the Methodist Episcopal Church, South, had sent a "stationed" minister to the area. He was well received and soon became an influence for future good. A Methodist Church was being built according to plan and other churches began to prosper. Although all ministers were not of the "stationed" variety no doubt all meant well.

By April of 1880 the population of the town was estimated at various numbers, even as high as 15,000. A federal census was taken that year and recorded 3,000 residents who could claim legal status of "one year in the State, six months in Carroll County, and one month in the community."

One may well question "how did so many people get to such a remote spot?" Wagons were the principal means of transportation, although many came in on the back of a horse. As large numbers of people continued to want to reach the place where the water healed, certain enterprising citizens began a daily stage service to and from Pierce City, Seligman, and Joplin, Missouri, on the north and Ozark and Fayetteville on the south. Travelers using this service were many as the *Times-Echo* for March 7th lists arrivals as 62 with 25 departures, and later the next day lists 100 arrivals with only

30 departures; arrivals outnumbered those departing so the town continued to grow.

With stage service in operation a daily mail delivery was now possible between Eureka Springs and those cities reached by stage. Mail connections could be made with railroads in all directions, North, South, East and West. Earlier in 1879 a local postmaster had been appointed. Likely it was his very first experience in handling mail and it soon became apparent that he was incompetent. Since daily mail service was a "must" a new postmaster took over and the post office was moved into what was known as the "Flat Iron" building where Spring and Center Streets converged.

Sometime during the 1880's a Mr. G. S. Tibbs, from Missouri, came to the community, purchased and began to operate the bath house built by the younger Jackson. Tibbs now started to ship Eureka Water from the Basin Spring in all directions. The *Herald* and the *Echo* had spread the healing news and hundreds of invalids who lived many miles away were reached by both the newspapers and Mr. Tibbs' advertising. After drinking of the bottled water most consumers desired to come and drink at the source. The curative properties of the water were now a well established fact with more and more people coming to be healed.

Even with both doctors and ministers to care for their needs, all was not continuously well in the City of Healing. During the summer of 1880 a severe epidemic of measles occurred, according to Professor Kalklosch, the early historian. Many left town to escape the disease but their places were soon taken by new arrivals. As would be natural in a community where the desire for physical healing was of prime importance many unscrupulous persons hoped to cash in on this desire of their unfortunate fellow men. Healers of all kinds were plentiful, competing with the legitimately-trained physicians.

The second winter for the lusty infant community was now in the offing and it turned out to be one of the most severe winters ever recorded. People had come from the northern states expecting to find a temperate southern climate and were greatly disturbed to find both cold and snow. Due to lack of suitable finishing materials many houses were not only poorly built but poorly finished. This added to the discomfort of the occupants and many returned to their homes or went on to warmer climates. Not to be daunted, many invalids continued to come and in spite of the wintry weather cures took place.

In January of 1881 a railroad finally reached Seligman, Missouri, reducing the travel by stage to a mere eighteen miles and replacing the old Nine Hour Line from Pierce City. Telegraph service was also brought in to a newly-established telegraph office and Eureka Springs was now in touch with the outside world.

By the summer of 1881 many of the temporary business buildings and makeshift houses and boarding houses were giving place to structures of a more permanent nature. A few business buildings were being constructed of the abundant stone quarried not far from the northern limits of the town. Some of these solid structures soon fell victim to the fires that raged in 1883 and 1888. New frame dwelling houses were often unique in that they were several stories high, it not being unusual to enter on one street level and exit at a higher or lower level. This continued to be a feature of many of the houses in Eureka Springs.

In addition to the building activity within the town proper, lots were being staked out on East Mountain and at the community at Dairy Spring. There thirty-one new house foundations had been laid in what appeared to be a real estate boom. This development was taking place around one of the finest springs in the area.

All during the month of November workmen rushed to complete the turnpike to Seligman. Improvement on this road made a new bridge across the White River at Beaver necessary and this new bridge was opened for travel the latter part of the month. Even during the road work parties of as many as thirty-five persons kept arriving daily by stage and by early December the city was full of newcomers. A large party from Neosho, Missouri, was also expected to come for the winter months.

After the M. E. Church, South, brought in a stationed minister and built a church others in the religious field soon followed until nearly every branch of the Protestant faith was represented. Each denomination was hard at work to organize a congregation and build their own church building.

While the churches grew and prospered the same could not be said of the schools. Private schools provided for such education as seemed necessary. Be that as it may, there were 1571 children of school age in Eureka Springs in November of 1881, and the *Arkansas Gazette* of that date records the fact that they were being taught by 12 teachers. The city received $3,000 yearly in State school funds but no attempt to provide a free public school had as yet been made and a stabilized school system was still in the distant future. Teachers were anyone who could or would teach and class rooms were in private homes or any building that could answer the purpose.

The transient population of the town continued to keep near the 15,000 estimate, and with these persons living under the primitive conditions of a construction camp it would not be surprising if the community exhibited some of the exuberance of such a camp. The many saloons now in evidence attracted characters desiring to raise a little hell and who accompanied the raising with yells and pistol shots. Considering the general conditions prevailing these occurrences were less frequent than could be expected. Even so Eureka Springs was a lively place. A letter written by D. Elmer Jones to the Carroll County Historical Society tells of his first view of the town in 1880 . . .

> ". . . it was jammed with people all seemingly making their way on foot towards the Basin Spring and its healing water . . . Down in the town nights were real noisy with some kind of entertainment going on in every block. Pianos and orchestras tried to outdo each other with noise."

In this confusion a few criminals were trying to prey on the innocent and afflicted but such officers as the City organization had empowered to do so were at hand to deal with law breakers and toughs.

It is almost with awe that one realizes that the town had not yet been plagued by a destructive fire, for most cooking was still over camp fires, and their lights flared and flickered in the early dusk as people prepared their simple evening meal. Houses were still in scarce supply and much of the food was prepared in the open, but the healing water was as plentiful as ever and even the threat of fire did not discourage the hope of healing.

During two and a half years the "Topsy" of the Northwest Arkansas mountains had "just growed" beyond anyone's wildest dream, providing anyone ever took time to dream of a future for the community. Soon a time of stabilization and real progress was to begin. Already the shadow of more new construction was falling on the town, with a new Opera House and a City Hall in prospect. Sufficient ground had been prepared for the continued growth and development of what would become a most remarkable community.

CHAPTER II

A Firm Abiding Place

In the autumn of 1879 by the time the leaves had left the trees, there remained little doubt in anyone's mind concerning the promising future of Eureka Springs. Life at the hilly settlement was pleasant and entertaining while every passing day brought improved health and vitality to suffering bodies which in turn brought uplifted spirits. Each new day also brought its share of newcomers who did not long remain strangers, as they were soon welcomed into the life of the community and in their turn extended the hand of friendship to those who followed them.

The site still had only makeshift tents, covered wagons and other temporary shelters. Thus far no attempt had been made to establish any governing rules or regulations as only good will and sociability prevailed among the people. The approach of winter made it necessary to provide more permanent housing, and thinking minds began to see the need for regulation in the affairs of the camp, particularly in regard to housing. Up to this time improvements had been made without regard to the size of lots, value of property or the location of roads and streets.

In mid-August, Hugh S. Montgomery, with the help of about twenty men, cleared away the trees and brush and opened up a road at the bottom of the gorge below Basin Spring. Business houses of every description were soon built along the road, wherever a man with an inclination toward business could stake out a building site.

These businessmen, being men of good judgment, together with Montgomery, put their collective wisdom to work seeking ways to incorporate the settlement into a town with a proper governing body. This move was deemed necessary to handle the future development which seemed bound to come.

The governing laws of the State of Arkansas necessitated the presentation of a petition to the County Court requesting the power to incorporate as a town. Accordingly, on October 8, 1879, a petition signed by twenty citizens of Eureka Springs was filed and the signers sat back to patiently await the granting of this authority. Previously the number of legal residents had not been sufficient to effect the incorporation which was now about to become a reality.

In the interim a committee of twelve men, which included Hugh Montgomery, his younger brother and ten others, was elected at a mass meeting of the citizens. This was the first council before which matters of dispute were to be brought for adjustment.

When the first arrivals at the Springs staked out their locations, they did so as close to the Basin Spring as possible, so apparently this area was to form the center of the new community. Now, the first order of business was to survey a townsite with particular attention paid to preserving the springs and their near vicinity for the use of the public.

In a book written by L. J. Kalklosch and published at Eureka Springs in 1881, he has this to say concerning the original survey:

> "The committee appointed I. N. Armstrong as Town Surveyor and gave him instructions to survey the town, making the lots 40 x 40 feet, streets thirty feet wide and eighty feet or two lots between streets."
>
> "It seems that this committee had no thought of a city of many thousands, and the inconveniences for the future they were creating by this survey of narrow streets and small lots. Reservations were made around the principal springs on which no one was permitted to build or place an improvement of any kind without permission of the Committee. As it was government land, all a person needed to become a free holder was to pay a fee of One

> Dollar ($1.00) to the surveyor, take a receipt for the payment, have his name registered in a private book kept by the surveyor's clerk, and he became a proprietor of one lot."

As quickly as the purchasers gained access to their lots, they began immediate and indiscriminate removal of almost every tree upon that particular patch of ground. Early photographs of the town show one bare hillside after another covered only with board shacks between the stumps of the once mighty trees. Row after row the shacks marched down West Mountain, through the muddy hollows and on up the eastern slopes. The only stands of timber that were left were the groves of pine within the principal spring reservations.

A reason for the senseless denuding of the land was never recorded and one may only speculate that the enthusiasm for erecting this city in the wilderness, a city dedicated to the healing of human ills, overrode any thought of preserving the abundant natural beauty of the land.

For many weeks that winter the Surveyor continued his work, and Kalklosch describes the result in this manner:

> "The . . . receipt of payment was generally recognized as sufficient right against all claimants to the same lot. In order to avoid speculation on lots, the committee passed a resolution that no party shall take more than two lots, and if not improved in a limited time, anyone may be at liberty to jump, confiscate or appropriate the forfeited lot to himself."
>
> Hence, no one could hold a lot without an improvement.
>
> "Surveying began at the Great Basin Spring. A large reservation was laid off, principally above the spring. Below were surveyed the first lots and registered as fast as they were established. The first street of the town was surveyed down the gulch a few rods below the spring, running north and south. A broad avenue connects this street with the famous Eureka (Basin) Spring. It being the first street in town, and for several months the principal thoroughfare; it was named Main Street. But owing to its low elevation and the law of gravitation, the water would find a level in the street, and as the immense travel created an abundance of mud, the street was nicknamed "Mud", a name without music or elegance."

Lot Number One on the south side of Main Street was the first surveyed for individual occupance and was entered by O. D. Thornton, a general storekeeper."

In concluding his account of the survey, Kalklosch indicates that Major Armstrong was perhaps not the most trustworthy of men, as follows:

> "The Surveyor was always followed by parties ready to pay the fee and register the lots, so that it proved quite a bonanza for him, especially when we recollect that he frequently "received payment" and gave receipts for the same lot from one to three times. Owing to several claimants on the same lots, frequent disputes arose, and the Surveyor thought he knew of a healthier clime for him than Eureka Springs, but not until he had reaped a rich harvest."
>
> "The disputes were generally referred to the invincible committee, which had power supreme to settle all matters of litigation. The lots were generally granted to those having the first "received payment" of the Surveyor, excepting when there was an improvement, which invariably held the lot. Appeals were not taken from this Court. Public sentiment always sustained its action."

Major Armstrong continued his work until the middle of the winter, laying out the principal streets of the town before moving on to a "healthier clime." The original governing committee, which had employed him, was superseded by another. This second committee dissolved without transacting any important business, leaving the infant community to fend as best it could without organized leadership.

In due time, sufficient curiosity was generated by the happenings at the Springs for the *Arkansas Gazette* of Little Rock to send a correspondent to report on what was taking place. This correspondent was the man who wrote under the by-line "Potomoc" and who was well qualified to report the situation. Somewhat a man of mystery, Colonel M. L. DeMahler traveled for the *Gazette* from 1878 to 1890. He made his journey principally on foot through every county in Arkansas, investigating the resources of the State. His first report concluded that the Eureka Springs development was a gigantic affair, as follows:

"The wonderful instances put forth in California, Colorado and Nevada were the products of mining excitements which may always be calculated to attract tens of thousands from all parts of the world. Conditions of economic growth, population and pre-eminence being altogether propitious to recovery from disease and debility, it therefore stands by comparison without a known rival in the history of man."

His dispatches concluded with an analysis of the waters and a list of those diseases for which they were considered beneficial.

Particular attention was given the townsite survey and the *Gazette* reported fifteen hundred lots surveyed by December of 1879, with five hundred houses completed and approximately three thousand persons in residence.

The large number of people which began to settle in Eureka Springs in 1879 and the succeeding two years were of the class generally termed "squatters." They settled on land which was designated in an earlier county survey as Section 15 and the south half of Section 10, Township 20 North, Range 26 West, in Carroll County.

The townsite survey and claiming of lots resulted in a peaceful distribution of land among the citizens and they were quick to begin securing their title against outside claimants. As yet it was a little known fact that during the previous August a group of speculators from Missouri, including a man named Alexander and one Northcutt had filed homestead claims at the land office in Harrison on the land where all of the major springs so far discovered were located. Apparently, it was their intent to speculate on these "healing waters." If the squatters knew of these claims, they evidently did not consider the filing as a threat to them and went ahead with their business of surveying the townsite.

Other shrewd business people also entered claims to the land, three of the more prominent being Franzisca Massman, Benjamin Woodruff and William Evans.

Before 1879, Mrs. Massman operated a sawmill on Leatherwood Creek. Her mill furnished a large portion of the lumber used in building the shacks which seemed to spring up over night to house the people of the new town. The name Massman was so well known in the area that the *St. Louis Republican* of September 11, 1879, told in their front page story of the "discovery of new and valuable mineral waters in Arkansas at a place called Massmans Mills" and went on to further report, "a constant stream of Missourians wend their way to this generous and inexhaustible dispensary of nature, and in every instance verify all that has been claimed for the waters."

With these hundreds of people coming into the area around the Springs, Mrs. Massman saw her opportunity to provide a seemingly endless supply of lumber for the construction of the countless homes and filed a cash entry on a good portion of Section 10. Evidently it did not occur to her that she wished to cut lumber off the same land claimed by the townspeople for their new homes and places of business.

One of the most colorful stories of early Eureka Springs concerns Mrs. Massman, and has been passed down by the children of men who dealt with her in the essentially male world of the lumber industry. It is told that in the days of free government land which had been surveyed and was waiting to be claimed by westward bound settlers, Franzisca Massman was always just "one jump ahead of the law" for cutting timber without authority to do so. Like her fellow lumbermen, she put her crews to work wherever trees were plentiful and showed small regard for conservation or wise use of the virgin forests. When a tree was cut down only the first eight or ten feet of "clear" lumber was used while the rest was left lying to waste and decay. In order to keep clear of the authorities —since it was a requirement that the land be improved—as soon as Mrs. Massman entered a claim on a choice piece of timber land she put her crew to work to cut down enough timber to build a two- or three-room shack, plowed the adjoining land, moved in a few household furnishings and sat down to supper there the same evening. Having improved and used the land, she had thereby "proved up" her claim and so secured the title to it. In this way, with the least possible outlay of time and money, she established a claim to the land which held until the timber had been cut and the lumber hauled away to be sold. Then the mill crew and Mrs. Massman moved on to another desirable location to begin the process all over again.

Another successful saw mill operator was Benjamin Woodruff, with two mills in the immediate area. He filed a cash entry on a large area of Section 15, again asking for land which was to be included in the townsite.

William Evans also filed a cash entry at the Federal Land Office on the Southeast Quarter of Section 10. The land he desired for himself was rapidly being settled by the "squatters" and later became that part of the city near the Dairy Spring known as Evansville. So named, no doubt, in honor of the prominent Mr. Evans.

The pending citizens petition for incorporation was dismissed by the County Court early in January of 1880 because there was still not the required number of voters resident in the proposed limits. Seven days later, a new petition carrying the names of seventy-one qualified voters was filed. It met with favorable consideration by the County Court and on Valentine's Day of 1880, Section 15 and the South Half of Section 10 became the incorporated town.

Simultaneously, the *Arkansas Gazette* received its first copy of T. J. Hadley's weekly paper *The Echo,* which carried the banner headline, "Eureka Springs to be incorporated."

The first election of town officers took place on April 6, 1880. Kalklosch, an eyewitness and participant in the birthing of the town, tells of the difficulties encountered in electing the first council:

> "It was difficult to find efficient men eligible to office, as the State Law requires a voter to be in the State one year, in the County six months, and in the voting precinct thirty days before being a legal voter or eligible for office. As a result of the election, E. Rossen of Carroll County, Arkansas was the choice for mayor; C. F. Hattenhauer for recorder, with Jasper Hooker, R. R. Pace, George Beavers, W. H. Jones and John Holden as town councilmen."

"The mayor soon received his commission from the Governor, the Council was sworn in and the mill for grinding out ordinances was put in operation."

It is noteworthy that the conglomerate mass of humanity which comprised the town got so far along with relatively little confusion. However, had it been possible to install proper authorities six months sooner, undoubtedly a better order of things would have been the result.

On May 10, 1880, Mayor Rossen made application at the land office in Harrison to enter as a townsite for the people of Eureka Springs the whole of Section 15, the South Half of Section 10 and a part of Section 14, for a portion of which he appeared as contestant.

Now another group filed claims to the mineral rights on all the springs. Seeing an opportunity to cash in on what appeared to be a bonanza, "The Blue Springs Mineral Company" was organized and filed their claim in July of 1880.

This filing divided the city into three opposing camps; first, the settlers who had purchased land after the first survey of the townsite; second, the speculators who filed homestead claims on the land upon which the springs were located and who were now regarded as imposters by the first settlers; and third, the miners who had filed claims on the mineral rights.

Thus began a bitter and frustrating battle which was to drag on for five long years of public meetings and legal proceedings.

Having filed their claim and feeling that they were within their legal rights to do so, the miners came in and began sinking shafts in various parts of the city. Many were near springs and one was started on the hillside above the Basin Spring. The miners now came to grief, as they struck water, and the townspeople feared that the water of the Basin Spring was threatened. An indignation meeting of the populace was hurriedly called. The unanimous feeling of those present was that the springs be protected at all costs and by any means. A motion to that effect was passed and a committee was named to call on the miners and demand that their digging cease, while other citizens went about filling up the holes already dug. Thus ended, for the time, the mining activity in Eureka Springs.

The long hot summer of 1880 dragged on and once again tempers flared as Mayor Elisha Rossen was accused of what were termed "gross improprieties" of office, and was impeached by his fellow citizens. A prominent professional man, John Carroll, was appointed to fill the mayor's chair until the next election.

At this time, the Blue Springs Mining Company was in litigation with Alexander and Northcutt, the agricultural claimants to the townsite. In April of 1881, the Land Commissioner rendered a decision adverse to the agricultural interests. Certain portions of the townsite were declared mineral in character and the claims of both townsite and mineral applicants were allowed. This decision was very satisfactory to the latter, who began preparations to continue their search for a paying mineral.

The municipal election in the spring of 1881 saw the citizens divided into four parties, each offering a full slate of candidates under the names of: "Peoples Ticket," "Citizens Ticket," "Townsite Ticket," and the "Independent Ticket." John Carroll headed the "Townsite" slate and was elected, as were his attendant council members. The council was well aware of the lack of money with which to run the municipality, there being no taxable real estate and little personal property to be taxed. The principal sources of revenue were the fines imposed for law violations, a business license tax and donations from public-spirited citizens. An occupation tax was also levied by ordinance such as:

> "One Hundred Dollars ($100.00) for each practicing physician, Fifty Dollars ($50.00) for each real estate agent and attorney, and Twenty-Five Dollars ($25.00) for every art gallery!"

The legality of such ordinances was much questioned—so the City Council passed a resolution not to enforce them until a legal opinion could be obtained from the State. The previous

Council had passed two very necessary ordinances, which remained in effect for many years. We are indebted to Kolklosch for their wording: Ordinance 10, Section 2.

> "All persons washing their persons or clothes in or above the basins of all public springs shall be guilty of a misdemeanor."

Section 3

> "The public springs are hereby declared free for public use except as hereafter provided. No person shall be allowed to water horses, mules, cattle or other stock from the public springs, nor to carelessly or maliciously remove, mutilate or destroy any of the appurtances of same."

The council also appointed a Board of Health, which drafted regulations governing all sanitary conditions, such as water supply, sewers and sewage disposal. This action was the result of a citizens mass meeting, which drafted resolutions calling for those regulations.

The most pressing problem, aside from local differences, continued to be the land case, as no decision had been rendered and the citizens were still in danger of losing their investments. Finally in March of 1882 there was more action on the land case, as the Secretary of the Interior reversed the previous decision of the Land Commissioners, declaring the land to be agricultural in character and remanding the case to the general land office. The commissioners directed the local land officers to take testimony and a hearing before the Register and Receiver at Harrison began September 4, 1882. Testimony was taken concerning the townsite which established the existence of a community before either the farmers or the miners arrived on the scene.

Mayor Carroll journeyed to Washington to intercede in behalf of the citizens and with the assistance of a Senator from Arkansas, it was finally determined that the land was mineral in character and the farmers claims to the gravel hillsides were not allowed. The application for a townsite was duly entered, and since no paying mineral had been discovered in Eureka Springs, it seemed very hopeful that the city would eventually receive its patent.

The decision of the Federal Land Commission was not handed down until July 19, 1883, deciding the question of priority of rights in favor of the city authorities. The farmers or agricultural claimants immediately appealed the decision to the Secretary of the Interior and another long year passed before his decision affirming that of the Land Commissioner was rendered. There was, however, one important exception which led to still further involvement and delay for the citizens of Eureka Springs. Portions of Section 10 within the corporate limits were conceded to the agriculturalists.

In continuing this history to its ultimate solution, it may be seen that much of the credit for the early progress of Eureka Springs belongs to the Honorable John Carroll. Appointed mayor to replace the earlier Rossen, then elected mayor in his own right in the election of 1881, he was able to control the political scene during 1880, 1881, 1882, when politics were often as blustery as the winter weather.

The infant community was indeed fortunate in having such a man to represent them in adjusting the land suit between the townsite claimants and the agricultural and mineral interests. Nevertheless, this litigation dragged on for five long years until its final settlement in April of 1885. This long drawn out business discouraged many of the citizens, as well as potential investors, and emptied the City Treasury of what small public funds existed.

Early in 1882, the population having sufficiently increased, Eureka Springs became a City of the First Class; at that time a census taken by the council showed a population of five thousand legal residents which made Eureka Springs the fourth largest city in Arkansas.

Back in November of 1881, the newspaper *The Echo* reported:

> "The council met yesterday and had quite a stormy session. The mayor informed them he would immediately tender his resignation to the Governor, who could either order an election to fill a vacancy in the office of mayor of the incorporated town or to elect a mayor of Eureka Springs as a city of the first class."

It is strange to note that the authority for a City of the First Class was received from the Governor of the State of Arkansas almost simultaneously with a refusal from the Federal Land Commissioner to accept the townsite application until all legal proceedings had been concluded in determining the character of the land.

This ruling did not deter the citizens of Eureka Springs from accepting their new status as a City of the First Class and proceeding accordingly. New powers accrued to the mayor and the number of aldermen was increased to ten, representing five voting wards.

On every hand the mayor and council met with difficulty in governing their city. Particularly, the area of finances consumed a good measure of their time, strength and imagination.

A closer look at the financial condition of the city during the five years before 1885 may be helpful in understanding the final outcome and the settlement reached with the Eureka Springs Improvement Company. The entry of this organization upon the scene marks the era of "the promoters," men who invested fabulous sums of money to publicize and develop Eureka Springs. Their investments made the new health resort more than a passing fad. It became instead a famous city with a promising future, so in the light of these results the individual fortunes amassed by these several men are of small consequence.

Goodspeed's History of Carroll County, published in 1889, tells the story of the early years in detail, as follows:

> "The immense expense necessarily incurred in street improvements and in pursuing the litigation to secure title to the territory upon which the city is built have severely taxed its resources. Prohibited from issuing bonds by the State Constitution and from assessing a tax higher than a certain rate, inadequate to provide sufficient revenue, the city council was forced to the unfortunate expediency of issuing city warrants at from fifty to eighty-five percent less than their face value. The amount of outstanding warrants on April 18, 1882, was $71,651.24; on April 1, 1883 the amount was $75,816.30; the revenue for the

intervening period being $36,679.10. This is a summary of the financial conditions at the close of the first year of city government."

It would seem that much of the indebtedness had been incurred without adequate returns and the Board of Aldermen had reached the place where definite action was imperative. Accordingly, in the following year they sought to effect a compromise between the city and the holders of this "scrip." In this, they met with only partial success, for a man named Samuel Ashley had purchased warrants approximating $46,000.00, and he refused to compromise on the terms offered by the city. Instead he instituted proceedings in the U. S. District Court for the recovery of this claim and as of the year 1889, Goodspeed tells us the case was still undecided.

Meanwhile, income was not forthcoming in amounts sufficient to lower indebtedness to any marked degree and the figure remained at over $38,000 on the first of April, 1884.

It was, then, in such straitened financial circumstances that the city authorities looked for the final settlement to the question of who owned the contested portion of land upon which stood Eureka Springs, by now one of the most exciting and famous health resorts in the United States.

In the meantime, several men of influence from St. Louis, Little Rock and New York, together with a group from both Texas and Eureka Springs, had organized and incorporated the Eureka Springs Improvement Company. This company was headed by the ex-governor of Arkansas, Powell Clayton, who had come to Eureka Springs three years earlier to make a home for his family. He immediately displayed a keen interest in the future of the community and invested heavily in various business enterprises of which he now controlled a good portion.

Now, the Eureka Springs Improvement Company, which was soon discovered to be the successor to the agricultural claimants, in February of 1884 instituted proceedings in the United States Court of the Western District of Arkansas to test the legality of the entire townsite title.

As previously noted, the city had no money and impaired credit. The citizens were disillusioned by the long years of uncertainity regarding their land titles and were generally agreeable to some sort of compromise, so long as such would settle the question for good.

Accordingly, the City Council requested a mass meeting of the citizenry at which Joe F. Ivey was appointed chairman of a committee to assist the Council in working out a solution. At the first meeting of this committee with the mayor and aldermen a proposition from the Improvement Company was reviewed and met with a most unfavorable reaction. Tempers worn threadbare by months of litigation almost brought about an abrupt termination of the negotiations. General Clayton now wisely suggested that the matter be "laid over" until after the annual meeting of the directors of the Improvement Company.

A month later, the committee again met at Downie Hall, this time with John Carroll presiding. It is not known why Chairman Ivey relinquished his position, but neither is it surprising when one considers the circumstances. This meeting with the Improvement Company went on for twelve hours until 4:00 a. m., when a basis for settlement was finally reached.

Once again the citizens gathered en masse and with a practically unanimous vote decided in favor of accepting the measures suggested. On April 6, 1885, a decree of the United States District Court was handed down ratifying the compromise, the main features of which were the following: The Improvement Company was invested with the title to a portion of Section 10 with the condition that deeds should be executed to the leaseholders thereon at the city appraisement, and that the Dairy Spring should be free to the public forever.

The title to the contested portions of Section 15, upon which were located the Basin Spring, Little Eureka, Maxwell or Cold, Harding, Califf, Sweet, Onyx and other springs was vested in the mayor, Archimedes Davis, the president of the Improvement Company, and John Carroll, by whom deeds should be executed to the lease holders at the city appraisement.

The churches were to receive lots without compensation, all spring reservations would belong to the city, and all property unclaimed within a specified period would revert without compensation to the Improvement Company. A commission representing all interests was provided for which was to have jurisdiction in the widening of streets, abatement of nuisances and removal of unoccupied houses. The company was granted the right to operate street car lines, also gas and water pipe lines, for a period of fifty years.

Goodspeed sums up this final settlement of the difficult situation in this way: "This compromise, honorable and just to all interests involved, removed the incubus of uncertain title, which had so long interfered with the prosperity of the city, while its provisions for public improvements insured a realization of those conditions which attract a desirable class of citizens."

Though the compromise itself might be considered "just" and "honorable," undoubtedly there was thought of little else than personal gain in the minds of Northcutt and Alexander in the beginning. Later, the same desire motivated the Improvement Company partners who sought to secure for themselves and thus control the land from which flowed Eureka's "healing waters." (Sufficient to leave to the imagination how vastly different the history of the community would have been had these men completely succeeded in all of their aims and ambitions).

CHAPTER III

THE DREAM BEGINS

The health resort at Eureka Springs came into being as the answer to hopes, prayers and dreams in the hearts of people who came seeking revived health and strength. The relief from suffering they received brought with it the promise of another chance to begin life anew—and to live that life in better ways than before. The twentieth century reader with his modern ideas and attitudes may scoff to see the new community heralded as the "Siloam of the Afflicted," but such it truly seemed in that simpler day and time. Some were drawn to the Springs in search of physical healing, some came in search of a new life—but all sensed in the very air about them the promise of invisible golden tomorrows, in what was to become a kind of earthly Victorian paradise.

From the earliest days of the community, townspeople had listened to the many promises of great things concerning the future that forward-looking citizens held forth for Eureka Springs. Now, these promises paled into insignificance in the excitement caused when a few men of great wealth began to advance their plans and schemes for the development of the resort. It was the aim of these men to attract not only the thousands upon thousands of suffering and afflicted, but also those wealthy world-weary persons who were seeking a place "to get away from it all."

These great designers and planners of the future resort were far removed from the fly-by-night schemers and the small plodding businessmen. The dreams they dreamed and plans they carefully made far excelled anything imagined by most of the townspeople, as well as by many of the civic leaders.

Beginning in 1880 and continuing for two decades, there existed in Eureka Springs the era of "the big promoter." Because of their activity the resort was to reach a peak in popularity, elegance and gracious living which began with their coming and ended as they went their ways to become involved in more interesting and sophisticated matters.

After researching newspaper accounts and public records, it cannot be said with honesty that the "promoters," the elected civic officials and the ordinary citizens worked together hand in hand. There were disagreements and sometimes daily encounters over one problem or another, but the building of the town progressed rapidly so that the time soon arrived when every citizen could look with pride upon what had been accomplished. To a great extent the promises of success and fame were to be fulfilled.

Foremost among the promoters were the members of the Eureka Springs Improvement Company, the organization which had been prominently involved in the settlement of the townsite case. The members of this company were also to form the nucleus of the Eureka Springs Railroad Company.

In 1882 the directors of the organization were headed by Powell Clayton, president, A. H. Foote of St. Louis, secretary, and Logan H. Roots, a prominent Little Rock businessman, was treasurer.

Since he was to be the most prominent figure in the early development of Eureka Springs, a look at Powell Clayton—who he was, where he came from, as well as the kind of man he was—will throw much light on several things which to this day are considered special features of the resort.

Almost every one who writes of Powell Clayton calls him the "carpet bag" governor of Arkansas. True, Clayton had been born in Pennsylvania and enlisted in the Union Army there. The fortunes of war brought him to the State of Arkansas, where he was stationed for the last three years of the war. Like soldiers often do, he met and married a local girl, Miss McGraw of Helena. At the close of the war he and one of his brothers purchased a large plantation for which they paid $53,000.00 in cash, and there he resided until 1867. Normally this residence would have made him an accepted citizen of the state, but Southern tempers continued high and much animosity was expressed toward anyone who had fought for the Union, particularly if they were born in a Northern state.

Far from deserving the term "carpetbagger," Clayton had been in the state long enough to be entitled to all the rights of a citizen, including the right to be elected governor. He was the first legally-elected governor of Arkansas following the reorganization of the State Government after the adoption of the Articles of Reconstruction, and it came about in this way.

Arkansas had joined with her Southern sisters and left the Union in 1861. Since it was a border state both armies see-sawed back and forth across the state until in 1863 the Confederate Army finally left for more important areas, principally Vicksburg. The neighboring state of Missouri continued to suffer Confederate raids until 1864, when it too was free of troops and both states could begin to consider their future course.

When the Confederate Army left Arkansas the civil government collapsed and President Lincoln immediately appointed Major General Steele, then Commander of the Military District of Arkansas, to administer both military and civil affairs in the state until such time as a new state constitution could be adopted and a civil government elected.

Those sympathetic to the Union cause desired to organize a state government with a constitution based on the recommendations sent out by the federal government to act as guide lines for those states who wished to rejoin the Union. These men began to hold small conventions at which they elected delegates to a Constitutional Convention. Soon such conventions became popular in the southern half of the state and large numbers of delegates were elected to represent those areas. When the convention finally met, these delegates were strong enough to dictate the working of the Constitutional Convention and turn it toward the ideas proposed by the defeated and deposed Confederates. In some haste they adopted a constitution based on the one previously in force with the addition of an amendment annulling the Acts of Secession, also a clause abolishing slavery and an amendment repudiating the Confederate debt. Under this constitution, the Convention appointed state officers beginning with Issac Murphy as Governor.

In the meantime, Major General Steele and his aides had not been idle, and spurred on by the desire of President Lincoln to hasten the return to the Union of those states willing to again enter the Union fold, Steele began to take steps to organize a convention to draft a new state constitution. To his surprise, he found a Constitutional Convention already in session. Appraised of this fact, President Lincoln thought best to let the state get organized and give the provisional government time to prove itself.

The senators and representatives of the Murphy Government (for such the provisional government was called) were refused seats in the Congress of the United States. Upon investigation, it was found that certain aspects of the Convention and its appointments were not within the context of such a convention, as specified by the government of the United States. During that period when it was hoped that the provisional government could be made to work, Major General Steele had been relieved of his duties with the Civil Government of Arkansas, which left the Murphy government temporarily in office.

By 1866 the government of the United States was also having trouble. President Johnson and Congress had reached an impasse and it was quite evident that those "never-say-die" former Confederates, who now called themselves Democrats, were in hopes to restore the old slave-holding regime in power. To do this, they needed the votes of the recently appointed members from Arkansas. So far they had not been seated, nor were they likely to be.

The Constitutional Convention had called for an election to ratify this provisional constitution and to give those appointed civil servants a legal status. Now a delegation of Democrats called on Powell Clayton and made an effort to influence him to become a nominee for one of the congressional seats. This honor Clayton respectfully declined.

In due course the election was held and the returns gave the ex-Confederates an overwhelming majority, putting them, in most cases, into national, state and local offices and confirming the Murphy government, as thus far it had not achieved the status of a legally-elected body, and those representatives to Congress had not yet been seated. Now a commission from the Murphy government was sent to Washington to lobby for the admission of the senators and representatives, but it returned to counsel patience, as it was the belief of the commission that the radicals (also known as the Republicans) would soon destroy themselves.

About three months later, the Congress of the United States enacted the Reconstruction Measures and almost immediately those who had pretended a policy of quiet peaceful submission to the federal government turned to the other extreme, and so began a time of anarchy and insurrection that was far from pretense. This was aided by a directive from Major E. O. C. Ord, now commanding the Fourth Military District of Arkansas, declaring the Democratic Provisional Government incompatible with the recent Act of Congress.

Loud denunciations by the Democrats who referred to these Acts as "unconstitutional, revolutionary and void" did not alter the case. When the government of the United States forbade the provisional government to reassemble, a step further could have been taken and it could have been disbanded, forcibly if necessary. The efforts of the federal government to be lenient with those states who like "penitent sinners" were being encouraged to return to the fold left the provisional government in Arkansas defiantly trying to exercise power which never did belong to it.

Powell Clayton, from the quiet of his plantation, had been made fully aware of the schemes the Democrats were promoting. He soon realized that unless some method was found to check them, any former Union man would not be able to continue to live in the state with any degree of peace and security.

Early in 1868, the Republicans became strong enough to call a convention of Union men in Little Rock. There a full ticket of candidates was nominated, headed by Powell Clayton for governor. Realizing his Confederate neighbors meant him little good he had been forced to take a political stand to protect his property and family. When the state election was held under the rules set forth by the Acts of Reconstruction, he was elected governor.

In his book, published in 1915 and titled *"The Aftermath Of The Civil War In Arkansas,"* Clayton begins with the ceremony which installed him as governor. The Murphy government had been allowed to continue in office until this time, so it was Issac Murphy who shared the carriage which took him to the inauguration ceremony and who turned over to him such perogatives of office as Murphy had continued to keep. These were practically nonexistent, but a certain formality was observed though Murphy was not especially formal.

In his first message to the Arkansas General Assembly, delivered on June 3, 1868, Clayton called for animosities and divisions to be laid aside and for every citizen to work for the betterment of the state. The message also covered such pertinent details concerning state welfare as registration and election laws, a state militia, immigration, banks, state indebtedness, education, state aid to railroads, the blind institute and a geological survey to ascertain the location and amount of such minerals and other substances as would be useful toward increasing the prosperity of the state. At the conclusion, he also mentioned the disorderly condition of the State Capitol and surrounding grounds and recommended a thorough house cleaning.

Nothing in this message could be construed as either radical or sensational. It was an orderly presentation of those affairs which would restore and promote the welfare of Arkansas, and during the first "honeymoon days" with the State Legislature many of his recommendations were enacted into law. Almost before the honeymoon got under way Clayton's troubles began. Even before his election that dark shadow which became the Ku Klux Klan had appeared to frighten and suppress. Now murder became the order of the day.

Naturally speculation has attributed the loss of Powell Clayton's arm to a war injury. In his book he explains his gun was accidentally discharged while hunting near Little Rock, and the injury was so severe it resulted in the amputation of his hand and part of his arm.

While he was in the hospital recovering from this amputation, a stranger came to the hospital urgently requesting to see him. On being admitted to his room, this man poured forth a tale of the activities, aims and organization of the Ku Klux Klan, and begged Clayton for money and assistance so he could take his family far from Arkansas. Since Clayton had heard enough of the stories about the Klan, he could fit them into the stranger's story and willingly advanced the funds necessary for him to travel. Soon the information Clayton had received proved only too accurate as one after another of the elected civil officials were gunned down, most of them being Republicans. Quietly the Governor began a full-scale investigation, but the assassinations continued, and as whole sections of the state succumed to fear and disorder, he issued an order for the organization of a State Militia. It took some time to perfect that arm of the law and make effectual use of it. Eventually those malcontents and outlaws who had been trying to take the law into their own hands, were either captured, killed or left the state for healthier areas. During this time the state was divided into four geographical areas—the Southeast, Southwest, Northwest and Northeast—and the efforts of the militia were mostly directed to those districts in the southern half of the state. Probably the sparse settlement and the mountainous terrain of the Northwest division helped to keep it peaceful and law-abiding, as the militia was never used there.

Now all the old hatreds and grievances of the Civil War days were fanned by the Democratic press as efforts were made to discredit Powell Clayton and remove him from office. Several attempts were made to kill him, but he managed to outwit his would-be murderers.

Finally under his constant diligence for the welfare of the state as a whole, Arkansas began to know a measure of peace and to achieve a measure of prosperity. As soon as it was possible, the Governor turned his attention to the schools. Education had never held a high priority in Arkansas and all of the schools had closed down for the duration of the war. It seems possible that the new State Legislature of 1868 had unwittingly voted for the adoption of an entirely new system of free schools. Spurred on by Clayton the next two years saw many new school houses built, and the school structure of the state revised, while school finances underwent a complete reorganization. This was accomplished in spite of the continual sniping by the Democratic press together with that section of the populace which being illiterate desired to preserve the status quo for the entire state.

The United States Government had set aside funds for the establishing of colleges in those states which could or would produce matching funds. Clayton greatly desired a state college for Arkansas and in spite of all the opposition his foes could bring forth, the requirements were finally met and a college was organized at Fayetteville.

While the legislative honeymoon was still on in 1868, the State Legislature also passed a bill, well protected by safeguards, which enabled the state to loan credit to railroads for construction purposes. At the time the bill was passed forty-five miles of dilapidated track was all the railroad Arkansas could claim. The first railroad bonds were issued in 1869 and by the autumn of 1873, there were three hundred miles of new track in operation. By 1874 the total mileage had been raised to four hundred forty-five miles, or sixty-three percent of all the railroad mileage in the state. Railroads meant prosperity for the whole state (but the opposition seemed unable to let the Clayton administration have any credit for the increased welfare of the state). From the time he first took office, every possible attempt, including murder, had been made to oust Clayton from the governor's chair.

In 1871, the Lieutenant Governor, a man named Johnson who lived in Huntsville, decided to add his efforts to those of others who were trying to get rid of Clayton. It became necessary for Clayton to go to New York City on business having to do with the state debt. Immediately his foes claimed he had left the state without due notification to the Lieutenant Governor. Travel between Little Rock and Huntsville being quite slow, by the time Johnson got the message and got to Little Rock, the governor had returned from New York City and was firmly seated in his official chair. When this attempt to eliminate the governor failed, impeachment proceedings were instituted in the hope the trial would drag on and on while the Lieutenant Governor took his place. It not being in Powell Clayton's nature to let anything drag on for any length of time, he soon rallied his friends and after relatively short proceedings the impeachment was vacated for lack of evidence. These proceedings were not entirely without a bright spot, for during the trial certain facts involving the state indebtedness were brought to light, facts which greatly strengthened Powell Clayton in his own party, so in March of 1871 he had no trouble being nominated for and elected to the Senate of the United States.

Now a charge of election fraud was made and the Democrats, being determined to discredit Powell Clayton so he would not be seated, were able to postpone hearings and obscure testimony so that a year went by before he took his seat as a Senator from Arkansas. Even then he felt (so he says) a marked coolness toward him as the lies told by his enemies were made so plausible.

At the conclusion of one term, Clayton had had enough. During the hectic days of the use of the State Militia his brother had been shot and killed, and he had missed being a target so many times a peaceful interlude seemed indicated. He could not stay out of affairs for long and assumed the presidency of the Little Rock, Mississippi and Texas Railroad.

While governor, he had (no doubt) assisted in the consolidation of the Little Rock, Pine Bluff and New Orleans with the Mississippi, Ouachita and Red River Railroad. This position could not have lasted too long for the record shows he was in Eureka Springs in 1880 associating himself with other men of wealth who were interested in developing the resort. It is possible he was attracted to the Northwest part of the state since it had always been peaceful and law abiding, even during the worst trouble in other parts of Arkansas. Two years later he brought his wife and family there to live, building a small hotel called the "Clayton House," where he and his family took up residence.

This establishment was located on Main Street not far from the road leading to Magnetic Spring, and the beautifully landscaped grounds came to be referred to as "The Park" by early residents. Beauty and a sense of order were always apparent in any endeavor Powell Clayton set his mind to. In later years, under other management, the name of the hotel was changed to Ponce de Leon and sometimes later was changed to the St. Charles House.

Another prominent member of the Eureka Springs Improvement Company was Richard C. Kerens of St. Louis. Born in Ireland and brought to America as an infant, he grew up to become one of the builders of America's railroads during the age of great railroad builders. After 1865 the railroads entered a period of rapid growth and Kerens was connected with railroad building in West Virginia and other parts of the East. Like General Clayton, he served his country in the Union Army and became an active member of the Republican Party. In the 1870's he began to take a prominent part in Missouri politics. Kerens was a man who enjoyed gracious living and was often entertained at the Clayton House in Eureka Springs by his friend, General Clayton. After the Crescent Hotel became a reality, his family spent many pleasant months there and at one time he intended to build a home near the hotel. Being of a deeply religious and sentimental nature, he built a Memorial Chapel for his family on the spot where he last saw his mother alive. Later the chapel became a part of St. Elizabeth's Roman Catholic Church.

It was only natural that these two men of such similar backgrounds should decide to combine their talents and capital to build a railroad to Eureka Springs, which they felt could become America's greatest health and pleasure resort. Their business partnership proved to be a long lasting one and their political connections were also rewarded in later years. When William McKinley sought the presidency of the United States, both men actively campaigned and after his election, McKinley appointed Kerens as Ambassador to Austria and Clayton was sent to serve his country as Ambassador to Mexico.

Another of the men originally associated with Powell Clayton in the Eureka Springs Improvement Company was Logan H. Roots. Well-born, well educated and trained from his earliest youth to accomplish what he attempted, Logan H. Roots early became a power in the state of his adoption. He was born in Perry County, Illinois, of a family of English origin who came to America in 1636. His paternal great-great grandfather was a Baptist clergyman who inherited what was considered a large estate, sufficient to enable him to devote his life to the work of the church without financial worries. His Grandfather was prominent in Illinois politics and his own father was able to afford young Roots the advantages of a college education. He matriculated at the University of Illinois where his business talent was soon manifest as he paid nearly all of his college expenses by buying produce in central Illinois, shipping it to the southern part of the state and selling it at a good profit. He was also an excellent student as he completed the course of study a year ahead of his class and put in the time as Principal of the Duquoin, Illinois, High School, returning to graduate, as valedictorian, with his class in 1862.

As soon as he graduated he enlisted in the Eighty-First Illinois Volunteer Infantry. Due to his business qualifications he was appointed quartermaster of the regiment and shortly afterward was transferred to duty in the Commissary Department of the Army. When Sherman "marched to the sea" Roots was in charge of all provisioning for those troops. He continued to serve in the Commissary Department until the close of the war.

When hostilities ended Colonel Roots was in Arkansas where he was stationed with the Federal forces. He soon purchased land near DeValls Bluff, Prairie County, and set up as a plantation owner. A few years later he was appointed Collector of Internal Revenue and held that office until he was elected to the Congress of the United States, one of the youngest men to ever serve in that august body.

In 1872 Colonel Roots purchased a controlling interest in the Merchants National Bank of Little Rock where as president he was prominent in banking circles until 1890, when he sold his interest and retired as president. It was once said of Roots,

> "Every enterprise which he considered to be for the prosperity of the State found him as a friend."

He also began the movement which resulted in the Logan H. Roots Military Post.

When Roots became acquainted with Powell Clayton is not recorded; however, both were staunch Republicans and their meeting was inevitable.

The fourth member of the officer group of the railroad was Arthur Hoyt Foote. He was born in Wisconsin of a family sufficiently prominent for his father to become a Flag Officer in the Federal forces, where his work in capturing Island No. 10 in the Mississippi on April 7, 1860, helped to open the river as far south as Memphis. Young Foote was about four years old at this time. After the War his family apparently moved to Erie, Pennsylvania, as Arthur Jr. attended school there, later going to work for the Marine National Bank of Erie in 1873. In 1878 he moved to St. Louis where in the course of his employment there he became affiliated with the St. Louis, Salem and Little Rock Railroad. When trains began to run over the new tracks to Eureka Springs he joined the organization as auditor and passenger agent. He became secretary of the new railroad in 1888. He also was secretary of the Eureka Springs Improvement Company from 1889 to 1891, as well as manager of the Crescent Hotel. He returned to St. Louis in 1892 and ended his association with those who had been instrumental in the promotion of the various affairs with which he had assisted.

The boom was really on when such men as these, together with those of lesser stature, started working for the future of Eureka Springs. On June 26, 1880, the Eureka Springs Railroad Company of Arkansas, a newly formed organization, received a charter. This company planned a railroad line to connect with the Frisco Railroad in Missouri, which would then make possible the establishment of a summer resort in Eureka Springs.

At that time the nearest railway connection was Pierce City, fifty-five miles to the north in Missouri. Visitors desiring to come to Eureka Springs by rail must necessarily endure a nine hour ride by stage coach after leaving the train at that point. To say the least this was discouraging, particularly to persons already in ill health.

The Frisco was rapidly completing its proposed route from St. Louis to points in Texas and had reached the town of Seligman, Missouri, by November of that year. Seligman, named for an important New York banking house—Seligman and Sons—was located near the state line about twenty miles from Eureka Springs and was connected to this new town by a winding wagon road. From Seligman train passengers still had a four- or five-hour trip by stage before reaching the resort.

It was this situation which the Eureka Springs Railroad Company hoped to correct by building a railroad from Seligman to Eureka Springs.

Approximately half of the proposed route between the two towns was in Missouri. This necessitated a separate charter which in three months time was secured under the name of "Missouri and Arkansas Railroad Company of Missouri." Powell Clayton was elected president of both the Arkansas and Missouri portions of the line. Clayton was not a stranger to methods of railroad organization. For a short time after his return from the Senate he was President of the Little Rock, Mississippi and Texas Railroad.

On February 27, 1882, the two proposed railroads were consolidated. Financial arrangements being well in hand other arrangements quickly followed pertaining to the use of Frisco rolling stock and the interchange of passengers and freight. At the time, Richard C. Kerens was elected president of the company, while Clayton became vice-president and general manager, so that it was his function to get the railroad built and in operation. The finances of the company now amounted to one and a half million dollars and Logan Roots was elected treasurer.

Surveying began in May of 1882 and proceeded swiftly. A contract for the construction of the eighteen mile line was awarded to the Jones and Cowen Company of Fort Worth, Texas, on their bid of $200,000.00. The crossing over the White River was located and the Delaware Bridge Company was given a contract to construct the two hundred fifty foot bridge. The actual work of clearing the land, blasting and earth moving began in August.

The route was to follow a narrow mountain valley along Butler Creek to the White River, dropping from an elevation over fifteen hundred feet at Seligman to about nine hundred feet at the bridge. Following the course of Leatherwood Creek upstream, the elevation rose again to one thousand one hundred fifty feet at the proposed site of the Eureka Springs depot.

Early the following year the line was completed and trains began to run as soon as the prevailing weather conditions allowed. A local newspaper, *the Eureka Springs Republican,* in the issue for January 25, 1883, reported:

> "Beginning February 1st regular through trains with Pullman parlor and sleeping cars will run daily to Eureka Springs. This convenience is not enjoyed by any other resort in the Southwest."

Two days later, the officers of the company, together with a number of the principal stockholders, gathered in the new passenger depot at Eureka Springs to celebrate the opening of the line. It was a gala event with many of the townspeople crowding into the spacious frame depot building to hear the speeches and also to shake the hands of the men who had brought the railroad to Eureka Springs.

It was the hope of those who were large investors in the new railroad to extend the line, of which the Seligman-Eureka Springs portion was the first part built, eastward at least as far as Harrison, forty-five miles away. Unfortunately, at this time Charles Rogers, a Frisco vice-president and close friend to Powell Clayton, died. Rogers had been a staunch supporter of the proposed extension, but other officials of the Frisco wanted no part of the extended line. This situation continued until 1892, when Clayton and Kerens learned of the rich yields of zinc and lead being mined in Boone and Newton Counties. They thought that a railroad would be financially successful, if built to ship ore from the mining areas. Patience with the Frisco being exhausted they went to St. Louis to try to promote interest among the capitalists there.

This promotion was successful and in 1900 the railroad was extended to Harrison by a new corporation, The St. Louis and North Arkansas Railroad Company. This company purchased the Eureka Springs Railroad, which had been a success from its opening to the end of the century. Directors of the St. Louis and North Arkansas Railroad Company now included more Eureka Springs citizens, the two most prominent being George West and C. W. Watkins, a former mayor.

This railroad, later known as the Missouri and North Arkansas, was to know a time of almost constant trouble; but for the time being, the residents of Eureka Springs were well pleased with it. Six trains a day made it possible for passengers to the resort to be connected with the population centers of the United States. Now those ill in health, as well as the world-weary, thronged to Eureka Springs, exactly as Powell Clayton and his far-seeing associates had predicted.

CHAPTER IV

THE YEARS OF GRANDEUR:

1885 - 1900

With the completion of the railroad bringing prospects of such a promising future the permanent development of the town began in earnest. Durable buildings with some beauty of design began to replace the hastily constructed and now shabby shacks. It soon became apparent that along with proper buildings, good streets and sidewalks, a central water supply and sanitation system, public transportation and better lighting and other civic improvements were now necessary. These would be followed by electric lights and that new-fangled invention, the telephone.

The Eureka Springs Improvement Company soon had a very large capital investment in Eureka Springs. Listed among its assets were several hundred acres of land within the corporate limits of the city secured through the townsite settlement.

Within a remarkably short time, the organization opened the limestone quarries north of the townsite, began operation of a gas plant, built the beautiful Crescent Hotel and put down street railway tracks through the main business and residential areas.

The syndicate-owned limestone quarries and mills were north of the city on the south side of the Narrows, the railroad crossing near the Beaver Community. At this point, the

White River is lined with towering limestone bluffs. An opening through this mass of solid rock had been blasted for the railroad to the bridge crossing the river. The quarries were located just a short distance away and at this point the syndicate cut and marketed a beautiful cream colored close-grained magnesium limestone. This is not only very durable but also very beautiful stone for buildings and monuments. Stone from these quarries was used in the Crescent Hotel, Presbyterian Church, the railroad depot and shops, the Ellis-Rosewater building, Palace Bath House, the Basin Park Hotel and numerous other important structures. Large amounts were also shipped by rail to various parts of the mid-west. Through his numerous Washington contacts, Clayton was able to secure contracts with the government of the United States to provide the stone for many public buildings in St. Louis, Kansas City and Springfield, Missouri. It is a matter of record that Federal Buildings in Harrison and Fort Smith, Arkansas, are built of this fine material, as well as the bridge across the Arkansas River at Fort Smith. The stone quarries proved to be a very successful operation for the Improvement Company, and continued so for many years until they passed into the hands of new owners.

The gas works, another operation of the Improvement Company, was granted a franchise under the name of "The Interstate Gas Company" by the City in December of 1885, and immediately began to lay gas mains all over town. The official ordinance passed by the City as regarding the franchise stated that the Company should erect a gas works of sufficient capacity to furnish at all times the amount of gas needed for use in the city and that the product must be equal to any standard gas of fourteen candlepower then being made and equal

> "to any coal gas now being made in Chicago or St. Louis, which shall contain no sulphur, no carbonic-oxide deposit or soot, or other impurities, but shall give a clear steady white light while burning."

The ordinance also set the amount which could be charged private consumers at $3.00 per one thousand cubic feet.

Less than a year later, fifty-six gas street lamps were placed on the main streets with special lighting at the Basin Spring Reservation. There the lights were placed in "the shape of a circle, with twelve lights equal to five gas lamps."

Again quoting from the ordinance framed by Mayor Archimedes Davis and the Council, the lighting and extinguishing of the street lamps was to be done

> "according to the regular moon tables, one-half hour after sunset and extinguished one-half hour after moon rise; lighted one-half hour before the moon sets each day of the year."

Lighting and extinguishing was one of the official duties of the night policeman.

In May of 1886, a reporter from the *Arkansas Gazette* visited the city for the purpose of collecting information for a feature article in that publication. He praised the beauty of Eureka Springs, but dwelt particularly on her "splendid gas-lighted streets."

A company known as the "Eureka Springs Gas Light Company" secured a franchise from the City in November of 1889, granting the right to establish an electrical system. The company began operation within a short time, but the electric lights were pronounced a dead failure by the local newspaper. The following year, the City Council repealed the franchise and electrical service was terminated for the time being.

In May of 1891, a franchise was granted to the Eureka Springs Electric Light and Street Railway Company giving them the right to construct a power plant and to furnish electricity to private consumers, also to provide street lighting and to operate a street railway. This company, which was connected with Powell Clayton's Eureka Springs Improvement Company, built a beautiful stone building to house the power plant near the railroad depot on North Main Street. Coal-fired steam boilers powered the generators which furnished the city with electricity. Private consumers enjoyed the new service, but several years were to pass before the electric street railway or the street lighting system came into actual use.

In the meantime, the City Council was working hard to supply other needs of the townspeople. The aldermen met on a weekly basis to administer civic affairs, but called meetings occurred almost daily. The various aldermen elected to the Council worked hard and devoted a great deal of time to organizing matters for the public good.

A Board of Health was appointed, the original members being Doctors Slaughter, Reese and Owen. It was their job to see to those matters affecting the health of the populace. The Board, with various succeeding members, served effectively and was instrumental in bringing about official protection of the principal spring reservations so that the water might remain pure and free from any kind of pollution. By official proclamation the duties of the Board were outlined as follows:

> "to secure the city and the inhabitants thereof from the evils of contagious, malignant and infectious diseases."

The work of this group must at times have seemed an uphill battle, people being what they are. In those days of no proper waste disposal systems, keeping spring water free from pollution was difficult, to say the least.

Credit must be given to these men who looked after the affairs of public health with such competence for the miraculous fact that Eureka Springs was almost free of infectious diseases. Throughout the years when it was so crowded with persons having such a variety of ailments the community suffered only one epidemic, that being measles, during the winter of 1880-1881.

When in the late 1880's the City established a Board of Public Affairs and later Boards of Improvement to effect water and sewage systems, prominent local physicians served with fellow townsmen in these endeavors. Doctors C. F. Ellis and J. B. Bolton were two of those most interested in securing an adequate supply of water for use in the homes of the citizenry, as well as an efficient sanitary waste disposal system.

Through the concentrated effort of many men, great strides were being made toward providing all of the facilities needed in a city of several thousand inhabitants. However, it seemed that for every progressive step forward, the City Administration was forced to take two steps backward in the area of finances.

For years, bills for the ordinary operating expenses of the city government had been paid by issuing "scrip". That is, city warrants were written without sufficient funds in the treasury to cover the amounts stipulated. These were given in payment of debts with the understanding that the holder might redeem them at some future date, when presumably funds would be available. Thousands of dollars worth of "scrip" were issued in the fifteen years following the chartering of Eureka Springs. Many business men sold or traded the "scrip" they held for varying amounts to others who were willing to wait for the time when the warrants would be worth dollar for dollar, thereby realizing a handsome profit from the transaction.

The debts incurred by the City during the years of the townsite litigation were crippling the plans for future development. It had been necessary for the City Council to borrow funds from private citizens with which to pay attorneys representing the townsite claimants in Washington. Adding to the accumulation of debts were the salaries paid to the mayor and aldermen. At that time the mayor received $600 per year and each alderman approximately half this sum. There being ten aldermen compensated at the rate of $3 per meeting, this added a substantial amount of indebtedness each year. In addition, a city clerk was paid $1,800 a year and the health officer received $1,000 yearly salary. These amounts, in the face of pressing needs such as good streets, an adequate water supply, a sanitation system and police and fire protection, seemed almost impossible to obtain.

Beginning in 1890, the City Council levied by ordinance a tax of five mills on all real and personal property "for the purpose of defraying the expense of city government." Although the population of the city was estimated at from 10,000 to 12,000 persons, only about 4,000 were legal residents and, therefore, taxable. The official Federal census for 1880 showed 3,984 citizens, and ten years later in 1890, only 3,706 were recorded. So, the City government faced a paradoxical situation; that of having to provide the necessary facilities for a city of many thousands with an income received from taxing only about one-third of the citizenry. The several thousand other persons lived in Eureka Springs for from three to six months at a time, while maintaining their legal residence in other states and cities. Whole families came; the well-to-do brought their numerous colored servants and set up housekeeping for the summer or winter months in rented cottages or in one of the numerous boarding houses. The necessary civic comforts of life must be provided for the duration of their stay in return for the few dollars rental paid to the landlord. The five mill property tax levied yearly after 1890 was all that the State of Arkansas allowed the Cities to levy for municipal purposes. It did not represent a great deal in actual funds but it was a help, and slowly the City began to catch up with itself in regard to finances.

One of the most pressing needs in a city of several thousand inhabitants and with such a large transient population was adequate policing. The town had elected a marshal yearly from 1880 through 1882. William Kimbrough, John Carroll, and J. J. Kirk had all served in this capacity. Then, Joe F. Ivey was appointed chief of police by the Council, although a municipal police department was not formally organized by ordinance until March of 1887. The marshals, and later the chief of police, had as many as three deputies or officers each, although the City was hard put to pay their salaries. In those early days, the work of policing the town was indeed difficult with the crowded conditions then prevailing, and having to enforce ordinances which prohibited everything from washing one's face, feet or clothing in the public springs to racing horses through the city streets.

The new town achieved effective law enforcement, but a much graver danger threatened the populace every hour of the day and night. The threat of fire was ever present in the busy crowded streets lined on both sides with house after house constructed of dry kindling wood. Up and down every hillside crowded the small flimsy dwellings.

In May of 1880, the City Council passed Ordinance No. 42, which outlined the duties and powers of a fire warden, and appointed Henry Marshall to the job. He immediately began to organize volunteers and also to purchase some primitive equipment. There is no complete record of this organization in existence, though the men of the "Bucket Brigade" evidently served well in the face of many obstacles. The local newspapers, in reporting fires either large or small, ever praised these men for their quickness and good work.

During the early days of the town no disastrous fires occurred. When Kalklosch wrote of it in 1881 he says:

> "During the early history, Eureka Springs had no fire of any consequence and only one serious windstorm which did minor damage."

Two years later on a cold November night in 1883, fire reportedly consumed seventy-five homes and business houses in a five acre area. This fire began at the foot of Mountain Street and burned up both sides of that street and Eureka Street. The origin was considered to be arson, as it began in a business building which was the object of a bitter dispute between a father and son. The wooden shacks clustered together on the hillside caught fire one ofter another and so many were burned that damages amounted to an estimated $35,000.00. The local bucket brigade arrived and made gallant efforts to contain the fire, but could do little to help with the poor equipment and the small number of volunteers on hand.

A second fire, even more deadly in its destructive force, swept through a part of the town in 1888. This conflagration began at the Hancock House near the Sweet Spring on Spring Street. That small hotel was burned to the ground as well as every building on Spring Street from there south to the Perry House adjacent to the Basin Spring Reservation. A few years later that beautiful hotel was to follow its fellow hotels in flames.

The ashes cooled quickly in the cold winter weather and soon the people were digging in, cleaning and commencing to rebuild. The citizens showed both faith and courage in rebuilding so soon after their loss, but wisdom also, for most of the new structures were of the native stone which proved to have greater resistance to the ravages of fire.

The next destructive fire was that of the sixty-room Perry House in 1890. This well known hotel stood where the Basin Park Hotel was constructed several years later. The fire swept across Spring Street and down the hill, burning the original Grand Central Hotel and every building between the two. The fire spread from one building to another until everything in the area south to the junction of Main and Spring Streets was consumed. The Grand Central Hotel, a frame building, originally called Conner's Hotel, and a popular stopping place on the stagecoach line from Pierce City, was soon rebuilt of brick and masonry. Other property owners took heart and rebuilt homes and businesses.

Later, a fourth fire, occuring about 1892, burned the intersection of Main and Spring Streets south to the junction of South and West Main Streets, near the Califf Spring. This fire destroyed two hotels, the Hughes House and the Western Hotel, along with several business establishments.

With the near completion of a water system in 1894, the citizens banded together in an effort to purchase apparatus for a fire company. By December of that year $1,000 had been subscribed to a fund to be used for the purchase of hose. The water system began operating on April 5, 1895, and eighteen days later the first company of the Municipal Fire Department was organized.

Two years later a special report in the *Daily Times Echo* described the fire department as consisting of a "Chief, assistant chief and three hose companies of twenty members each, all well-trained men." The three hose houses were located in different parts of the city, so that a quick response to an alarm of fire would be possible.

Many of the fine hotels which served the early visitors to Eureka Springs went up in flames, and when others took their place they were larger and of a more permanent type of building. By the late 1890's the number of visitors coming to the resort had noticably slackened off and the newer, larger buildings were adequate to entertain the traveling public. So, it is only in the accounts of the fabulous crowds which once converged at the Springs that we learn of the many fine hotels which burned and were never replaced.

The municipal water system, which was so important to the town for fire protection and good public health, came into being through a period of about five years time. During the summer of 1889, a number of citizens petitioned the City Administration to do "something" about securing an adequate supply of water. On September 6th of that year, the council passed an ordinance creating improvement districts which encompassed the entire corporate limits. Two districts, each taking in about half of the area, were for water improvements; the others for the purpose of developing a sanitary waste disposal system.

The resident property owners within these specified areas approved the measure by their vote, which empowered the City to levy a tax against them for the purpose of paying off the ad valorem bonds with which the project was to be financed. An assessment of 7.85 percent on the dollar of property value was agreed upon for these improvements.

In January of 1890, the council appointed a Board of Commissioners for Water Districts No. 3 and No. 4. The Board was to oversee the entire operation, including the responsibility for collecting the special taxes on property, planning the new water systems, considering bids, awarding contracts and all other pertinent details.

The Board members elected Powell Clayton as their president, with Dr. C. F. Ellis as secretary. W. M. Duncan became treasurer of all moneys collected and paid out for all improvement districts, both water and sewer. The other members were W. R. Baker, Z. P. Freeman, D. F. Putnam and J. Congdon. The Board was to serve for the duration of the project and vacancies were created only by the death or resignation of a member. J. Congdon died within three months after the formation of this Board, and John Carroll, that intrepid town builder who now reappeared upon the scene, was appointed to fill the vacancy. Surely, it would be possible for such a body of men to accomplish great things for their fellow townsmen.

According to the complete account of their actions, neatly written by Dr. C. F. Ellis and filed in the City archives, the Board began to meet immediately and frequently. Their first action was to employ a tax collector, who began his duties at once.

A number of men served in this capacity over the next few years, some for only short periods of time, but the money came in steadily. There were only a few instances when the Board of Commissioners had to resort to the courts for non-payment of an assessment.

The Board employed John W. Riley as city engineer. His duties included locating a feasible source for the water supply, planning the overall system and submitting estimates as to the probable cost. First estimates submitted were $54,536.00 for the water system and $51,500.00 for sewage improvements. It was soon found, however, that these estimates were most unrealistic, particularly the one for the proposed water system.

The Board continued planning, while the amount of taxes collected grew larger, but it was not until March of 1893 that anything of major importance to the public occurred. Then the City Council set aside by ordinance five acres of land in Section 16, part of which was still unclaimed public land, the rest having been purchased by the city for the waterworks site. This location took in two mountain sides and the narrow hollow between, and was a short distance southwest of the corporate limits. Several springs were within this area, the largest flow of water coming from what was called Sycamore Spring, located in the very center of the proposed reservoir. A short distance away was Saucer Spring and at the head of the hollow was Arsenic Spring, so called, not because of any chemical content, but for the peculiar taste and color of the water. On the top of the mountain just above the spring was the large saw mill originally operated by Benjamin Woodruff.

Old-timers claimed that the water of Arsenic Spring was slightly colored and flavored by the oak sawdust of Woodruff's mill. Nevertheless, the entire site offered the largest and most consistent supply of pure spring water available in the area.

In April of 1894, the Board of Commissioners recommended to the Council and Mayor Z. P. Freeman that Water Improvement Districts No. 3 and No. 4 could only legally lay mains and install fire plugs. It was necessary to establish a new district which would take in the entire city, and which could then build the reservoir, water works, standpipe and other necessary items. This was accomplished by an official ordinance creating Consolidated Improvement District No. 5.

A month later, the board contracted with the Ralph E. Brownell Company of Chicago for the complete construction of the water system and issued the ad valorem bonds with which to finance it.

Brownell's contract specified the construction of a masonry dam and sluiceway across the hollow just below Sycamore Spring. The dam was to be twelve feet high and approximately one hundred fifty feet in length. A stone boiler house large enough to accomodate two boilers fifty-six inches in diameter and sixteen feet high was to be built. Two steam-powered pumps capable of furnishing 500 gallons of water per minute at a height of four hundred feet, using eight hundred pound steam, were to be installed. Brownell was also to construct a standpipe of iron, twelve feet in diameter and one hundred feet in height, located at the top of the mountain and connected to the pumping station with a ten inch water main. He was also to install six-inch and eight-inch mains all over the city and provide forty-three hydrants. All this work was to be accomplished for a total cost of $75,000.00. The contract was quickly signed and work began immediately, to be completed within a year's time.

The stonework in the dam was as beautiful as any seen in the buildings of downtown Eureka Springs and the gleaming new standpipe towered over West Mountain. The tank had a capacity of 83,000 gallons and the water stored there had been pumped approximately 1,000 feet straight up the mountain side. The area around the new standpipe was landscaped to some extent and soon became a popular picnic spot for local people, as the standpipe also became a landmark which could be seen all over the surrounding countryside.

The pumps which carried the water to the mountaintop were steam pumps, operated by engines fired with wood. Once the system was in operation, the board found it necessary to purchase wood in large quantities, several hundred cords at a time. By official city ordinance this wood was required to be a mixture of black oak, black jack and hickory in equal amounts. After a few years, the engines were changed to coal and required a car load every two weeks.

The Brownell Company laid a network of six-inch and eight-inch water mains throughout the city and private consumers were connected to the system as quickly as possible.

The Board of Commissioners proposed water rates, which were approved by the Council and Mayor W. R. Hardesty. The consumer had the choice of paying a set annual fee according to certain ratings or to have a water meter installed, then to pay for the water usage at the graduated rate of 5c per one hundred gallons (using one hundred to two hundred gallons daily) down to 2c per hundred, using 4,000 to 10,000 gallons daily.

A private dwelling of four rooms or less, not using the meter, was required to pay $4.00 yearly plus 75c extra for each additional room. If a "bathing tub" was located on the premises, an extra fee of $3.00 was collected. In the business district, offices of professional men, where one washbasin was installed, were charged $5.00 per year. A dentist or barber could get by with only a $6.00 annual fee, provided he too had only one washbasin. Hotels and rooming houses paid $1.00 per room per month, plus an extra $4.00 for each watercloset installed.

Livery stables which offered their clientele the service of washing buggies and carriages were charged $1.50 per horse stall per annum.

With city water now available the municipal fire department was able to furnish better fire protection. If the party whose house was burning already used city water in the dwelling or on the premises there was no charge, otherwise a charge was made for the use of the city water used to extinguish fires.

The beautiful new reservoir was referred to as a "pond" by the local press who declared that "pond water" by any other name was still unfit for human consumption. The Board of Commissioners stood by its accomplishment and its members who were medical men testified to the purity and safety of the city water. As the majority of the people continued to drink water carried from the springs, the complaints faded away and the new water system sufficed for several years for other household uses.

The sewage disposal system instigated in 1890 was also completed about this time. Apparently the Board of Commissioners of the Sewer Improvement Districts hired local workmen to lay the pipe after City Engineer Riley completed a plan locating a network of mains throughout the corporate limits. Private lines were connected to this system which terminated approximately one half-mile north of the city limits. The outlet at that point emptied into a stream and the effluent was carried away down the gorge. It was to be ten years before a septic tank and sewage disposal plant would be built.

Through the foresight and sound engineering principles adopted by the Board of Commissioners of the Improvement District, the water and sewer systems they planned and installed proved adequate for many years. At no time during the years was there ever a major epidemic and only one threatened water shortage. This shortage occurred in a year of practically no rainfall, which even the best of engineering could not prevent.

About 1900, local businessman and president of the Board of Trade, B. J. Rosewater, in addressing a meeting of citizens praised those leaders who had

> "found a way to provide sewer and water facilities in spite of the fact that the city suffered from lack of money and obstructed credit,"

because the laws of the State of Arkansas forbade the issuance of bonds for such purposes or the levying of more than a five mill property tax.

Through the first twenty years of the existence of the town the streets remained unpaved, although much effort was put into encouraging property owners to build sidewalks and gutters in front of their business establishments.

The streets were very poor indeed, as Main (Mud) and Spring Streets were merely trails along the hillsides. The street work had been done originally by volunteers and the Council had soon passed an ordinance stating that all able-bodied men who had lived in the town more than ten days must contribute a certain amount of manual labor to street improvement. This ordinance was at best difficult to enforce and proved ineffective toward providing better streets. The situation went on for many years, not without numerous protests from the local press about the terrible condition of the city's streets, either oozing mud or clouded with choking dust according to the season of the year.

In 1887, the Council and Mayor F. M. Lawson succeeded in passing an ordinance regulating the building of board sidewalks throughout the city. It was required that each place of business build such a walk connecting with his neighbors on either side. All walks were to be six feet wide and provided with a railing in dangerous spots where the surface was high above the ground on the off-street side.

Early in 1892, the Board of Public Affairs was created by ordinance, with a prominent citizen being appointed as chairman. Naturally, Powell Clayton chaired this group of distinguished citizens interested in the general welfare of the community. To this group fell the responsibility for planning improvements, such as the proper placement of dwellings and business establishments, developing streets and sidewalks, building retaining walls and approving the purchase of material and equipment for use in these projects. A. R. Sayles, Z. P. Freeman, Dr. C. F. Ellis, L. P. Badger and B. F. Putnam were members of this Board and served in this capacity for a number of years.

In June of 1892, Mayor W. H. D. Brown and the Council set up an Improvement District encompassing the principal sections of the town for the purpose of grading, widening and paving the streets. The Board of Public Affairs then undertook the task of seeing that the plans were carried out. Men were hired to work the streets and some improvement was made, although the streets remained unpaved until many years later. The Board was very strict, however, on property owners, seeing to it that sidewalks were completed as quickly as possible in the business district.

During the summer months, the streets were sprinkled daily to keep down the dust. This was accomplished by hauling a tank of water mounted on a mule drawn wagon through the streets each morning to wet down the hard packed earth. This method was at least partially effective during the dry summer months, but nothing could be done about the mud caused by winter and spring rains.

Complaints about the condition of the streets began to die down as soon as the mule drawn street car line was completed from the depot through the busiest part of town, as most folks would rather ride the cars than walk. Besides, no one really could complain about a small inconvenience such as poor streets in a city which had so many wonderful things to offer visitors, as well as the other conveniences enjoyed by the townspeople.

Public transportation in Eureka Springs was first provided by privately owned horse drawn vehicles, such as the tally-ho. These rigs were present to meet incoming trains and also carried passengers to and from various points in the city for a small fee. From 1891 until 1899 this manner of transportation was replaced by mule-drawn street cars. These cars operated on a line of tracks from the depot up the long grade called Hillside Avenue, where it intersected with the main line of tracks, which began near the Basin Spring and followed the wide, pleasant street called the Boulevard to the Assembly Grounds and the Crescent Hotel, ending at the top of Mountain Street. This business was owned by the Eureka Springs Improvement Company and proved to be very popular with visitors to the city.

In 1899 the city was introduced to electric cars on this line, a franchise having been granted to the Eureka Springs Electric and Street Railway Company, another part of the Eureka Springs Improvement Company.

The new electric cars had a seating capacity of approximately seventy-five persons and ran from 8:00 A.M. until late at night. The conductors were paid the munificent sum of $1.00 per day for their services.

It was often said that in no other city on the continent could there be found a street railway that led such a winding course around and up the mountainside as did the one in Eureka Springs.

The *Daily Times Echo* once printed the information that from the railroad depot up the mountainside to the intersection with the main line at the Crescent Spring, a little more than one-half mile, the ascent amounted to one hundred and one feet, or a little more than two hundred feet to the mile. On the mainline from Main Street up to the intersection of Mountain and Owen Streets, there was an ascent of sixty-seven feet with the terrain being fairly level from that point on around Spring Street and the Boulevard to the car barns just beyond the Grotto Spring.

> "Here commences a most charming and tortuous ascent and a feat of engineering that has challenged the admiration of many scientific men who have visited the resort. The roadbed had to be graded around the mountainside at angles that would seem ridiculous were they anywhere else than in this unusual mountain range and one car will be only a few yards from and above the other, and apparently moving in the same direction, when actually they are headed toward opposite ends of the line."
>
> "These ends, however, are only about three hundred yards apart, one end resting in the valley while the other is at the mountains peak."

From the location of the car barns to the Crescent Hotel there was an ascent of approximately one hundred forty feet.

The main line of the railway was 2.16 miles long and the depot line 0.53 miles. This total plus the siding made three miles of track.

The equipment and service of the street railway was considered to be better than that to be found in cities much larger than Eureka Springs, and the citizens were indeed proud of the entire system.

Several years before the electric street railway became a reality, the resort excelled many of its sister communities by acquiring another modern convenience—that new-fangled invention, the telephone.

The first telephone system installed in Carroll County went into operation at Eureka Springs in May of 1895. Alexander Graham Bell had developed this miraculous instrument of communication about fifteen years earlier, but only a few of the larger cities in the state preceded Eureka Springs in making use of it. The new exchange was known as the J. W. Hill Telephone Company, with offices located on Hillside Avenue. The switchboard had space for only one operator and was connected to twenty-five telephones. The original operator was Miss Mae Starr, who held the position for many years. There was only one lineman, Sam Richardson, and to him fell the responsibility of attempting to set poles and keep wires in operation up and down the rocky hillsides.

The owner, J. W. Hill, also operated the Crescent Livery Stables, which furnished riding horses and vehicles daily for the guests at the many hotels about the city. It is said that Hill had once seen a telephone in operation, presumably while attending the World's Fair in Chicago in 1893, and decided that such an instrument would be very useful to his livery stable. Use of this system of communication between his business and the hotels would save sending an employee around every day to find out how many horses each would be needing, at what time, and so on. For this reason the first switchboard installed took care of only those calls made to the livery stable, but very soon several local citizens became interested. They persuaded Hill and his associates to obtain a franchise from the City, so that the whole community could be served. This was quickly accomplished and a substantial number of subscribers were soon making use of this innovation in communication.

The *Daily Times Echo* in an issue during August of 1898 reported the completion of direct telephone service between Eureka Springs and the world via Fayetteville and Monett. The community had taken another giant step forward in providing for the needs of both citizens and visitors alike.

Throughout the last decade of the nineteenth century, both the daily and weekly papers devoted column after column to praising the joys of living in Eureka Springs, together with the unsurpassed beauty of the surroundings, both natural and man made.

Among the most beautiful and unique features of the landscape, then as now, were the miles upon miles of stone walls holding the hillsides at bay above private dwellings and commercial buildings alike. Everywhere it was possible to dig or blast a narrow shelf on the side of the mountain, people built homes. The stone walls held the earth and kept it from washing or crumbling. They also provided enclosures which were filled with good soil for level lawns and garden spots, and all along the meandering footpaths walls began to appear as trails were widened and filled to make proper streets.

The majority of these walls were put up in the late 1880's and early 1890's, utilizing stone brought from the Beaver quarries. They were constructed of cut stone blocks of varying sizes laid without cement, this being done by skilled local workmen under the direction of the Board of Public Affairs. Contracts are on record for various sections of walls within the city and much of the work was done by the Waldrip Brothers, talented stone masons. In some instances, arched stone bridges were built crossing the stream which flowed along Main Street joining the walls on either side.

The building of walls went on steadily on both East and West Mountain, so that by the turn of the century the newspapers reported: "Miles of retaining walls have been built." As far as is known no attempt was ever made to actually measure the combined length of the walls, but the total has been estimated at more than forty miles.

The result is an engineering feat of the highest order and might very well have been initiated by the Honorable Powell

Clayton, then Chairman of the Board of Public Affairs. He was a trained engineer, and while research can not prove the fact, it is possible that the honorable gentleman had either seen such walls in his native Pennsylvania or had heard descriptions of the miles of stone walls built in Mexico using the same type of construction. Many of Clayton's friends had fought in the Mexican War and it is almost impossible to travel any distance from Mexico City without finding acres of terraces held in place by walls of gray stone. Even if he had not yet been there in person, it would have been easy for a man of Clayton's ability to work out the proper method of laying up the stones so that the walls would stand for many decades. When in 1897 Clayton was appointed United States Ambassador to Mexico, he undoubtedly saw the forerunners of his walls which were unique to Eureka Springs.

These miles and miles of stone walls, some beginning to be overgrown by the wild honeysuckle and clematis, added their own touch of beauty to a city whose inhabitants dwelt in ever-increasing charm and elegance. No city in America could offer more in the way of comfort and convenience, as the tireless efforts of many men had borne fruit in public facilities and a strong business community which promised only continued progress for the future. Eureka Springs began the twentieth century in grand style with a celebration of the twentieth anniversary of the city. The *Times Echo* devoted editorial comment to the past and the present, contrasting the beginnings with the many great changes accomplished in such a short space of years.

> "Settled as the foundation of the mountains among which nestles the City of Magic Waters is the fact that during the years since the discovery of the famous springs, thousands of cures that have seemed little less than miracles have been wrought here by the waters and climate. Thousands of visitors come here annually. This is a wide awake little city, having all the needful necessities—such as substantial business blocks, water, sewer, electric lights, electric street railway, police and fire departments, fine hotels, bath houses, schools and many beautiful residences."

CHAPTER V

THE DREAM FALTERS

Whether Eureka Springs owes more to the capitalists who invested liberally in her successful development or to the ordinary businessman who through years of effort built a stable business community is a moot question. The first twenty years or so seem best summed up by J. L. Russell in his book *Behind These Ozark Hills.* Mr. Russell, who was well acquainted with the people and with the growing pains of the early community says:

> "While the effort might have been doomed to failure without General Clayton and his associates, who liberally invested their capital and paved the way, there were hundreds of others to whom scarcely less credit is due, for they stood in solid phalanx with their shoulders to the wheel through thick and thin."

Although every responsible citizen had a share in making the town prosper and grow, still Clayton's was the name which was heard most often in connection with the development of the community. It was sometimes spoken in a respectful manner, but more often uttered in anger by those individuals who could not see the tremendous advances being made because of the blind spots of prejudice and suspicion they harbored. General Clayton was indeed a man who struck varying responses from those with whom he came in contact. Probably no other person in the history of Eureka Springs encountered so much bitter opposition, while all the while he was able to drive his endeavors ahead at full speed. Clayton was agressive and he had a vision for the future of this resort. The vision led him into opposition which very nearly became open warfare on several occasions. However, Clayton seemed to thrive on opposition.

About the time of his move to Eureka Springs in 1880, Clayton, motivated by a wish to help old friends who had served with him in the Union Army, had two of them join him. One was Major J. W. True of Illinois, who came immediately and was soon followed by J. W. Newport. The three men were close friends and each was afforded the opportunity to enter into his chosen work in the new town.

Looking for information on the life of J. W. Newport before he came to Eureka Springs is like looking for a needle in a haystack. Cora Pinkley Call in her *Pioneer Tales of Eureka Springs,* published in 1930, gives a partial sketch of his career after he arrived. Where he was born, educated and grew to manhood is unknown. His first appearance is after the Civil War when Powell Clayton invited him to come to Eureka Springs and join with him in the development of the city. Apparently the two had struck up an acquaintanceship during the War but subsequent events seem to bear out the fact that the friendship, if such it was, was not a close one. Neither did Clayton exhibit his usual good judgement in choosing those with whom he wished to associate himself.

At what point their friendly relationship became ruptured is not a matter of record. It would be enlightening to know more about the character of the man who left almost as much of an imprint on Eureka Springs as that made by Clayton, but in a different manner. Undoubtedly there were those in the new city who were unhappy and dissatisfied over the land settlement, even though it was a great relief to most to have what seemed at the time to be such an amicable agreement. Just why a man invited to come to share in the good things of the community should expressly align himself with those disgruntled individuals which nothing could be done to satisfy will always be a question.

Major True also came to Eureka Springs at the invitation of General Clayton. According to earlier stories he must have been born in central Illinois, as one story says he was a hostler for Lincoln. Another tells of his attendance at one of the Lincoln-Douglas debates where he became acquainted with a Miss Marshall of the free state of Kansas. The friendship ripened into courtship and in due time she became his wife. The record states that True served with General Clayton during the Civil War and that they became friends and the friendship bore fruit when Clayton invited the Major to come to Eureka Springs and participate in the development of the new city. After Powell Clayton went to Mexico as ambassador he tried to keep in touch with Major True. In a letter to a friend in Eureka Springs in October of 1899 he inquires as to whether or not the Major ever visited there. In this letter Clayton writes as if Major True had some kind of position which required that he travel over the State of Arkansas. True was a dedicated Republican and was now in a position where he could keep his political ear to the ground. In the same letter Clayton warns his correspondent that "Newport and his gang will try to put up a job on the Republicans," so the differences of opinion were political as well as personal and continued even after Clayton went to Mexico.

Not many years passed before the people who knew Clayton began to choose sides. Those who were friends of the General aligned themselves with him, and since many were considered to be of a high social standing they were soon nicknamed the Silk Stockings. This group represented mainly the business and residential area along Spring Street and West Mountain and wished to see that part of the town grow and develop.

At that time, Main Street was the important center of business for the community. The street was lined with numerous business establishments from the intersection with Spring Street just below Basin Spring to the railroad shops and depot at the north corporate limits. A number of warehouses were located between the depot and a flouring mill situated where the muddy Main Street intersected with a trail leading to Magnetic Spring. Within the short distance between this intersection and the road leading up Mill Hollow were located three general stores, a boarding house, a small hotel, the Clayton House, a blacksmith shop and a riding stable. The Siedel Brothers had put up a substantial block of business buildings at Mill Hollow road fronting on Main Street; next to that was a feed store and wagon yard and across the way was another grocery store. Any spaces left between business establishments were quickly filled with small shacks which, beginning at the street level, continued up the bluffs and on up the sides of the mountain on either side of the creek. The Grand Central Hotel was built on this street, as were the Landaker House and numerous retail stores. On toward the south where the street ran close to Spring Street, but on a much lower level, were situated buildings which sometimes housed three different businesses, reached from both the upper and lower streets and from a path or steps leading up the steep hillside between buildings.

The people of this area and those of nearby East Mountain formed themselves into an organization called the Mohawks, for the mutual protection of their part of town and their business investment there. The general feeling prevailed that the Silk Stockings wished to see progress in their area at the expense of the Main Street neighborhood.

Clayton's friend, Major True, sided with the Silk Stockings while his other friend, J. W. Newport, aligned himself with the Mohawks and became their very active and able leader.

The rivalry between these friends and their respective followers became such that what one proposed the other opposed. As the years passed and Clayton's power grew in both partisan politics and civic affairs the enmity increased. The local newspapers also joined the affray, choosing sides, and the *Daily Times Echo* of July 30, 1891, devoted the entire front page to the constitution of the Royal Order of Mohawks.

The stated objectives of the new organization were dedicated to promoting the general welfare of the people by bettering their conditions morally, socially and politically. The Mohawks declared war on rings, monopolies, trusts and "bossism" at local and county levels and laid the blame for certain unfair and discriminatory legislation to: "men of the different parties who seem to work together under the leadership of Powell Clayton." Further, the Mohawks held no brief with certain "corporations" who according to unidentified informers, "obtained control and became owners of the land and homes of the people—without fee or reward." These same "corrupt influences" were also accused of getting thousands of dollars of the people's money with which to build a railroad into the city, then in fact bringing the facility only to the corporate limits in order to escape taxation. The Mohawk constitution raged at length and in rambling fashion about "corporations goading men through long continued law suits into compromises and depriving them of sections of city property." These same unidentified persons, allegedly working under the direction of Powell Clayton, were accused of removing landmarks, making illegal surveys, changing the assessors books in accordance with such surveys, then raising assessments "in dark rooms, hidden from the people." The final thrust at these "designing men" accused those of different political leanings of having gained such control as to have placed in public office "men who were not the choice of the people."

The Mohawks apparently found fault with every endeavor General Clayton promoted, from the townsite settlement, which involved his Improvement Company, through the building of a railroad, to meddling in politics, local and otherwise.

The newspaper account of the Mohawk organization ends with a high sounding pledge: "To strive to secure harmony and good will among all mankind and with brotherly love among ourselves. To maintain our laws inviolate, to assist the poor and the laboring classes, to lighten their burden by making it equal upon all, to emulate each other in this labor and work and to hasten the Good Time Coming."

Only a few newspapers of the 1890's are available for research, so it is not known how long the Mohawks, with their single-minded purpose for being, continued in existence. However, it was probably dissolved within a short time, as General Clayton left Eureka Springs in 1897 to assist William McKinley in his successful bid for the presidency. At this time his fellow citizens were sufficiently in accord to tender him a very elegant farewell banquet.

With Major True also gone from Eureka Springs the way was left open for the cultivation of the reactionary ideas advocated by Newport, ideas which did little to help the community work toward the high goals to which the city was dedicated. Evidently Newport did not have the inclination to work with those seeking the development of a community where the well-to-do and world-weary would be assured of an appropriate welcome.

It is apparent that after General Clayton left that Newport's popular support grew. He spent his time and what money he could attract in trying to build up Main Street as the central business street. During the years he served as postal clerk, assistant postmaster and was one of the procession of mayors that went through that office in the early years. As late as 1910 Newport was still a public figure trying to promote discord. He had by then got himself elected to the school board and the most trouble that body ever had was when Newport opposed the hiring of Mrs. Barnett as a teacher. The wife of Professor Barnett, she had taught twenty years in the Eureka Springs schools and Newport thought that was long enough and he opposed renewing her contract. Both of the Barnetts had made such a great contribution to the cause of education in Eureka Springs that this time Newport didn't succeed in his disruptive tactics. Eventually Newport went into the grocery business where he ended his career.

Whether the charges of the Mohawks against Clayton were true or false cannot be determined with any degree of accuracy, and there were certainly many prominent businessmen and civic leaders who considered it an honor to be considered a friend and associate of this controversial man.

Two men remember Clayton with respect and gratitude; one a member of the town's poorer class and the other a prominent newspaper man from a neighboring community. In 1882 Amos J. Fortner was brought to Eureka Springs a helpless paralytic child in the arms of his father. Fortner recalls that property values in those days were based on the proximity to one or the other of several springs. Consequently, the well-to-do citizens lived on the lower levels, while their poorer counterparts dwelt on the mountain tops, literally "looking down" on their rich neighbors. His own family lived in various uninhabited shacks, rent free, but having to move frequently as the Improvement Company razed one after another.

Fortner also felt that the city owed a great deal to Powell Clayton, as he was chiefly responsible for the picturesque beauty. Fortner says, "he (Clayton) had a vigorous program of creating beauty out of the motley array of shacks that dotted the hillsides. Of course, he made enemies with some property owners." He also recalls the frequent moves his family made and of how Clayton would tell his parents of some other house in which they could live rent free, until it in turn, was torn down. He says: "At one time, when my father was out of town, Mr. Clayton even paid the expenses of our moving. But he was in a hurry that time. He wanted to immediately start clearing the ground for the erection of the Crescent Hotel and our shack was on the spot where the hotel was to be built. Oh, how I hated to leave that hilltop."

In writing of General Clayton and his efforts for the betterment of Eureka Springs, J. L. Russell, author of *Behind These Ozark Hills,* says:

> "He not only set up effectual means of unraveling the tangled situation with reference to land titles, but it was not too long before he had a locomotive screaming up the canyon, announcing that the ambitious resort was connected with the outside world by bands of steel . . . For years the colossal movement went forward, making the government-backed Hot Springs look sorry."
>
> "Everything necessary for the maintenance of a modern city was either quickly instituted or blueprinted with a confidence that left no shadow of doubt as to the outcome.
>
> "Whatever else may be said of General Clayton . . . it must be admitted that he was at least a near-great man. Honesty compels the people among whom he spent so many years to look upon him as their greatest friend and benefactor. He did more looking to the development of this area than any other man or set of men, for that matter."

Suffice to say, that the threads of the history of the town are tightly interwoven in the life of General Powell Clayton.

Carpetbagger, politician, capitalist, a man both hated and revered, he put his mark upon the "City that Water Built" and along with the other builders of the town, most of whom are long since forgotten, left today's residents a goodly heritage of grandeur achieved—even if only for a little while.

PART II

CHAPTER VI

People: Hopeful and Confident

During the first turbulent days of the development of the new city, it soon became apparent that many were determined to stay and a feeling of civic pride began to emerge. While the dusty streets were thronged with those who were ill and those who were both ill and destitute, among them also were men who had considerable means at their disposal. Men such as these could well afford an investment in the future of the community. With them stood others, literally hundreds of men ready to stake their more meagre resources in whatever the outcome might be. All willingly left the past behind and with great expectations began establishing new lives in what came to be called "The City that Water Built."

The lives and times of many of the prominent early settlers have been chronicled many times over, yet there were those lesser-known individuals who through their ordinary daily lives added color to the story of Eureka Springs.

Charley Birk hauled pine knots to the campsite in 1879. The wood sold for 50c a wagon load and Birk couldn't haul it fast enough. One day a friend asked him why he didn't claim some of the newly surveyed lots and settle down, but Charley Birk replied, "No, this will all blow over by cold weather and they'll be no one here."

The Charles Husseys came to the campsite, saw its possibilities and went right back out again to the nearest town to purchase lumber. They brought in the first load of lumber hauled into Eureka Springs and it was used to construct a business building. The Husseys found it no easy task to bring that wagon loaded with lumber down over the extremely steep East Mountain road into the campsite.

Hussey was a building contractor by trade, and erected many of the business houses in the growing community, including Powell Clayton's hotel, the Clayton House.

The town's first dealer in general merchandise, O. D. Thornton, started his business with a wagon load of goods. Thornton unhitched his wagon on his newly acquired city lot and began business. Soon the ladies came to buy his calico cloth and Thornton cut the yardage for them with his pocket knife.

In 1883 Clarence Spear arrived to open a billiard parlor which proved to be a great success. There were many men about with nothing to do each day but drink the water, and billiards was a most pleasant way to pass the time.

Like Charles Hussey, W. I. Sanford was a building contractor, and many early settlers turned to him for a shelter from the elements. Sanford and his men worked day and night throwing up the small wooden houses as quickly as possible. Later Sanford took up stone work and many of the permanent and beautiful stone structures were of his workmanship.

The first photograph studio was a small gallery on wheels brought to town and operated by a little woman named Mary Harris. This wagon studio could easily be moved about, but was usually settled on a lot about half way up West Mountain where Mrs. Harris enjoyed a thriving business.

A very new bride, Mrs. W. R. Hudgins, came to the new town in 1879. Her eyes widened at the sight of the crowded campsite. Soon she watched houses being built over night. One of these houses became her home. Over the years the houses were changed and became more beautiful and livable and for some seventy-nine years Mrs. Hudgins remained and grew old with the town.

Among the crowds seeking health at the Springs was John Dickens. He came an invalid and being healed stayed to become the town's first blacksmith, surely a hard and physically demanding business.

Way down in Polk County, D. H. Hopper heard about the "boom." He immediately sold his farm and stock, loaded his family into the wagon and set out for Eureka Springs. He stopped to camp in South Eureka, and there he stayed, setting up a grocery business.

Desperately ill with malaria fever, Dr. J. H. Smithers came to the town in 1881. He procured a room at the Kansas House, then spent all of the next day sitting near Basin Spring, drinking cup after cup of water. From that day on he improved and Smithers, who "holds a degree as a physician and chemist," set up in business—as a tailor.

Colonel C. J. Betten arrived in Eureka Springs on a stretcher, his only luggage a suitcase carrying his "burying clothes." The colonel died thirty years later after years spent in an active business life in his adopted community.

The Cochrans, husband and wife, built two beautiful stone houses on Armstrong Street. Hattie Cochran made the Basin Bath House famous with baths and later on with electrical treatments. A branch of this same family, the Hughes, built the Western Hotel, most popular in its day before the great fire of 1888.

The "first modern boarding house" in Eureka Springs was built by Captain and Mrs. Davey on Owen Street. Both came here on the advice of their doctor but continued in good health and carried on a successful business for many years.

The first woman doctor arrived in the community in 1880 and practiced for more than fifty years. With her husband, who was also a doctor, Pearl Tatman, in the words of an old timer, "told us how to use the water for health—and took care of us when sick."

Among those first settlers were many other individuals representing a wide variety of backgrounds and ancestry.

Goodspeed's *"History of Carroll County,"* published in 1889, lists many of the more prominent citizens of the day. Very likely the town would never have succeeded had it not been for this type of public-spirited citizen, and it is fitting that a few of them be remembered.

During the first decade of its existence, the city seemed to be filled with promising young professional men.

The Honorable John Carroll was an exuberant, stalwart Irishman as quick with a smile as with a display of temper. At a time when the young town needed intelligent and imaginative leadership, this very capable man arrived on the scene. Not yet fifty years old, he had behind him as varied and fascinating a career as any of the well known heroes of the Old West. Son of a Confederate soldier and grandson of a hero in the Battle of New Orleans, John Carroll carried on in the tradition of these men. Reared on the Frontier, he received his education by his own personal efforts, mostly among the Cherokees in the Indian Territory. During the Civil War he raised three companies for the Confederate Service and was made Captain of a company under General Price. Later he received a Colonel's commission and continued to serve without receiving any injury until the war ended. He served for many years as Sheriff of McDonald County, Missouri and also as U. S. Marshal for the Western District of Arkansas. This district included eighteen counties of the State plus the five civilized tribes of the Indian Territory — the Chickasaws, Choctaws, Creeks, Cherokees and Seminoles. It is said that during his years of service as marshal, seventeen of his deputies were killed. Desiring to engage in a quieter life, Carroll moved to Eureka Springs and went into a general merchandise business.

He served as mayor for four years and in 1884 was admitted to the bar and practiced law as a member of the law firm of Carroll, Glitsch and Vandeventer. In October of 1885, he was again appointed Marshal for the Western District of Arkansas.

Henry Glitsch, born in Hesse Darmstadt, Germany, came in 1880 to be the first solicitor in the new town and was prominently connected with the townsite land suit. Glitsch, whose maternal grandfather was on Napoleon's staff at the burning of Moscow, had himself led an interesting life before coming to Arkansas at the age of thirty-two. In 1863 he enlisted in the Twenty-first Pennsylvania Cavalry of the Federal Army and served until the end of the Civil War. Immediately after returning home, he entered Pennsylvania College at Gettysburg to begin the study of law. For the next several years Glitsch led the life of a schoolteacher and practicing attorney in Pennsylvania and later in Arkansas, coming to Eureka Springs by way of Harrison. Three years after his arrival he entered into partnership with a newly appointed member of the bar, John Carroll, and a man named Vandeventer to form the law firm of Carroll, Glitsch and Vandeventer.

Archimedes Davis, third mayor of the city, was also an attorney, having come to Eureka Springs to establish a practice as soon as the settlement was open. Davis was a native Virginian of Welsh and English ancestry. Here was another young man of breeding, intelligence and good education putting his many talents to work for the good of the young community.

The March 8, 1882, issue of the *Daily Echo* reported there were thirty physicians in the city at that time, and it is true that the first medical society in the county had been organized here the previous year. Doubtless, the credentials of some of these men would not bear close inspection, but for the most part Eureka Springs was well supplied with reliable physicians.

One of the more prominent of these was J. O. Drucker, M. D. Trained in the Jefferson Medical College of Philadelphia, he arrived in the city in 1880 and set up a practice. For a number of years, this worthy member of the profession was seen in Eureka Springs only during the summer months, as during the winter he enjoyed a flourishing practice in St. Louis.

A fellow member of the medical profession was Dr. William Johnston, who also began to practice in Eureka Springs in 1880. During the Civil War, Johnston was a surgeon in the

Eighty-eighth Indiana Volunteer Infantry and one of the youngest medical officers in the Army. He became a prominent member of society in Eureka Springs where he helped to organize the Presbyterian Church. He also served as secretary of the town's first Board of Education and later became a leader in the Republican Party in Northwest Arkansas.

Another early arrival was Dr. William Reese, said to be the grandson of a hero of the Revolutionary War. He came to Eureka Springs in February of 1880 and immediately entered into a flourishing practice. Dr Reese soon became extremely active in public affairs, being appointed to the original Board of Health, and was a great asset to the young community. Politically, he was listed as an old line Whig, but with the dissolution of that party he had become a Democrat.

Another medical man who found a permanent location in Eureka Springs was George P. Young. He had barely reached the age of thirty-two and was indeed a young man when he entered into practice of surgery and chronic diseases. Dr. Young soon had a lucrative practice and invested in extensive property holdings to become one of the most important citizens in the community.

It seems that one essential factor in the proper development of a budding community is the press, for through reading the daily or weekly paper citizens are drawn together in a common purpose directed toward the betterment of those factors of community life in which all equally share. Eureka Springs was well endowed with newspapers and editors whose own lives were as colorful as the headlines they printed.

Andrew B. Adams, editor and proprietor of the *Daily and Weekly Echo,* came to the community in 1879, the year of its founding. A well educated man who taught school before learning the printer's trade, he is listed by Goodspeed as being descended from the "fine old Virginia-Adams stock." Adams was barely twenty-eight years of age when he came to Eureka Springs, but he had spent several years previously in publishing various newspapers on the midwestern frontier.

Another publisher, Colonel George Sweesy of the *Eureka Springs Times,* had also led a life of adventure. During the

Civil War he served first in the Second Iowa Cavalry and, after a time spent in Libby Prison, became a member of the Missouri Forty-first Infantry, leaving the Army at the close of the war with a Lieutenant Colonel's commission. Colonel Sweesy published two newspapers in Kansas and one in Indian Territory called the *"Indian Chieftan."* His political leanings were Republican and his *Times* advocated the principles of that party as strongly as did Mr. Adams speak for the Democrats in the *Echo.*

Providing for the needs of the people of Eureka Springs did much to promote the continued development of the town, and during the first decade of its history several young men built up outstanding business establishments.

A native of Tennessee, Joel G. Breeding arrived in 1879 and started a hardware business. The historian tells us that "Mr. Breeding is a very successful businessman and is one of the prominent and reliable citizens of the county." He was a member of the town council for four years and was also active in the townsite land settlement.

Another arrival early in 1880 was John Hamilton, formerly from Alabama, of Irish and German descent. Young Hamilton was a popular addition to the retail merchants of the town and was elected City Clerk in 1882. From this post he went on to the position of County Circuit Clerk and later became postmaster at Eureka Springs.

Twenty-six year old J. W. Hill established the Eureka Transfer Company and Crescent Stables during the year 1881, and a few years later was described as having "the largest capital investment of any single individual in the city." Hill had been an orphan, earning his living as a $15.00 a month farm hand and store delivery clerk before coming to Eureka Springs, where he purchased a team and carriage and started a transfer business. A year later he added another team and from then on his business grew steadily. Within four years he built the Crescent Stables, a beautiful native stone building having a capacity for fifty-three horses, and was constantly using forty horses in the business. In addition, Hill had contracts with the railroad, Eureka Springs Improvement Company, the mail service and express company, as well as enjoying an extensive livery business. Two years a widower, the successful Mr. Hill was probably a much sought after member of society in the infant town where social affairs were of the utmost importance, even from the very beginning.

The romantic figure of Captain John Tobein, tragically wounded in the War Between the States, entered upon the scene in 1880. Tobein, a German, had been in his adopted country only ten years at the beginning of the war, when he joined the Forty-Third Illinois Volunteer Infantry. While in service he received injuries from which he had never fully recovered and came to Eureka Springs in search of healing. Captain Tobein stayed on to become one of the most successful merchants and prominent citizens of his adopted community.

F. A. Pickard, the first city clerk elected by the town, was another young man with an interesting background. A descendant of one of the Mohawk Dutch families, he served in the Seventy-Second New York Infantry with the Federal Army during the Civil War. Wounded at the Battle of Gettysburg, Pickard was taken to David's Island where he recovered and was given charge of the hospital there until the war ended. He had been wounded previously and had been captured and spent three months in Libby prison before the Battle of Gettysburg.

For many years after the war ended Pickard taught school on the Kansas frontier, but in 1881 came to Eureka Springs to establish a business dealing in fine furniture.

Captain Joseph Perry was the son of an Englishman who had been a lifetime hotel man. At eighteen young Perry opened his first hotel on the Hudson River, which was the first of a succession of fourteen caravansaries across the frontier. He developed hotels in Kansas, Missouri and Colorado, moving to Eureka Springs in 1879 because of failing health. When Perry regained his health, he firmly resolved not to leave the life-giving fountain and built the beautiful Perry House within a hundred feet of the celebrated Basin Spring. He was considered a great asset to the town because of his fine reputation throughout the West, and his Perry House did much for the upbuilding of the community.

It becomes apparent as one reads of the citizens who were responsible for the phenomenal rise of Eureka Springs during the decade following its founding, that these were young adventurous business and professional men. While many of the large influx of new residents were either infirm, old, or both, the civic development revolved around capable young men of both mental and physical strength. Of the fifteen men just reviewed, a half dozen of them were just barely in their thirtys, four were not yet thirty and the remaining five had just attained two score and five years. The young town had young leaders and at that time the future held nothing but good fortune and success for them and the community they served.

While the majority of the business and professional men were intent on building a strong and healthy business climate in Eureka Springs, at the same time such a large gathering of strangers in a new town could not but hold some who were interested more in lucrative schemes involving the fast turnover of money with the investment of small effort on their part.

The endeavors of these individuals are also of interest for they added their part to the unique community life of Eureka Springs through the 1880's and 1890's.

Through the early years, several men operated successful businesses devoted to the shipping of Eureka Springs water to points all over the country. This provided the health restoring benefits to those who could not come to stay at the Springs.

Not all were successful in their endeavors, though flourishing for a time. A news note of January of 1882 advises that the Eureka Springs Concentrating Company located at Basin Spring had received a "patent as sole manufacturer of hair restorative, eye water and Eureka Springs soap," all purporting to contain the particular healing qualities of the water from that spring.

About this time there was a widely published claim that "ninety percent of the cures of Eureka Springs were brought about by the Basin Spring water," so it is not difficult to see why this company, located on the premises of the Basin Spring, was favorably received for a time.

In an atmosphere so full of hope and with such concentration placed on cures for all ills, it is not surprising that a few men and women who felt less than a scrupulous regard for the truth should make an effort to profit from the unfortunate individuals who were more eager to believe the gaudy claims of unreliable healers than of those who enjoyed a good reputation. Fortunately, only a few questionable healers left a record of these misleading claims. In the July 6, 1900, edition of the *Daily Times Echo* a Professor and Mrs. Ault advertised the cure of "all diseases without the use of knife or poisonous drugs." The Aults guaranteed good health to all comers and for a fee applied "Magnetic Healing." Their advertisement did not make clear the method entailed, nor did it state whether or not the waters of any of the springs were incorporated in the treatment.

The same paper carried the announcement of the Magnetic College and Sanitarium. The grand opening of this institution took place on June 18th and Dr. Thomas Tooney assured a cure "for all curable diseases" through the use of "vital magnetism."

In an adjoining column was the notice of a certain Mrs. Decker who "reads the mind of an absent person by holding his photograph in her hand." This generous offer was made as a free test of her "strange science" with which she effected healing of the sick.

One of the more prominent of the early merchants, Herman Siedel, suddenly discovered that he was gifted with a natural healing power and had been successful in curing rheumatism, paralysis and similar afflictions by "Natural Magnetism." He offered his services to those afflicted with such diseases, and by newspaper accounts met with excellent success. Since Mr. Siedel was a most respected citizen, his claims were never greatly doubted.

Just before the turn of the century, drug addiction had taken a sudden upturn all over the United States. At that time the possession and use of opium and morphine was legal. Cough syrup was consumed by the gallon, though purchased by the bottle, and one of the chief ingredients of cough syrup was opium. Morphine could be purchased for 25c a pill, and it was believed that one in every four hundred persons was a drug addict.

Small wonder that newspapers were full of advertisements of establishments offering to cure both the liquor and drug habits. Elsewhere is a copy of the advertisement for such a sanitarium run by Dr. Lennox, who in 1904 purported to cure the problems of alcoholism and drug addiction at his sanitarium near Magnetic Spring. Apparently, the water of this spring was a prominent part of the cure. It is not known how many persons brought their troubles to Dr. Lennox, who probably also relieved them of considerable cash for such a miraculous cure.

How varied were the lives and personalities of the first townspeople. They poured into the town from every direction. It would be an impossible task to list all those who came in various stages of poor health seeking relief, or the healthy ones searching new beginnings.

It is enough to say that many who came stayed, married, raised families, established businesses and in myriad ways helped bring about a community upon which they could look with justifiable pride as home.

CHAPTER VII

EDUCATION FOR EVERYONE

When people came to the area of the Springs in Northwest Arkansas in 1879 they usually brought their families, including children. Those who stayed soon began looking toward some method of educating them. The newcomers were mostly from states other than Arkansas and at first were not fully aware of the lack of educational facilities within the state. These facilities were meager and scarce.

It is not the purpose of this story of the schools in Eureka Springs to dig deeply into the history of education in the state. It seems necessary, however, to provide a bit of background before going into how the school problems were handled when sufficient numbers of children of school age arrived at the Springs.

The federal government had made efforts to assist the Arkansas Territory to establish public schools as far back as 1829. Each township was allocated a section of land for the support of education. These were to be rented and the rental used to establish an educational fund. These sections brought in a very low rental and in 1829 the federal government passed a law permitting the land to be sold and the money invested in such a way that the income could be used to finance public schools. Even by combining the money from both sales and leases there was not enough to support a public school system. The majority of the citizens considered that when a child was old enough to go to school it was old enough to work and their help was needed on the farms. Many early settlers had a low opinion of education and no compulsory school attendance law had ever been passed in the state. The Federal census of 1860 showed more than 23,000 white persons in Arkansas who could neither read or write. If it was considered foolish to educate white children it was worse than foolish to educate the colored. When the War began the few private and semi-public schools that had struggled into existence were soon closed.

When the War ended the federal government again renewed the effort to help the state to establish an educational system. Now the effort was greatly hampered by the deep antipathy regarding the education of Negroes. The Freedmans Bureau succeeded in establishing a few day-schools but the masses of children of either hue were not reached, although it was a first step toward education for everyone.

In 1868 the State Legislature elected by the people under the Reconstruction measures passed and tried to put into effect an ambitious program for education in Arkansas. It was so much more ambitious than any program ever proposed previously that it is doubtful if the legislators really understood what they were voting for. Various excuses are put forward for the failure and breakdown of the program for by 1874 it had broken down completely and the schools, all except those supported by private funds were closed. The most logical reason for the failure was undoubtedly the deep seated resistance to public education for the masses.

The Constitutional Convention held in 1874 wrote new laws limiting the powers of the state, county and municipal governments to tax and spend. Money could not be used for anything but absolute necessities and education was not considered a necessity . . . yet. It took many years for the ideas to develop that education was necessary for personal advancement.

Due to the inept financial methods used by the state government, Arkansas was bankrupt in 1879 and the state debt amounted to $115 for every voter, so the outlook for education in the new community was far from hopeful. When in 1880 the need for public schools was finally established in Eureka Springs the state could provide only $3000.00 a year for their operation. With over 1500 children of school age no advanced arithmetic is needed to find it amounted to less than $2 per child per year. Even with that much help it took the school district long years to build up adequate financing for the schools. The state wide situation contributed its share to the slow development of all schools, but Eureka Springs proved more fortunate than other communities when in the 1890's their most pressing needs were met by a generous minded citizen, who not only provided funds to keep their schools open that year, but later gave sufficient money to build a fine red brick school house which served the needs of the community for many years.

Public notice was first called to the situation in the Eureka Springs schools by the *Arkansas Gazette* in the issue of November 12, 1888, when it stated there were 1571 children of school age in Eureka Springs being taught by 12 teachers. The town had been in existence for nearly ten years but during that time no grade or enrollment cards had been kept and classes had been held in any building that could be made available and taught by anyone with sufficient interest to do so. Several small private schools had been organized by parents, disturbed over the lack of educational facilities for their children, but they did not become permanent.

Since records are not available the story that seems to be closest to the facts is told by Miss Nellie Mills who graduated from the Eureka Springs High School in 1890, one of a class of three, having the distinction of being the first to graduate from that institution of learning. Beginning school in 1880 her memories of what it was like to attend school during the early years are fairly reliable, as she wrote them down for publication before 1940. During the intervening years the neighborhood along Main Street and the vicinity of Mill Hollow changed so completely that the places where she went to school can not be found, nor can the house she lived in.

If legend can be relied on, the legend places a school, a good sized one-room school building, near the entrance to Mill

Hollow before 1880 and credits it with being an Indian School, taught by a Mrs. Stubblefield. When Nellie took her McGuffy's first reader in hand and started to school in the fall of 1880 it was to this school that Nellie went and there she learned to read. She recalls a picnic there in the spring of 1881 so she apparently attended school all of the winter of 1880-1881. She says there was also a school further "up-town" taught by a Mrs. Jack, but the location is uncertain, though it could have been near the Landaker Hotel, as a Mrs. Jack is mentioned as having taught in that vicinity.

In the fall of 1881 Nellie moved to a three story building farther up the mountain, but still near Mill Hollow. According to her this building was actually built for a school building and while she does not call it by name it probably was the Soldier School. It agrees with the account of the early schools which appeared in the *Carroll County Historical Association Quarterly*. This building was used as a school for ten years. Nellie remembers the Christmas program at this school, but seems vague as to when she left it to attend elsewhere. She next recalls trudging up West Mountain to attend the Comer School located near the site of the Episcopal Church. How many terms she went there she fails to say as she goes on to tell about the three or four terms she attended school in four different buildings on Spring Street. She mentions the Nixon Building, the Carey Building and once again back to the Nixon building, as well as a term in a building where the Penn Memorial Baptist Church was later built.

In 1885-1886 Nellie was trudging up West Mountain to still a different school, the Lamar, which she locates on the site of the present Christian Church. The next year a superintendent was hired as there were now several schools scattered throughout Eureka Springs. While they had moved about considerably by 1889 they seemed to have permanently settled into place, one on East Mountain, the Clay Street School in South Eureka, opened in 1883, and the Lamar. School had been held in many other buildings, but was of such short duration it is not necessary to try to locate them. However a school occupied a building on Owen Street several hundred feet west of where Elk joins it; also another was on Benton just off Main. When wealthy visitors brought their colored servants with them while vacationing, the needs of the children were met by a school for colored, located down on German Alley near the present site of the Perkins Lumber Yard. This is the school Nellie Mills refers to as

> "another school on Howell, down the mountain from the Harding Spring."

Teachers were fairly faithful, for Helen Putnam, Laura Mellon, Mrs. Jack, and Mrs. Stubblefield were among others who carried the teaching load for most of the ten years Nellie was in school. For the term of 1886 and 1887 a superintendent of schools was hired, but Mrs. Stubblefield replaced him before the term ended.

The year 1888 was one of crisis for the Eureka Springs Schools as the Lamar was closed for lack of funds and the other schools shared the same fate. In order to continue her education, as she planned to become a teacher, Nellie Mills went up to Kansas to attend school. What others did is not of record, neither is the way the residents solved their problem. By 1889 they had recovered sufficiently to organize the Eureka Springs School District to try to bring some order to the chaotic conditions of the educational scene. At once the School District found it had neither money nor buildings in prospect.

On May 20, 1890, the new District called an election and a five mill tax was levied on each one hundred dollars of taxable property. Property values at that time were not in the higher brackets so sufficient funds were not forthcoming with which to build a school building. An existing frame structure was made available and public school in an organized school district was started.

By some stroke of good luck Professor C. S. Barnett was employed in 1890 and he immediately began to bring a semblance of order to the disorganized school system. The school work was systematized and different grade levels established for the first time. Up to this time no grade cards had been issued and no attendance records kept. Due to the fluctuation in the population 105 might be enrolled in a school at the beginning of the school year, and 35 left at the end, not one of whom had been enrolled at the beginning.

Soon Professor Barnett began to organize exhibits of school work and provide festivals and public entertainments which helped to arouse the public to the needs and abilities of the younger generation, and led the citizens to make their struggle to see that the schools took their rightful place in the community.

Three pupils had shown sufficient advancement to be admitted to work of high school level, so the Eureka Springs High School was organized in time to graduate its first class in the summer of 1890. One of the members of this class was Nellie Mills who had returned from Kansas to complete her education at home.

Problems still continued to disrupt the orderly advancement of the school system though many things were tried to solve them. In his report on the schools issued in December of 1890 Professor Barnett says:

> ". . . it was ruled at the last meeting that all non residents and residents over and under school age should pay tuition. Notices have been sent to all persons considered non residents. The rates of tuition in our Public Schools are as follows: High school per month $2.00; Grammar school per month $1.50; Intermediate and primary per month $1.00. Tuition fees are charged non residents in almost every school of which we have any knowledge, and our visiting friends should not be aggrieved . . . when they know that much of the money for the support of these schools comes from local taxation. We are justly proud that our Schools have gained favor, not withstanding our inefficient buildings, justly proud that our own people do not send their sons and daughters away . . . to be educated until they have finished our public school course, and with not a little pride . . . notice that almost 100 pupils are enrolled from a distance. We have enrolled 714 children during the months of our present school year . . . we now have eleven teachers employed and no school with less than 50 pupils in attendance, except the colored school."

This plan must have been put into effect for in the "School Notes" in the *Times Echo* of January 5, 1891, Professor Barnett reminds—

"non resident pupils will please see the secretary . . . Dr. W. W. Johnston, this coming week to make arrangements for tuition."

Even with this rather precarious assistance, as it was almost impossible to sort out the transient pupils and enforce the idea of paying tuition, the schools continued to have a hard time financially. The many scattered buildings where school had once been held were abandoned as the results of Professor Barnett's efficiency. They were not suitable for educational purposes in the first place and Nellie Mills recalled that "sanitary conditions were superlatively deplorable."

In July of 1891 a citizens mass meeting was held for the purpose of raising funds with which to build two additional rooms on to the existing frame structure. Tax funds had not been sufficient for this purpose and in fact were proving inadequate to keep the school in operation. More pupils were attending school and more class room space was badly needed, but in view of the financial situation the schools might have to close. This crisis was met by the help of a man who could be called one of the greatest benefactors toward the cause of education Eureka Springs was ever to have. A banker from Chicago, W. H. Reid, vice-president of the Illinois Trust and Savings Bank, had spent some time in the community for his health and had built a beautiful home not too far from the Crescent Hotel. He had become quite interested in the future of the town and now came forward with a gift of $2,500 to the school district which enabled the schools to keep open.

Continuing his interest in the Eureka Springs school system, a short time later Mr. Reid gave the school district $25,000 with which to build a permanent school structure. This red brick building was completed and ready to start the school term on September 3, 1892. To honor Mr. Reid for this generous gift the school was known as the W. H. Reid School and is still standing. Located a short distance off of Prospect Avenue, it was used for school purposes for over fifty years. The first class graduated from the Reid School in 1892. There were now three public school buildings, the new W. H. Reid

School, the Soldier School on East Mountain and the Clay Street School in South Eureka. School was now continuous for nine months of the year and the schools were all graded.

So much for buildings, but it takes more than four walls and a teacher to make a school. Equipment is necessary and in the beginning this was practically nonexistent. The "library" consisted of an 1845 edition of Websters Unabridged Dictionary, and of course the back was missing. Under the directon of Professor Barnett the pupils went to work to raise funds for books, and even for a piano. It took many entertainments and lots of hard work, but eventually sufficient equipment was obtained.

The effort to upgrade the teachers had also been successful and of the thirteen teachers employed the greater number were Normal graduates. A plan of special incentives had been put in effect to induce teachers to attend Normal School in the summer to earn educational credits.

At first none of the high schools in the state were accredited, i. e., had their credits accepted as entrance requirements to institutions of higher learning. When Nellie Mills desired to enter the Southwest Missouri State College her credits for the two year high school course in Eureka Springs were not acceptable and the Arkansas State Board of Education would not acknowledge them so they could be transferred. By this time Professor Barnett had so impressed the State Board that the credits earned in Eureka Springs were finally allowed and the High School placed on the list of accredited schools.

In a remarkably short time great progress had been made. When the Chicago World's Fair opened in 1893 the exhibit of the Literature Course from Eureka Springs won first prize as the best exhibit of its kind.

The October 3, 1897, issue of the *Daily Times Echo* made the statement that Eureka Springs had the best schools in the state. There were 18 members in the graduating class that year.

The *Daily Times Echo* for May 4, 1904, issued a special report on the schools which filled most of the paper. Faculty and students were both given credit for their many achievements. During the year a special exhibit of English Composition was sent to the Louisiana Purchase Exhibition. This exhibit not only won first prize, but attracted much attention. A special case was designed for the exhibit by Professor Barnett and built by the W. O. Perkins Lumber Company. Later this exhibit was shown in the Educational Building, Arkansas Division, at Saint Louis. When other and larger communities gave Eureka Springs their attention and admiration it gave the local school pride in their achievements and also fostered pride in the community to have such outstanding schools. Back in 1902 a news note mentioned that there were 108 pupils attending school on East Mountain, so that school was not being neglected.

The school system occasionally sponsored civic endeavors. One was a campaign to kill as many flies as possible with a prize of $1.00 to the pupil who killed the most. A more interesting project was the Gurney League Program. A man from Saint Louis, James Gurney, had organized this League to help promote the love of Nature and its beauty by planting flowers and shrubbery around school grounds, at home or in any space that could thereby be made more attractive. Soon over 300 of the school children were taking part in the program or over one half of the 600 student enrollment. At one time Mr. Gurney purchased property on East Mountain with the idea of establishing a sort of a botanical garden, but this dream was never realized, though Eureka Springs did profit by the efforts the school children made toward its beautification.

When failing health made it necessary for Professor Barnett to leave the school system he had spent thirty-eight years in bringing it to a high level of excellence. All the local newspapers gave him great credit for his years of devoted work. The schools of Eureka Springs got off to a slow start, but once a direction had been decided upon a system of education was established which provided a firm foundation for the present school system.

When the last Commencement exercises were held in the W. H. Reid High School, participants looked back with nostalgia to the past and toward the future with hopes yet to be realized. High praise was given to both teachers and students in the account of the Commencement exercises and in the Alumni edition.

Parochial schools never seemed to obtain a firm acceptance in Eureka Springs. Several were in operation in the early years, but only two are remembered, one in Harding Gulch, later Howell Street, and the other near the site of the red brick Reid School on Fairmont.

From the early days various business colleges offering the advantages of courses in typing, shorthand and bookkeeping made their appearance on the scene. Usually these colleges had rooms in the upper story of one of the multiple story business buildings along Spring Street. They flourished briefly and did not attract a sufficient number of students to achieve any kind of permanence.

A news item in the December, 1925, issue of the *Flashlight* advises that the Highland Business College turned its lease and furniture over to the stockholders for liquidation. How many other schools of that kind met the same fate is unknown.

The year 1890 had been a year of great vocal activity in the educational program of Eureka Springs, as a project for establishing a college came under discussion for the first time. These projects often require many years for fulfillment so it was not until an advertisement for Crescent College appeared in the August 7, 1908, issue of the *Eureka Springs Flashlight* that the college project began to bear fruit. Back of this advertisement was the plan to move Maddox Seminary from Little Rock to Eureka Springs, so Crescent College began life as Maddox Seminary. The school needed more space, better and more modern buildings, and the big stone Crescent Hotel was not being used as a hotel at that time. The president of the Seminary, together with several prominent businessmen of Eureka Springs, decided to utilize the building and location for a college. An advisory board was created and among those chosen for the board were R. C. Kerens, Dr. C. F. Ellis, C. A. Fuller (then mayor), Dr. R. G. Floyd, B. J. Rosewater, John DeBoise (then Municipal Judge), and Julius Labsap.

The first college term began September 23, 1908, with a nine member faculty prepared to teach mathematics, science, languages, English and history as well as primary and preparatory work to boys and girls from ages six to fourteen, according to the advertisement in the *Times Echo.*

The original prospectus of the College states that "Eureka Springs is a city of 6,000 inhabitants with a steadily increasing population." It goes on to say:

> "The municipal solidity and improvement, the social, culture, and morality not to mention the healthful location, are unsurpassed."

The prospectus continued with praise for the beauty and convenience of the building and location. One of the conveniences mentioned was the nearness of the Carnegie Public Library, then in the planning stage.

The College Yearbook for 1911 shows many changes in both the faculty and the curriculum for the coming year. A school of speech and a conservatory of music were being added and more stress was placed on athletics. The year before, in 1910, the girls basketball team won the Southern Basketball Championship which provided the needed incentive to increase such activities. Local newspapers carried accounts of the basketball games with Drury College of Springfield, Missouri, and the Neosho, Missouri and Eureka Springs High School teams. The physical education program also included tennis, bowling, hiking and horseback riding. The horse back riding was very popular if pictures of the participants in this sport can be relied on.

The tenth anniversary annual was a handsome leather bound book and from it one learned that the cultural aspects of college life are being stressed, also it is learned that a School of Business and a Domestic Science Department are being added.

The graduating class had 15 members and the total enrollment was seventy five girls, with the majority from Texas and Oklahoma. It did not mention the charges for tuition for that year, but in 1912 it was $375.00 a year, including room and board. Additional fees were charged for electives such as music, expression, voice, the School of Business and other special courses.

In spite of such auspicious surroundings, a good curriculum and faculty, the school did not grow and prosper and in 1924 it was decided to close. Some of the citizens felt the school was a great asset to the community and that every effort should be made to keep it open. By this time R. R. Thompson had become associated with Crescent College and he tried hard to rally local support to keep the school in operation. His efforts were in vain and so after only 16 years, a brief life span, the school was closed.

For the next six years only rumors such as Eureka Springs can produce were heard about the College. There was some substance behind the talk, for the February issue of the *Times Echo* for 1930 carried an impressive advertisement to the effect that Crescent College was to be reopened with an imposing faculty headed by A. Q. Burns as president. The paper did not go behind the scenes and show how this was to be accomplished or who was responsible for the resurrection. The faculty was most distinguished with Grady Cox heading the Conservatory of Music and C. Harry Ellis in charge of the Art Department. Junior colleges were just beginning to come into favor and the school was now organized as a junior college. With such a splendid start the success of the venture seemed assured. Scanning local newspapers for the years 1930-31, it seemed to be a period of great activity for Crescent College. In the winter of 1930 an Alma Mater Society was organized to promote interest in the school. News items about the newly organized college continued through the year 1931. In April of that year the College Drum Corps presented a program at Fort Smith, and in May the faculty participated in the dedication of the Covered Bridge Studio. During the next months the depression moved in to discourage and hamper all activity. So it was with Crescent College and in 1933 its doors closed again . . . for the last time.

Another brave attempt to attract and keep institutions of higher learning in Eureka Springs was the Interstate Summer Normal Educational Assembly. An old map of the Eureka Springs area for about 1890 shows the location of the Interstate Summer Normal Educational Assembly in what later became Harmon Park. A large outdoor auditorium, seating 3,500 people and affording ample stage space, had been built at this location. The summer normal session was organized to offer better training advantages for teachers and was considered superior to those of any other Normal School in the United States.

Now that she was a teacher Nellie Mills attended that first assembly for five weeks, July 14 through August 26, 1891. The president of this Assembly was Powell Clayton, whose finger was in any pie which would promote the prestige of Eureka Springs.

In her little booklet *Other Days at Eureka Springs,* Nellie lists each program and describes those of special interest. Educators from many states came to lecture, and conduct classes in English, history, mathematics and other subjects of interest to country school teachers. The day in the sun for the Interstate Summer Normal School was brief, as it was held only one year, but it provided incentive for other educational programs.

From this Assembly came the Carroll County Teachers Association formed in Berryville the next year. This Association met for three days in Eureka Springs in 1892.

That same year a State District Normal School was permanently located in one of the public school buildings. The school was in session for five months each year. Later, due to changes in the educational pattern of the State, this normal school was discontinued.

Another normal school opened in Eureka Springs in September of 1906, according to the February, 1907, issue of a magazine, *The Beautiful Ozarks,* published by Giles E. Miller. A handsome picture and the accompanying write-up refers to the Arkansas Normal College. The second term was ending, according to the story, so it must have opened in September of 1906. The building shown was the so-called Magnetic Spring Hotel. As late as 1904 advertisements for the cure of the drug and liquor habit also showed pictures of this building. When the metamorphosis occurred cannot be substantiated, but according to the story in *The Beautiful Ozarks,* the college was chartered by the state and empowered to confer the usual degrees. The president was W. T. Shepherd, M. A., M. S., and PhD. . . . truly impressive credentials for the day and age. Also, so stated the publicity, students from Illinois, Michigan, Missouri and other northern states were in attendance and several bachelor degrees were to be conferred in June. Among the activities mentioned were a dramatic club and literary society. The story neglected to state how many were in the student body or who were the members of the faculty. Due to the dearth of material available for further research it is not known how long it endured, but it is hoped all went well, though the lack of additional information relative to the activities of a school of this type seems to indicate that its life span was comparatively short as were so many other efforts in the educational field in Arkansas.

The 1927 session of the State Legislature provided for four normal schools in the state. The Commercial Club of Eureka Springs made a determined effort to have one located in their community but were not successful.

The story on schools would not be complete without mentioning the part the School Board played in the local school picture. The School Board was organized in 1891 with J. C. Gordon as the first president. The school system was just beginning to get a good start under Professor Barnett when the School Board was organized and so the two began to work together to improve the schools. Like many other civic leaders they had to learn their duties since it was their first effort at helping direct the educational progress of a community.

They must have learned well as no matter sufficiently discordant to be of news value made the newspaper until July, 1910, when one of the members of the Board required three columns of newsprint to call attention to his opposition to rehiring Professor and Mrs. Barnett to teach school. He was upset by other school problems, but getting rid of Mrs. Barnett seemed to be his principal aim. Both professor and Mrs. Barnett had devoted twenty years of effort to try to upgrade the school system so his attack did not meet with success, and the Barnetts continued to teach. Otherwise much credit accrues to the School Board for their part in the steady progress made in the school system.

Old school mates tend to enjoy meeting to recall what time has made into rose colored memories of their school days. So it is with the alumni of the Eureka Springs High School. As early as 1894 the High School graduates organized an Alumni Association which continued to meet yearly as they welcomed the members of each year's graduating class to their numbers. Elsewhere it has been mentioned that three students graduated from the two year high school course in 1890. They were joined by six others in 1891, three in 1892, ten in 1893, and twelve in 1894. The time was to come when the Alumni Association numbered its membership in the hundreds and continued to hold yearly banquets as a high light of each school year.

In 1910, the "Old School Mates Association" was organized to

> "bring together each year in annual session all those who attended school and helped to settle Eureka Springs. All those attending school before 1890 are eligible for membership."

The last meeting in the records of this organization was dated 1928.

Schools in Eureka Springs kept pace with those in other communities of comparable size. Money continued to be in short supply for school needs and changes in the nature of the city reduced the number of pupils enrolled. In spite of such handicaps students continued to graduate and go on to the colleges and universities of their choice secure in the knowledge that their early training compared favorably with that of other schools in the state.

CHAPTER VIII

SOCIETY: FASHIONABLE AND BENEVOLENT

Hotels and Hotel Society

The spring mud of 1880 had scarcely dried on the wagon wheels, nor had the summer dust settled along the trails which passed for streets, before it became apparent that the new community of Eureka Springs was to be an exceedingly social one. Persons who were benefitting by their sojourn at the Springs wanted to meet with others who were experiencing benefits for mutual discussion of both ailments and treatments. Folk from the same far away states also liked to meet with others from home and compare experiences. These early visitors to the infant community did not come in order to make a hasty fortune, nor for purposes of establishing a permanent residence. They came seeking healing of ills their flesh had long been heir to, and when able, to enjoy the climate and beautiful surroundings. The earliest photographs show pretty, well dressed women and stalwart men in city business suits lounging on the rocks and logs close to the springs.

During the summer of 1881 the *Arkansas Gazette* sent a reporter to write up the new wonder of "water that healed." Under the byline of "Potomoc" he comments on the "amounts of good clothing worn in the community" and pays special tribute to the ladies "whose dress, grace and street manners, beautiful complexions and beauty rivaled those of Little Rock."

Soon the hotels with their spacious verandas and parlors began to appear and replaced the logs and rocks as favorite visiting spots. The first hotels were either built as close to a spring as possible or as far up the mountain side as feasible, in order to provide a view.

One of the earliest hotels was the Hancock House. Built in 1880, it later became a mecca for those who returned to not only drink again of the water but to exchange tales of "the way it was" in the early days.

Among the many hotels which appeared and disappeared through the years was the Clayton House. This was Powell Clayton's first venture as a hotel man. Another early hotel was the Grand Central down on Main Street, built by Captain John Carroll and opened in 1883.

Cutter's *Guide to the Eureka Springs of Arkansas,* published in 1884, claims the Perry House as the only first class hotel in the city. The same publication lists thirty additional hotels and rooming houses offering rates for room and board from $8.00 to $10.00 weekly. Others offered accomodations from $3.00 to $5.00 weekly.

After the Perry House, the Cutter *Guide* rated the Southern and the Hancock House next as to elegant appointments and congenial surroundings. Others recommended were the Kansas Hotel near Harding Springs, the Monroe House downtown near the Basin Spring, the Mitchell House, Mountain House and Richmond House. Several of these hotels were destroyed in the fire of 1888, among them also a Hotel Silver and the Hancock House. About 1890 the Grand Central Hotel suffered a disastrous fire and was later rebuilt of brick.

As fire continued to wipe out one and another of the frame hotels, others were built to take their place. The most noted of these was a huge stone structure called the Crescent Hotel built in 1886.

The *Daily Times Echo* carried advertising in 1890 for the Southern, the Lindell, the Mansion House, Pence, Landaker, Piedmont, St. James, Thach Cottage, Wadsworth and the Crescent.

Altogether, over fifty hotels of various sizes made their appearance in the town during its first fifty years. Only the

Crescent, Basin Park and one which began its career as the Wadsworth, later becoming the Allred, and still later doing business as the New Orleans, survive.

The first hotel to achieve social distinction was the Thach Cottage Hotel. It began as a four room cottage away from the lower street levels but only a short walk up the hill from the Harding Spring. It very quickly grew and grew and grew until it had one hundred very genteel rooms and was surrounded by spacious verandahs. During the 1880's and the gayer 1890's it was one of the most prosperous of summer hotels with guests returning year after year to enjoy the familiar family atmosphere. Food was abundant, served family style, and regular guests had their regular places at the tables. The menus were hearty and a lingering memory noted warm peach cobbler as the all time favorite dessert. After the Crescent was built, the Thach Cottage may have slipped a bit, but it continued to enjoy a goodly measure of popular support until it too fell victim to fire in 1932. This fire was probably caused by faulty wiring and not only the hotel, but an adjacent church, a twenty room apartment house and a residence were destroyed. While the building was a loss, the many pleasant memories of early times in Eureka Springs could not be destroyed.

The crooked, hilly streets, inadequate fire fighting equipment and lack of a sufficient water supply system let many once prosperous establishments go up in flames.

What was to be the showplace of Northwest Arkansas appeared in 1886. The Crescent Hotel was the brainchild of Powell Clayton and the group of men who formed the Eureka Springs Improvement Company. Securing twenty-seven acres of wooded mountain side, a setting was provided for a hotel of the type of architecture popular in the 1880's and known as American Gothic. The architect responsible for this palace in the wilderness was Issac S. Taylor. The stone used was quarried from the nearby quarries at Beaver.

A feature of the spacious fireplace in the lobby is a large stone carved with the names of Powell Clayton, Logan Roots,

D. A. Nichols and others as a permanent memorial to those who helped bring forth such a lusty child.

The grand opening was held on May 21, 1886, and was attended by four hundred guests from far and near. Jesse Lewis Russell, in his book *Behind These Ozark Hills* tells of the opening of the Crescent as attracting nationwide attention. The guest of honor was no other than James G. Blaine, then Republican nominee for President of the United States. The *St. Louis Globe Democrat* of that date lists some of the distinguished guests from over the state and describes the elegant evening attire worn by the ladies. The wife of the Chief Justice of Arkansas, Mrs. S. R. Cockrill, wore jet-trimmed black velvet and diamonds. The wife of a United States Judge, Mrs. H. C. Caldwell, was equally elegant in brown silk entraine, while the wife of the Treasurer of the State appeared in black lace and diamonds. Brocaded satin and very elegant diamonds was the choice of Mrs. Judge McClure and Mrs. W. G. Whipple made her appearance in beautiful black lace enhanced by diamonds. Very rich black velvet with a court train was worn by Mrs. Logan Roots and Mrs. E. N. Van Harten appeared in brown lace sprinkled with daisies and diamonds. The young ladies were in no way eclipsed by the matrons, as Miss Laura E. Brown was attired in golden brown silk with rhinestone ornaments; Miss Jean Goughbrough appeared in white satin with crystal trimmings and Miss Annie Kimbrell, daughter of Judge Kimbrell of Dardanelle, wore lace trimmed pink with a handsome corsage. Generally acknowledged to be the belle of the ball by the Little Rock newsmen, the costume of Miss Mary Newton was of marvelieux with a plush embroidered front panel and garniture of ostrich tips and diamonds.

Gentlemen attending from Little Rock included Col. Logan H. Roots, Major W. E. Woodruff, Judge H. C. Caldwell, Judge John McClure and E. N. Van Harten. The list of Eureka Springs guests is not available, but it surely included the flower of society from the gentlemen who were instrumental in the organization through the top social strata of townsmen.

During the Victorian era, the Crescent was famous for its gracious Southern hospitality. An army of white coated

Powell Clayton

The Crescent Hotel, a "castle in the wilderness", built in 1886

The Summer Auditorium at the Assembly Grounds — 1890

The original lobby of the Crescent Hotel

The Basin Spring Park and Southern Hotel, about 1895

The Basin Spring Park after improvements
by Board of Public Affairs — 1890

The Pence House hotel on The Boulevard — 1890

The popular Chautauqua House, across the street from the Pence.

The Thach Cottage Hotel, fashionable during the 1880s and '90s

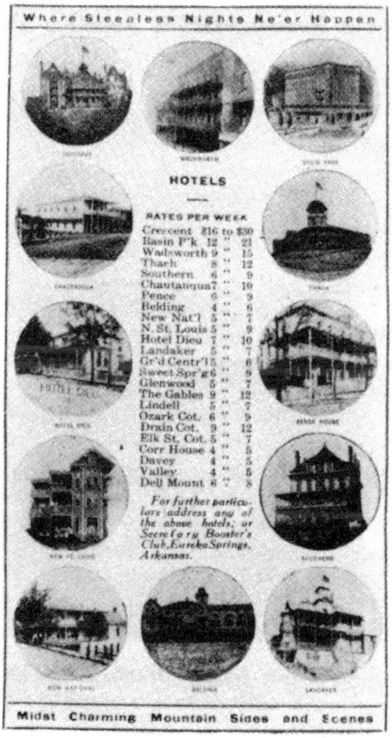

Some of the early hotels and rates

The beautiful Rosewater-Ellis building, about 1898

The Crescent Livery Barn, built 1884

The Basin Park Hotel, nearing completion, 1905

Looking up Spring Street — 1910; Basin Park Hotel entrance at left, Rosewater-Ellis building at center, Flat Iron building at right

Salisbury's Band, Basin Park Band Stand, about 1890

Barbecue crowd at the oil derrick, 1921

servitors catered to the slightest whim of each guest. Meals featured the true Southern cuisine and tall frosty mint juleps were to be had at all times, served on the shady porches and walks.

Orchestras played for evening dancing and a boardwalk ending in a shaded summer house helped promote many a romance.

The guest season slacked off during the winter months, but the coming of spring was always celebrated with a ball. These balls were gala events, but the one in March of 1900 was especially festive. A colored string quartette, also the Harrington Mandolin Club from St. Louis, were imported to entertain the guests. A partial guest list, which also described the gowns worn by the wives of the distinguished guests, mentions Mrs. Dr. Ellis in black silk decollete, Mrs. Mellier in black satin with lace applique and Miss Mellier in white net over white silk.

Balls were not the only entertainment provided by the Crescent for the amusement of guests. Picnics, tally-ho rides, street car rides, horseback riding and hiking were pleasant diversions. A tally-ho or carriage ride out to what was then known as Sanitarium Lake (Lake Lucerne) ending in a picnic was part of the program provided. The tally-ho was a sort of coach drawn by four horses and having places for as many as thirty-five persons to ride comfortably. Not only the hotels, but the livery stables advertised tally-ho rides to Berryville and to other more scenic attractions.

Horses for riding were in plentiful supply, as both the hotels and the livery stable could supply guests wishing to take advantage of this form of exercise. Often as many as seventy-five riders would be in a gay party making their way along a mountain trail. The ladies were especially elegant in their long skirted riding habits. Faces were well protected by hats and veils which shielded delicate complexions. At first women rode the fashionable side saddles, but by 1910 they appeared in divided skirts and more western appearing hats. English saddles were usually the choice of the men.

Sometime in the early part of 1904, the Citizens Electric Company put a fully illuminated street car in service for street car excursions. Several trips were made each evening in the gaily decorated trolley with its hundreds of twinkling colored lights. Often bands or orchestras accompanied these rides, which were very popular with the guests of the hotels, including the Crescent.

As all dreams must end, so did the opulent dream called the Crescent Hotel. The big stone pile was never big as a money maker, but the Frisco Railroad decided to take a chance and took it over on a five year lease in 1902. The hotel had been in operation sixteen years and was in need of a face lift. The well known St. Louis architect, Guy Crandall Morimer, was called in for some remodeling and $50,000.00 was invested in improvements and new furnishings. At the end of their lease, the Frisco did not renew and in 1908 Crescent College took over for nine months of the year, the hotel being open only during the summer.

In 1932 Crescent College closed its doors and the building passed from hand to hand until 1937, when it fell into the clutches of Norman Baker. A book about Baker and his activities shows him to have been in serious trouble with the government at the time he purchased the hotel. His history was far from wholesome for a doctor, but since the final outcome of his troubles was still in doubt, possibly the building was sold to him in the hope that it would be profitable to him and to the community. It was the Crescent's darkest hour, for Baker turned the once beautiful interior into one of the strangest hospitals in hospital history.

Professionally, Baker was a protege of the notorious Dr. Brinkley of Texas, but his ideas of interior decoration were his own. Purple paint was liberally applied to the once beautiful lobby and tasteless signs appeared in the long corridors. Between his purple walled office and the lobby was a large panel of bullet proof glass and the office was tastefully decorated with two tommy guns hanging within easy reach. Rumor spoke of a secret stairway from the office up to the roof. Baker had ensconsed himself in the apartment formerly occupied by Powell Clayton—in fact the governor's suite—and such changes were in marked contrast to the former beauty. To carry out his purple theme, Baker dressed to suit the decor—wearing orchid ties, wrote with purple ink on orchid stationary and rode in an orchid-tinted automobile.

In 1940 the law caught up with Baker, one of the many charges being that of using the mails to defraud. Even in the three years Baker had been in residence, almost irreparable harm had been done to a once elegant interior. What was the showplace of Northwest Arkansas stood vacant until a group of hotel men from Chicago saw the possibilities of the building and its beautiful location and tried to restore it to its former grandeur.

Another grand hotel opening took place on July 1, 1905, when the Basin Park Hotel, with great fanfare opened its doors to the public. Promoted by W. M. Duncan and his associates, this eight story stone structure was adjacent to the Basin Spring just a short way north of the intersection of Spring and Main Streets. Built against the steep side of the mountain, an exit to terra firma was provided on every floor. The restaurant on the second floor, the ballroom and a roof garden soon became the settings for lavish dinners and dances. Old programs, as well as news stories, attest to the high order of entertainment and service provided. Invitations to special events often requested full dress, so evenings were formal though gay.

After 1907, dances were regular summer events at both the Basin Park Hotel and the Crescent. These hotels had their own orchestras for several years and also imported larger ones for special occasions.

Like the castle on the hill, this hotel also changed ownership several times, but always continued in its role as a hotel. As the years took their toll of both the building and its furnishings, many of the public rooms were closed. The restaurant moved to the ground floor and the lobby was reduced in size. Rates were kept very reasonable, but the many modern motels built along Highway No. 62 left the once glamorous hotel a bit less than glamorous. This is the hotel that Robert Ripley once featured in his "Believe It Or Not."

In the autumn of 1908 the numerous affairs of W. M. Duncan destroyed his once prosperous business empire and the Basin Park was leased to the managers of the Crescent. They proposed to operate the two hotels independently. This was the first of the many changes in ownership and management for this popular hostelry. Finally it came into the capable hands of C. A. Fuller, where it remained for many years.

The third of the hotels still in business began as the Wadsworth and later became the Allred. This was built in 1902 by W. S. Wadsworth, one of the prominent early settlers who built several outstanding business buildings. The three upper floors fronting on Spring Street were enhanced with wrought iron balconies reminiscent of the deep South. For some reason this hotel never achieved the publicity or popularity awarded either the Basin Park or the Crescent, but continued as a hotel under the name New Orleans.

The stone carving on the front of the well built stone structure just around the corner of Spring Street from the Sweet Spring says, "Palace Bath House 1901." Baths of water from the Harding Spring were provided in the lower floors while the upper stories were guest rooms. A spacious lobby and parlors were on the Spring Street level. While once popular because it was so close to the Harding Spring it never enjoyed the success, even short lived, of the other hotels.

For the first fifty years the hotels of Eureka Springs made a large contribution to the social life of the city.

Club and Fraternal

While many of the clubs and fraternal organizations used the hotels for meetings, luncheons and banquets they also met in the homes of members and in halls provided for that purpose. Some of these organizations are of especial interest because they were products of the time and the place. One of these, the Invalids' Association, was not for purely social reasons though some social benefits accrued.

The now rare little magazine *Points* for the first quarter of 1900, has this to say about the Invalids' Association, and they quote from an earlier newspaper *The Register* for 1881,

> "Tuesday the 29th of November, 1881, the regular meeting of the Invalids' Association convened at the Elk Street M. E. Church. Long before the hour for opening (2:30 P. M.) the church was crowded to its utmost capacity."

Following this is a two column report of the proceedings giving the names and personal testimonials of twenty-one people cured by the waters of Eureka Springs. The diseases with which they were afflicted run the gamut from asthma to spinal disease, also cancer.

In a news story in April, 1883, the proceedings of an election of officers is given. Officers were only elected for six months as ordinarily when a visitor was cured he went back to where he came from to tell his or her story and encourage others to try the "healing water." From its first meeting the relating of testimonials of healing was the principle object of the association. The members not only provided hope for other health seekers, but expressed gratitude for finding a source of healing. *Cutter's Guide to Eureka Springs* published in 1884 says meetings were held twice a month and sometimes oftener. He also relates how

> "Visitors who had been cured or benefitted by the use of these waters—after relating their case history would express gratitude for their healings in a most demonstrative manner and were as happy as new converts at a religious revival."

The happy results of cures by the magic waters often encouraged other sufferers to remain long enough to be cured and not to rush away discouraged. How long this most interesting and useful association continued to hold meetings is not a matter of record. No other organization ever served the same purpose and one can but wonder had it continued to spread the healing message if the later story of Eureka Springs might not have been different.

It wasn't too many years until the healing qualities of the water, while remaining the same, were less emphasized than the resort qualities of the community. People continued to come and possibly one of the oldest organizations devoted to sponsoring tourism and keeping the tourist happy was the Tourist Club. Legend says it began when two families both desiring to hold picnics met at their chosen site the Magnetic Spring, only to be rained out; one family was from Iowa and the other was from Nebraska. Planning for another day, they were joined by about 30 others and so the Tourist Club was born. The real name was The Tourist Social Hour Club and everyone staying in Eureka Springs from a few days to many weeks joined this unique club. Talent from all over the United States participated in the impromptu entertainments which were held in various places. The Opera House was a favorite place, but so were the spacious hotel parlors, and needless to say every entertainment was well attended.

An old treasurer's record of The Tourist Social Hour Club and an envelope of pictures are all that remains of this once active organization. The treasurer's record of the Club is for March and April of 1919 and shows that 68 persons paid 25 cents dues at that time. While the purpose of the club was mostly to have a good time, when the opportunity came civic enterprises were given aid as well as encouragement. The Tourist Social Hour Club disbanded in May, 1935, and the funds left in the treasury were donated to Harmon Park.

The small card which was passed out to all visitors sums up their reason for existence.

"How do you do, Friend Tourist,
How do you do?
We'll do the best we can,
Stand by you like a man
How do you do, Friend Tourist
How do you do?"

A special song, "Ode to Eureka Springs," was used to open the meetings which were always boosters for the community.

In the city of Eureka Springs, where
    crystal waters flow,
There is healing in the waters that
    will cleanse from every woe;
There you'll see all faces smiling, as
    you daily come and go
On the streets of our city so fair.

CHORUS

Glory, glory for our friendships,
Glory, glory for our friendships,
Glory, glory for our friendships,
    Forever, evermore.
There you'll see the Ozarks crested
    with the flower and the vine,
You will see the people coming from
    the states, and every clime,
To drink the waters freely from the
    springs that are divine,
On the streets of our city so fair.

CHORUS

Here we drink from pure Magnetic
    From our Harding and the Sweet
From the Basin, at the Circle, where
    our friendships are complete,
And our joys made everlasting, by the
    charming ones we meet,
On the streets of our city so fair.

Written by W. J. Moore

This was usually sung to the tune of "The Battle Hymn of the Republic."

An association which was most unique for its time and which was not for purely social reasons was the Ladies United Relief Association, though it too undoubtedly provided certain social benefits in the mutual satisfaction of the members. Mrs. Powell Clayton was life president of this association which was organized in 1886 and whose aim might be said to be that of the old song, "to rescue the perishing, care for dying." From the earliest times many people came to Eureka Springs without visable means of support or without any skills they could use to make a living. These people were in need of help and the gallant ladies organized to do what they could to relieve the suffering caused by poverty.

According to Nellie Mills in her little book *Early Eureka Springs*, her mother was a member and met with other ladies on Tuesdays to spend a large part of their time mending and altering the large quantities of used garments given to them. At that time Mrs. Clayton was in residence at the Crescent Hotel where she no doubt found a good supply of little worn clothing discarded by the guests. More strenuous work than sewing also took up much of their time. The town was divided into districts and one, and sometimes two, members were assigned to each district to visit and investigate cases of destitution. Complaints were reported at the weekly meetings and discussed by the members before action was taken. The case load was heavy and a small charity hospital was opened and operated for a short time. So many cases applied for help it began to be suspected that paupers were being sent to Eureka Springs to keep neighboring communities from taking care of their responsibilities so the hospital was closed.

In 1897 General Clayton was appointed ambassador to Mexico and Mrs. Clayton had to leave her beloved LURA. By that time the members had been actively engaged in their good work for nine years. No available record was left of those years, but a secretarys' book was started in 1895 to report activity which continued after Mrs. Clayton's departure. The book showed members visiting the destitute and providing living quarters, food, clothing and medicine where needed. They also helped indigents to locate relatives who were willing to give them a home and provided the fare necessary for them to make the trip away from Eureka Springs. Burial was also provided for those whose families were unable to help. The County Welfare was poorly organized and the influx of people had strained the resources of Carroll County to the limit. The County Judge decided on the help necessary and did as much as possible, but as ever, with the poor, it was not enough.

The load of indigents grew heavier than usual and without the encouragement and resourcefulness of Mrs. Clayton the ladies became quite discouraged. Meetings were so poorly attended it was voted to disband the club.

Apparently they couldn't break faith with Mrs. Clayton and her high ideals and Mrs. W. S. Wadsworth continued her determined encouragement, so they went back to work again, caring for the sick, keeping shoes on bare feet and also sending as many as possible back to where they had lived before their Eureka Springs adventure. The ladies finally disbanded on April 7, 1896, so they said, for all time. Providing clothing, shoes, food, shelter and medicine for those too old, ill or worthless to do for themselves was a large order for the 13 active members left in the once large organization.

But the ladies couldn't stay disbanded, so on November 24, 1896, they reorganized with the original members who had voted to disband increased to the number of 27 and with 16 honorary members. Once more they pledged themselves to relieve the suffering winter brings to the unfortunate. The case load was taken up again and they also tried to get the Carroll County poor farm to do its duty toward the indigent. Men, women, and children often came to Eureka Springs expecting to be looked after and maintained like the lillies of the field. Children were sent out on the streets to beg in such numbers that in February of 1898 the County Judge ordered a survey to determine the number of children so used.

The LURA owned a small house, Turlock Cottage, which was used to house respectable poor and they tried to keep it in decent repair as well as occupied by decent people. Tenants provided the good ladies with some interesting problems, but the good judgement of the club members usually prevailed. Many of the single women came to Eureka Springs for no good reason, good for themselves or good for the community. Women of this class were referred to as "chippies" by the ladies of LURA, who sent them on their way as soon as possible, though not letting them starve in the meantime.

The secretary's book for the LURA breaks off in March 1899. Once again meetings had dwindled down to only 6 or 7 members while the churches and county were in a better position to handle their responsibilities. So, one of the most interesting and colorful clubs of Eureka Springs was no more. Among the many supporters besides Mrs. Clayton, who had continued to send money from Mexico, was W. H. Reid of Chicago, whose interest in Eureka Springs extended to its unfortunates. Funds had also been raised by socials where ice cream, lemonade and other digestables were sold. The handful of women who contributed their time and sympathetic labor to the club for 13 years could only reap their reward elsewhere than in the town they assisted so unselfishly.

It is hoped the angels recorded that during the existence of LURA no child in Eureka Springs who needed shoes ever went without, as the shoeless ones ever found a soft spot in the hearts of the members of the association.

The Ladies Union Relief Association was not the only local organization having a humane purpose. A Humane Society was organized on October 26, 1896, to detect and punish anyone guilty of cruelty to animals. No record is left of the extent of their work, but the large numbers of horses and mules used for hauling supplies and produce over the mountain roads probably provided them with sufficient interest until the railroad and later the automobile made the major part of their work obsolete.

When a few people decided to remain permanently in Eureka Springs and to organize as a city they also began to organize chapters of the lodges and/or fraternal organizations to which they had previously belonged in other locations. Some of these clubs only lasted a short time, others have continued active through the years. Apparently the first lodge to organize was the Knights of Pythias which started in 1880. They were followed by the IOOF in 1881. The F and AM Spring Lodge No. 386 and the Eureka Chapter Royal Arch Masons were organized the same year. These lodges were followed in 1885 by the Knight Templars and the Eastern Star.

In 1888 the Independent Order of Good Templars organized, but soon disbanded as their regalia and other lodge paraphernalia proved too expensive.

By May 31, 1890, the GAR (Grand Army of the Republic) Post, Sons of Veterans, YMCA, WCTU and the Farmers Alliance were all meeting regularly, as were the ex-Confederates. The Farmers Alliance was an organization which planned to assist the farmers. Another organization, the YWCTU, made a brief appearance in 1889.

The Maccabees and the Lady Maccabees, the Modern Woodmen of America, the Redmen and the Rebeccas (the distaff side of the IOOF) had all been organized by 1894 and soon all of the major lodges and fraternal organizations were holding meetings.

As the town developed, so did the social scene, and soon clubs with no other aim but to have a good time or to elevate their thinking appeared.

The popular literary society known as "The Fortnightly" was organized on the 24th of January, 1894. Membership was limited to 50 and Mrs. Chas. E. Davis was the first president. A yellowed, undated clipping records the second annual banquet of this club at the Thach Cottage Hotel. Members and guests totaling 64 persons were served with turkey, ham, salads, fruits, ice cream, cake and coffee. Dinner was followed by an elaborate program of toasts and responses and ended with musical numbers. Since these were very well prepared the evening was considered a literary and musical treat. Another clipping, undated, in an old scrap book records that the purpose of the meeting was for the election of officers and that the president was re-elected for the seventh time. This meeting was at Avarana, the summer home of Mr. and Mrs. W. H. Reid. The Club membership numbered ministers, doctors, and business men and their wives. From the tone of the clipping it was evident that the membership had made good progress in amiability.

During the next ten or twelve years numerous small clubs were organized, some to play cards as the Whist Club, some to sew as the local chapter of the Needlework Guild and at least one to read current books. In 1908 a Shakespeare Club dedicated to the study of works by the ever popular Bard of Avon, was organized. They gave many elaborate programs featuring readings by the members from both the tragedies and comedies. In this way a culture-hungry few were able to satisfy their longing for great theatre.

Outdoor activity also came in for a share of social gatherings. Dedicated to the sport of hunting and trap shooting one of the early clubs was "the Trap Shoot and Gun Club." They owned their own clubhouse and grounds and not only enjoyed the keen competition afforded by the sport, but some very sumptuous feasts which pleased both members and guests.

The Modern Priscillas were organized in January, 1908. Their original book of bylaws has been preserved. Their object was to "create interest in Art needlework and to promote and strengthen the social relations between members." The membership was limited to 20, new ones being added as vacancies occurred, but all were to be from the young married set. Refreshments were to be served only once a month, and on that occasion the hostess was permitted to invite guests. Once a year a gala event for husbands and two other friends of each member was to be given and refreshments for these affairs were to be provided from club funds. Club meetings were to be treated in a secret fashion and members could be dropped for repeating either the business or the conversation which took place during meetings.

At the first meeting on January 23, 1908, the constitution and by-laws were approved with Mrs. R. G. Floyd as organizing president. At the January 30th meeting, the name, "Modern Priscillas," was adopted and at the February meeting, green and white were selected as the club colors and carnations as the club flower.

When the first anniversary came it was celebrated with a party. These parties were to become events for which invitations were eagerly sought after and which were the high lights of many social seasons. The first one of these elegant affairs was held at the home of the C. A. Fullers; another affair given by the Fullers was a rook party. Twenty-six Modern Priscillas and their John Aldens partook of refreshments of fruit salad, finger sandwiches, creamed chicken and relishes followed by apricot sherbet and cake. Mrs. Fuller carried out her hostess duties in a corn-colored charmeuse with a small train and a lace overdress. The house was a bower of white carnations, the club flower.

Since the members were all young women, an occasional meeting was devoted to welcoming new babies and entertaining older ones. The members adopted the historic Priscilla costume of Plymouth times and wore them on special occasions.

So the organization went on through the years. Their funds were principally used to purchase patterns for the use of the members. Eventually there is a time when patterns have accumulated to the point where a new one is needed only now and then so it was voted to use the extra funds for charity, if approved by a 2/3 vote of the members. The rest-room opened in the central part of town was the first project to receive a donation.

In the early part of 1914 the club voted that each member buy a book which would be circulated among the other members, so that during the year each member would have an opportunity to read it. Thus a sort of lending library was started.

The Carnegie Public Library building had finally become a reality, but books were lacking and a library is incomplete without books. So, at their meeting of May 14, 1914, the Priscillas decided to "do something" for the library. Earlier they had voted to give a one dollar prize, to be awarded by Professor Barnett, to the school child killing the most flies in a fly extermination campaign. Help for the infant Library was next.

After much discussion and a delay while the ladies waited to see the results of a benefit the P.E.O. was giving for the local band, a committee was appointed to meet with the Library Board. The purpose of the meeting was to determine what was required by the City in the way of assistance to the Library. After hearing the report of this committee, permission was requested and received to hold an ice cream social in the newly completed Library building. The proceeds were used to establish a fund with which to purchase literature for the childrens section. A total of $14.00 was used to buy especially selected childrens books and it was further decided to add additional books to this section whenever funds were available. It was also voted that each Priscilla join the Library Association. Later a low table and six low chairs were placed in the childrens room; also additional books were added from time to time.

The United States was now at the brink of War and Red Cross work replaced embroidery. The once elaborate luncheons were replaced by simple buffets with an occasional box lunch making an appearance. By 1916 all of the members were too busy to plan the elaborate banquet of former days and the annual dinner was given at Thach Cottage Hotel.

Later in 1916, the Library requested additional help and a pop concert was given in May which eventually provided more editions of juvenile books for the childrens room.

War work continued to take precedence over social events until 1919 when embroidery made a comeback as an afternoon's occupation.

The Library again became a matter for concern and a plan to buy reference books finally produced a single volume in 1920.

It wasn't until 1924 that the poverty in Eureka Springs was brought to the attention of the Priscillas. How they responded was never made public.

The important fact about the Priscillas was the change in the completely social character of this butterfly club to a sober organization ready and willing to assist with civic problems when called upon to do so. In 1925 they were in cooperation with the Woman's Club to give an entertainment to raise funds to be used to help equip the Domestic Science Department of the High School.

The Woman's Club was organized in 1906 as the Magazine Club. It changed its name in 1917 and in 1921 became a member of both the State and National Federation. The members first became active in a civic enterprise when it was proposed to build steps up the mountain side adjacent to the Sweet Spring. Taking the initiative, they hired an architect from Rogers who designed the three flights of steps and two landings each with a stone bench. The steps were completed in 1925 at a cost of $700.00, mostly raised through their efforts. Other activities included luncheons honoring former residents who had made contributions to the early life of Eureka Springs, and also helping to sponsor the free public rest room.

During 1925 they also began to discuss the idea of purchasing a building for a permanent home. These plans were eventually realized with the purchase of a building across the street from the Palace Hotel.

The P.E.O. sisterhood is another well established society. The exclusive membership of this group is composed of the foremost leaders of the community in philanthropic work. The local chapter was organized in 1891 and while the aims and objects of this sisterhood remain secret from the world, the personnel of each local group bears witness to the noble aspirations and high ideals of the order.

With such substantial organizations in the forefront of the social scene, only progress could result. Many of the good things enjoyed by visitors to the city were made possible by the foresight, dreams, and hard work of the womens' organizations. They had a good time too, and brought the mountain town a measure of sophistication lacking in many other towns of larger size.

The Veterans of Foreign Wars did not come on the local scene until 1919. Promoted by Colonel C. D. James this group of World War Veterans was an active participant in both civic and philanthropic endeavors.

Public Entertainment

At a very early date it was recognized that good legitimate entertainment would have to be provided for those visitors whose health permitted them to enjoy concerts and shows. Plans for an Opera House had been made in 1882, according to a story in an issue of the *Echo* published during that year. It was eventually built on Main Street, just north of the intersection of Spring and Main Street. After the opening of this very pleasant opera house, theater as well as opera, lectures and concerts added to the social scene. A photograph published in 1905 shows a spacious auditorium which could seat approximately 300 people in comfortable chairs. Flanking the stage on either side were large boxes. The stage was 18 x 24 feet with a proscenium arch 25 feet high. A stage of this size could accomodate large scale scenery so that the larger productions of the better stock companies and road shows could be shown. Before the foot lights came on, the auditorium was flooded with the light of 200 electric lights. This beautiful and well-equipped entertainment center was under the operation of W. M. Duncan.

Just what gala event opened the Opera House is unknown, but advertisements in May, 1900, newspapers herald the appearance of the Chicago Stock Company. Other events over the next years included a production of "Way Out West", then a popular drama. The Miller Bryan Dramatic and Vaudeville Company also brought their troupe to town and Santinelli, the hypnotist appeared.

Sometime in November of 1908 the Morgan Stock Company presented "Lena Rivers", one of the most repeated dramas in every stock company repertoire. A few weeks earlier "Parsifal" had played to a full house.

One of Mrs. E.D.E.N. Southworth's plays, "The Hidden Hand", was given on February 3, 1909. Mrs. Southworth was a well known novelist and this dramatization of her work was undoubtedly entertainment of a high order.

During the month of February, 1910, a Scandanavian comedy drama "Ole Peterson", was on the boards, and on February 17 the Marlowe Dramatic organization presented an entertainment.

In addition to the offerings of commercial theatrical companies, the social scene was further enlivened by the recitals and concerts given by the faculty and students of Crescent College after it opened in 1908. Often these entertainments were quite elaborate and a great deal of hard work went into their production. The Opera House stage was also the scene of music and speech recitals given by pupils of the many private teachers then resident in Eureka Springs. The Opera House continued to be a center for live entertainment until the movies became popular. Late in 1917 the Opera House began to show movies and continued to do so until it was dismantled.

When Chautauqua became a popular form of summer entertainment, the Summer Auditorium became the focal point for large crowds of people who flocked to the lectures and musical events. Often the seating capacity of 3500 was well filled with men and women who came to hear the outstanding speakers of that time.

Chautauqua season usually lasted two weeks with devotional exercises conducted in the mornings by pastors of the various denominations. Afternoons and evenings were given over to entertainment. The season for 1904 began on July 17 with a talk by Eugene V. Debs. In 1894 Mr. Debs had made headlines with his "Debs Rebellion" against the Pullman Company of Chicago. His philosophy made him in great demand as a speaker and also gave him an opportunity to promote his radical ideas. A sympathetic party met Mr. Debs at the train and escorted him to the Wadsworth Hotel where he rested until time to go to the auditorium. Unfortunately no record as to how his ideas were received survives. Neither was the balance of the program for the week, but the second week offered many other attractions.

On Monday the afternoon entertainment was a piano recital by Miss Lash, while on Tuesday, Dr. C. H. Brough gave a lecture. A dramatic recital by Miss MacDougal was scheduled for Wednesday, to be followed on Thursday by a Grand Musical Concert. Events doubled up on Friday with a lecture, "Castles in the Air", at 11:00 A.M. and with Governor Bob Taylor presenting "The Fiddle and the Bow" in the evening. Saturday's grand finale was an old time Fiddlers Contest.

Chautauqua as an intellectual force continued through the First World War and then disappeared not only from Eureka Springs but from all of the South and the Midwest. During its finest years it had provided the best of music, lectures and sermons, usually by the people most noted in their fields, for the edification of the intellectually undernourished countryside.

When the Chautauqua faded from the scene a natural successor was the Lyceum Lecture Series. Instead of a two weeks program of events, single events given in a series once a month for several months, attained great popularity. Chautauqua booking organizations were converted to Lyceum Bureaus where local organizations such as Woman's Clubs, Rotary Clubs, or other civic groups could, for a small fee, obtain the services of lecturers, musicians, and even small performing groups for single performances. The first Lyceum Series in Eureka Springs was sponsored by the Woman's Club.

It is unfortunate that one of the worst enemies Eureka Springs had in the past was fire. The many destructive fires have burned gaps not only in the landscape, but in the day by day history as chronicled in the daily newspapers lost in those fires. For a time it was the custom of the daily and weekly papers to devote space to continued stories and bits of news not relative to the comunity, rather than to the social events and day by day activities of the local citizens. Because of this, much of real historical interest as to what people wore, ate, or thought is lost. Undoubtedly it was correct to list the healing of all the "ills that flesh was heir to" and to give full credit to the healing waters; still it would be interesting to know more of the human day by day events in such an unusual city.

The well know local reporter, Annie House, kept scrap books, but failed to keep the date on the stories she clipped. She reported events as she saw them for some 65 years and many prove most entertaining. We are indebted to her for the account of the first celebration of the birthday of Robert E. Lee as celebrated in Eureka Springs.

After the State of Arkansas declared the birthdate of Robert E. Lee a State Holiday, a grand public celebration was held at the Basin Park Hotel. This took the form of a public entertainment arranged by Professor C. S. Barnett, in co-operation with the faculty of the Eureka Springs Public Schools. Hailed as the "grandest event of its nature ever to be given in the city" and before "the most cultured throng ever gathered in any city," the program was so exceptionally good, an attempt at description seemed beyond the pen of the reporter; an impassioned description then follows. The Basin Park Orchestra began the program with a selection, "National Airs", which mingled the music of both the North and the South. Readings and songs followed in rapid order until Professor Barnett announced that Miss Bebe Brown would sing "Just Before the Battle, Mother." Now—

> "There was a hush of expectancy, and the expression which fell from the notes of Eureka's Queen of Song thrilled every heart and dimmed every eye. Miss Brown forgot the audience before her and every note reached the heart strings of her auditors with the same passionate sentiment with which they issued from her beautiful throat. Many there declared that her rendition was the sweetest ever heard and her voice the most wonderful."

There were several more numbers on the program which reached its climax with Miss Brown singing "The Last Rose of Summer."

Tributes were then given to General Lee in the form of both prose and poetry, and the event concluded with the singing of "Hail Columbia." It was predicted that future celebrations would have a hard time to equal this one which "reflected great credit to Professor Barnett and the faculty of the public schools, under whose auspices the program was given." Other programs were given as the years came along, but none ever equaled the first celebration of General Lee's birthday.

Music played a large part in the public entertainment of visitors to Eureka Springs. The first band was organized in 1886, according to a letter to the Carroll County Historical Society written by D. Elmer Jones, one of the original bandsmen. His account says the most prominent druggist was a b-flat coronet player who had to have someone to play with. This band marched with the local militia company and Elmer notes they looked "mighty nice with their glistening instruments and nobby uniforms." The militia company is described by J. L. Russell in *Behind These Ozark Hills* as "Captain Joseph M. Hill's company of 'Light Guards', a real military unit set up at Eureka Springs when everything was going wild with excitement at the then uncontrolled booming resort."

D. Elmer Jones goes on to tell of his being a charter member of the band organized in the middle 1890's by Pete Brown. With two members of the original band as a nucleous, they soon built up to 34 charter members, although by the time they had practiced long enough to get a job, their number had dropped to 18. They called themselves the Big Brass Band and got a job playing an hour long concert in the Basin Park Bandstand. This band began the yearly custom of daily, and later, weekly concerts in the park during the summer months.

The Eureka Springs Military Band was also organized and both bands played concerts in Basin Park and out at the auditorium on the assembly grounds. By 1890 concerts were also given by Salisbury's Band, a local organization.

Apparently it was difficult to keep a good band organized as the population was constantly changing. Competent musicians would come to town, sit in awhile and leave with others equally competent not always available to replace them. Thus, over the early years many fine bands were organized, gave concerts for awhile, and just faded away.

Stewart's Band was yet another of the local bands which played for concerts in the Basin Park during the summer of 1904. During the years many visiting bands were scheduled to play there and also for dances at both the Basin Park and Crescent Hotels. In addition to the local bands mentioned previously, several other bands were written up in news items such as the one concerning a concert given at the Opera House in February, 1904, by the Woodmen of the World Band. A few years later, in October, 1909, Brown's Coronet Band had reorganized and was preparing to give summer concerts.

In 1915 a new band stand was built in Basin Park to give a more festive appearance to the annual concerts given by both local and visiting organizations.

Undoubtedly the most exciting performance by any band was the one given in 1928 at the new auditorium across from the Basin Park. John Philip Sousa brought his world famous band to Eureka Springs by special train for this musical event. This band toured the United States that year playing not only in major cities such as Chicago and St. Louis, but in many smaller towns, and Eureka Springs was fortunate in being one of them.

So it was from the earliest times that a "Concert in the Park" was a weekly part of the summer season in Eureka Springs.

Private Parties

There was no dearth of elegant private parties in the early days of Eureka Springs. When private homes were constructed in sufficient quality and quantity, the matrons of the city were always most gracious and generous with their hospitality. Visitors who came and spent several weeks in residence at a hotel were frequently guests at private luncheons, teas, and dinner parties. Often after being the recipient of these favors the departing guest would give a large dinner at one of the hotels as a thank you. No expense was spared for either menu or decorations at these affairs with palms and cut flowers being used in profusion. Both hostess and guests appeared in elaborate new toilettes and even special costume affairs were given. The gay nineties were just as gay in Eureka Springs as in the larger cities, and manners and clothing just as elegant.

In 1910 several social events were chronicled in a small magazine *Points* which was devoted to the social scene. A reception was given by Mrs. Dr. Floyd for her visiting sister. The ladies were beautifully gowned, according to the reporter, and their costumes appeared to the best advantage against a background of palms and cut flowers.

That same year, Dr. and Mrs. Charles Davis celebrated their silver wedding anniversary in their home on Crystal Terrace. Mrs. Davis appeared in cream crepe de chine trimmed with white lace, worn over white silk. A guest, Mrs. Sayles, was gowned in a black and white satin skirt, the black waist trimmed in black lace. Another guest, Miss Carrie Hawley, was attired in green and white silk and Mrs. Melone wore pink silk with white lace, while Mrs. Wadsworth's gown was of tan cloth with pink silk trimmings and pink roses.

Another silver wedding anniversary shared the months spotlight when Mr. and Mrs. W. S. Wadsworth entertained for 150 guests in rooms banked with flowers and palms. For this auspicious occasion, Mrs. Wadsworth appeared in white and pink silk trimmed with real lace.

While the foregoing accounts present a somewhat limited picture of the social life in a community where the primary purpose was healing, it shows that large amounts of optimism were always in the foreground. Great joy and relief often followed the healing of serious ailments and helped to create an atmosphere in which social events could flourish. This, together with the great beauty of the surrounding landscape, helped to promote such beauty as could be made available in each life.

So in the "olden days" Eureka Springs was gay, sociable, and with no lack of either cultural or more mundane entertainment.

CHAPTER IX

SIN . . . AND SALVATION

During the early days in Eureka Springs sin was never on the rampage as it was in the mining and cattle towns of the West. Sick people came to Eureka Springs hoping to be healed, while adventurers flocked to the mining towns hoping to become well-heeled. During the early part of 1879, when the first of the sick and helpless began to arrive, ministers also arrived to care for their spiritual needs.

It took a few weeks after the crowd began to gather before word reached the outside world of the "easy pickin's" to be made in this gathering of people having a single purpose, the healing of infirm flesh. These people were eager for just one thing, so were unsuspecting of what else might befall them. When the word did get around, it wasn't long before every type of lawlessness was to descend on this bonanza, especially after a saloon opened to dispense that type of liquid which bolsters false courage and encourages false cheer.

The first step was to provide curbs for the wrong doers. Those desirous of maintaining order formed a Citizen's Committee which in turn appointed law enforcement officers and a court was set up with His Honor, the Mayor, as judge. Only a short time had passed since the community had seemed like one big happy family at a Camp meeting; now signs of strain were beginning to show.

Early in 1880—

> ". . . the first victim to feel the iron hand of the law, in the person of T. Mallett was soon brought before His Honor, the Mayor, found guilty and sentenced to pay a fine of $500.00 with one year in jail for 'drawing a pistol as a deadly weapon.' This seemed rather austere of His Honor, but no doubt he meant to make an example of the first case, in order that others, in the language of the German 'might look a little out'."

Notwithstanding the Mayor's rigid decision, other cases were soon numerous and his court presented an interesting appearance and in many respects an unpleasant one.

A letter of reminiscence to the *Carroll County Courier* written in 1930 recalls conditions in Eureka Springs in 1881. By then just two years had elapsed since the first draughts of healing water had been quaffed at the Basin Spring. The writer stresses the fact that drinks of a different kind, together with gambling, were now available seven days a week. Up in Kansas the Governor had declared war on the rum sellers and gamblers of that state and some of them moved down to the Springs. At that time the correspondent worked at the drug store next door to the Hancock Hotel and lived at the Grand Central Hotel down in the Gulch, as he called Main, also known as Mud Street. The lawless characters from Kansas were soon sent on their way or drifted on to greener pastures, as Eureka Springs never had the allure of the wide open cow towns such as Wichita or Dodge City. Before they departed shootings occurred with some frequency and a forty-five strapped around the hips was a standard accessory for the well dressed man at that time.

Drinking and gambling are usually accompanied by other evils, and steps were now taken by the forces of law and order to eradicate at least one of them. The Palace Theater was being turned into a dance hall, so they arrested the proprietor. It was bad enough to run the theater as a variety show,

> ". . . but as a dance hall where lewd women, drunken men and reckless boys congregate for their drunken revels and shameless orgies makes it necessary to supress the Theater."

The demise of the Palace was noted in a news item.

> "Hereafter the Palace will be known as The Academy of Music," (A rose by any other name.) Since seventeen saloons were running full blast at the time the dance hall was probably not greatly missed.

To take advantage of the saloon situation, and possibly to try to impose curbs on it, an ordinance was passed in December, 1881, putting the license fee for a saloon at $400.00 a year.

It may not have had any bearing on the situation but a news item for December 26, same year, takes note of the free distribution of bread to anyone in need.

Going on into 1882 and using that year as an example, one finds the Chief of Police and his officials had their work cut out for them. Police Court was held, sometimes daily, and at least every fourth day that summer, with E. R. Ray presiding. It was to be another year before a jail would be built to hold offenders, so they were brought directly to Court, tried and fined for their wrong doing, and released. The most numerous charge was "drunk and disorderly," for the saloons selling "demon drink" were now well established in Eureka Springs. Offenders were fined $10.00 and sent on their way on receipt of payments. Assault and battery and firing off pistols in the streets were all common occurrences and drew fines of $25.00 for each offense.

It was about this time that gambling also became a civic problem. On June 5, 1882, the police cracked down on these undesirables and in a single day closed two saloons, arrested four men for running gambling houses and brought to Court seven individuals caught gambling in these places. A few days later five more persons were tried and convicted for permitting gambling in their saloons. All were fined and set free to continue their normal business pursuits until the police could again discover illegal activities taking place.

Naturally certain women were attracted to the saloons and gambling houses and naturally the civic officials considered them to be undesirable influences in the community.

A number of women were fined for visiting and drinking in saloons, and during the summer more than a dozen were convicted and fined for "keeping houses of ill fame." In those days it behooved a gentleman to consider carefully the company he kept, for several men were arrested and fined $15.00 each for being caught walking along the street with a woman of ill repute.

Lawlessness was off to a good start and as in the frontier towns of the West it took the forces of law and order time to organize in sufficient numbers to establish a law abiding community. As soon as possible the city was well policed and the all-seeing eye of the law was alert to even small misdemeanors, as when a certain Mr. Smith was arrested, tried and convicted for "carrying and using a bean flipper within the city."

During the next several years improvements were made in the handling of miscreants. A jail was built, but most cases of a serious nature were sentenced to the County Jail at Berryville. The tone of the community gradually quieted down as the more responsible citizens built homes and business establishments. Only scattered locations were scenes of lawlessness. One of these had always been the freight yard on top of West Mountain in the 16th Section. (Later in 1894 the water standpipe was put there, and by that time the character of the neighborhood had changed).

In the December, 1891, issue of a local newspaper a news story points to conditions at this yard. Teamsters changed their horses there and found lodging nearby. Apparently this spot was the scene of several other kinds of activity besides changing horses. The miscreants had long defied the law and boasted that they could not be arrested. People living near the freight yard finally complained of a particularly noisy shooting affray, so the Constable, Harris by name, gathered up a posse. They went up to the freight yard and convinced the characters responsible for the disturbance that they could be arrested. Taken before the presiding officer the four women and fourteen men made a sorry sight, especially the women. The Justice recommended that they be got rid of in some way, "as they were a disgrace to the Christian Comunity. Every drunken freighter looks them up and they go on a tear." Fines turned out to be less harsh than words; one man was fined $5.00 the others $1.00 each. The four women were also fined only a dollar a piece. All of the men but two paid their fines, the other two and the women couldn't come up with even that small amount, so they were hauled over to the County Jail at Berryville. The young women had previously figured in police action as had some of the men. The arrests were designed to be a warning to other freighters who of necessity were tough, as freighting called for toughness.

An advertisement in the same newspaper priced whiskey at $2.00 per gallon. One of the ingredients of disorderly conduct appeared to be both cheap and in plentiful supply.

Turlock Cottage was in the vicinity of the freight yard, which still kept its disreputable name as late as 1896. For many years the good ladies of The Ladies Union Relief Association often donated or rented the cottage to indigents. This year they were keeping a close watch because of the occupation of some of the occupants who occasionally proved most undesirable. This was especially true of certain unattached females. The ladies of the L. U. R. A. called them "chippies" and sent them on their way whenever they were found in residence.

Several years before this in 1880 a young man arrived in Eureka Springs who surprising as it seems, became one of the respected citizens of the community. Surprising in view of the attitude toward the saloon business which then prevailed. Born in Clarksville, Johnson County, Arkansas, Robert J. Gray was one of the few early arrivals who had the good fortune to be a native of the state. When he was thirteen years old his parents had taken him along on the six months trek to California and he stayed eighteen years. The call of his native hills brought him back to Arkansas where he began a merchandising enterprise. In 1880 he came to Eureka Springs and engaged in the saloon business. During the next seven years he devoted his time to this and other matters which gained him sufficient prominence to be elected vice-president of the Citizens Bank where, some time later, he acted as president for a period of six months. Newspaper advertisements also show him as a partner in Freeman, Gray and Company, dealers in produce and stock. Mr. Gray was a comparatively young man when he began business in Eureka Springs and in spite of all the agitation against strong drink he was able to attain a sufficiently secure business position in the community to become a banker. This was a switch from the usual saloon to gutter routine. However, one rarely heard of a saloon owner who reached such depths, only his patrons.

Naturally the public desire for law enforcement and the deeper desire to cure the evils which made such enforcement necessary, called forth any number of reform organizations. Since drink seemed to be responsible for a majority of the lawlessness, most of these organizations were designed to warn of the evils of drink before it became a habit.

One of the early attempts was made by the Young Women's Christian Temperance Union. The W.C.T.U. was gaining national prominence and these young women desired to appeal to the youth before habits were formed. Evidence of their efforts to further the cause of temperance is found in the yellowed pages of a notebook kept by the secretary. According to this book a general organization meeting was held in May of 1886 to enlist those "willing to pledge themselves to total abstinence from all liquor." While all of the twenty-four original members were women, men were welcomed as auxiliary members provided they too signed the pledge. Eventually three men did this in time to be called charter members. Besides urging on all and sundry strict adherence to the temperance pledge, the organization provided interested nonmembers with bouquets of flowers in an effort to turn their thoughts to higher joys.

A library of books on temperance was started and a scholarship fund begun. The money was intended to pay for a scholarship to an unspecified school for some young convert. Evidently this intended good work did not exactly prosper, as the worthy group found it necessary to reorganize in 1887 and again in 1889. The notes made by the secretary ended in

1891 and since the book still had many blank pages on which to continue, it is assumed that interest in the good cause ran out as apathy and discouragement ran in. Their efforts had lasted about five years and died not on the vine, but because of it.

Although the Young Women's Christian Temperance Union could not prosper, the older organization, the W.C.T.U., could and did. The original Women's Christian Temperance Union was organized in 1874 at Chautauqua, New York. In the beginning it shared the jokes and jibes of the emerging Women's Sufferage Movement, but by 1879 it had become a power in the land. Small wonder that an active chapter was organized in Eureka Springs which continued active as long as the consumption of liquor in the community continued to be at a high level.

Another temperance organization was the Neal Dow Club. A native of the State of Maine, where he owned many mills, Mr. Dow found that his profits were considerably less when his employees lost time over too generous portions of the cup that cheers. He decided to see what he could do to put a stop to this drinking. His work was so effectual that in 1856 the State of Maine voted itself dry, the first state in the Union to do so. For years temperance clubs bearing his name were organized all over the East and Midwest. In 1880 he ran for President on a Prohibition ticket. It was during this campaign that a Neal Dow Club flourished for awhile in Eureka Springs. Election over and Mr. Dow defeated, the club was never heard of again.

The cause of temperance was served in a more practical manner in Eureka Springs when a Dr. Lennox proposed to establish a cure for the whiskey and drug habit at the Magnetic Spring Hotel. The advertisement in a local newspaper in 1904 offers

> "Liquor habit cured in One Week. Morphine, opium, cocaine and all other drug habits cured in fifteen days. You need not pay one cent until cured. No hypodermics, no confinement, no sickness, no pain."

Just how it was proposed to rout these habits is not known, nor how long this haven of refuge stayed in business. It is quite likely the coming of prohibition made the venture unprofitable.

Women all over the United States pursued the Cause of Temperance with unremitting zeal. Every woman able to speak at a public meeting did so and the more effective speakers traveled up and down the land giving lectures to promote the Cause. Eureka Springs was not neglected, for in July, 1904, the local Temperance Legion sponsored a talk by Mrs. Mary Hunt and later the same month a large audience heard from Mrs. Nannie Curtis on the evils of drink. Probably such a determined effort could not be sustained through the years, and in spite of all efforts at the local level saloons continued to keep open and enjoy good business. During 1908 there were six saloons licensed to sell liquor.

The agitation to remove such places from Carroll County met with success in both Green Forest and Berryville. Editorials in their newspapers pointed the finger of shame at Eureka Springs for letting the saloons stay open. Both towns bragged of being out of debt as well as having rid themselves of saloons. The editorials spoke of Eureka Springs and its $40,000 indebtedness as though it were caused by harboring such establishments. Probably the debt was incurred to pay for local civic improvements that neither of the other towns cared to afford.

From the *Eureka Springs Times* for January 7, 1908, we learn that an election for new City officials occasioned much angry activity and resulting publicity on both sides of the saloon question. Petitions were circulated both pro and con and accusations as to the extent of political involvement in the affairs of the City by the saloon owners was well hashed over. However, no great changes resulted, although the effects of all those temperance lectures were beginning to be felt.

The echoes of the crusade which Carrie Nation had been waging across the United States and over in the British Isles also reached Eureka Springs, although Carrie had not yet made an appearance. When she finally did arrive her visit was on the mild side. She was beginning to be both old and tired. Mrs. Nation's zeal had outlasted her strength, so her visit was not a "smashing" success. When she came in 1908 she proposed to establish a temperance school and purchased property for that purpose. Her plans did not interfere with the local saloons; they were open for business as usual. In February of 1910 the six saloons as well as the three pool halls were allowed to renew their licenses. In June of 1911, Carrie Nation died, after a six months illness, and with her died some of the more drastic efforts to abolish saloons. At the national level the campaign for prohibition continued and in 1919 prohibition became the law of the land. Finally Eureka Springs went "dry" and sin, at least so far as "ardent spirits" were concerned, was never the same again.

Prohibition as a national law was a great shock to many as the provisions of the law began to be put into effect. Those determined not to be deprived of their liberty to drink what and when they choose began to investigate ways in which the law could be circumvented. During the early 1920's stills were set up in several locations deep within the wooded hills which encircle Eureka Springs and soon the making of moonshine whiskey became a business, even though an illicit one. The law on both local and federal levels did its best to stamp out this unlawful activity and succeeded to some extent.

The laws enacted to enforce national prohibition proved to be unworkable and after a fair trial of approximately twelve years, the law was repealed. When this happened the sale of liquor was turned over to the states for regulation and soon became a game for politicians. After long years of effort, decency and law and order prevailed within the town of Eureka Springs except for an occasional "cutting scrape" when two quarrelsome citizens would take the law in their own hands and try to settle their differences with knives. Most citizens went about their affairs in a peaceful and law abiding manner.

All the long years while the battle for the bottle was being fought the forces for good were not dormant.

Unlike the Western frontier towns, where Christianity did not make its formal appearance upon the scene until well after the "forces of evil" had taken hold, the Gospel was preached in the summer of 1879 to the first families camping around the Big Spring. Those who came to be healed of bodily ailments by the waters also needed the solace and encouragement of religion. Visiting ministers could issue their call "to come and be saved" from any convenient rock and the atmosphere of a camp meeting prevailed. Kalklosch writes in *The Healing Fountain,* his eye witness account of the early beginnings, how:

> "Ministers of the Gospel also found their way to the new Silvan and preaching was a common occurrence. People were impressed with the necessity of drinking also of the water that Christ shall give, that shall be in them a well of water springing up into everlasting life."

From neighboring communities and more distant towns the ministers came. For the most part they were active and intelligent men representing various denominational leanings. They labored earnestly in their chosen work preaching by day or night. This early ministering to the needs of the people in a spirit of Christian love helped provide a climate in which all religious beliefs could be welcome.

As the months passed and people began to build permanent dwellings, the ministers sometimes preached from unfinished houses, but more often the Good News rang out from "the great temple sheltered only by the canopy of evening."

Throughout the first summer life continued to be a picnic in a very literal sense, and it was not until the first frost came, bringing with it the falling leaves of autumn, that people began to plan for survival through the cold and snowy months of winter. While the summer warmth remained the people gathered for preaching, sitting comfortably about on the hillside, while the minister borrowed some large rock for a pulpit upon which to rest his well thumbed Bible.

Soon the traveling preachers moved on to make way for the "stationed" or permanent pastors sent by various denominational groups "to collect and feed their flocks". The Methodist Episcopal Church, South, is credited with sending the first "stationed" minister to the new town in November of 1879. The following February the Methodist Episcopal Church (Northern Body) sent their man. Both groups organized within a short time and began work to secure church buildings, in the meantime holding Sunday School classes and meetings in any available spot. The first house of worship for the Northern Methodists was situated on Elk Street and there the congregation gathered from 1880 to 1926 when the building was sold. The members disbanded transferring their affiliations to the M.E. Church, South, and continued as a part of this congregation. The other body of Methodists met in various buildings on Eureka Street, also above a store on Spring Street and on Pine Street not far from Thach Cottage. In 1900 a new building was erected near Harding Spring and this building remains in use to the present time.

In the *History of Carroll County,* Goodspeed tells that the Christian Church (Disciples of Christ) is among the oldest religious organizations in Eureka Springs, and further states that the first sermon ever preached in the settlement was delivered by a minister of that denomination. Subsequent events did not bear out this first beginning as the congregation was not organized until 1889, when they met in a little white frame chapel near the Thach Cottage Hotel. A second congregation of this denomination met on Mountain Street in a building which had housed the Emanuel Baptists for awhile. When Thach Cottage burned, so did the little white church. Fortunately it was insured and the insurance was used to pay off the debt on the Mountain Street church when the two congregations united.

Several persons representing Presbyterian leanings came on the scene by March, 1882. They called their number together at the M.E. Church, South, for an organizational meeting. The Reverend Mr. McElwee had been holding Presbyterian services for more than a year and during 1881 had preached in a large tent, which could accomodate 300 people, at the corner of Mountain and Spring Street. The worshippers sat on hard wooden benches; even so attendance was good until the cold weather forced the services to discontinue.

When the Presbyterian organization meeting was held in the Methodist sanctuary representatives of the Northern,

Southern and Cumberland bodies were present. An agreement was reached to unite in one organization and then become attached to "Which ever of the bodies offered the most liberal assistance." The organization which resulted was composed of 28 members; four were Cumberland, four Southern, eighteen Northern and two Congregationalists. They became connected ecclesiastically with the Ozark Presbytery North.

This newly organized body continued to hold services in the tent for yet another summer and provided floor boards and chairs to contribute to the comfort of the parishioners. A store building on Short Street was the next meeting place and the group set about resolutely to build an edifice as soon as possible. The "Ladies of the Extra Cent Society" put their collective initiative to work, as Christian women are prone to do in time of need, and raised $1400.00 toward a building fund. In 1885 the Eureka Springs Improvement Company donated a lot to the Presbyterian effort, but only on the condition that a stone building be constructed on the site.

Apparently this restriction was an early attempt at city planning and zoning. The final townsite settlement between the City and the Eureka Springs Improvement Company stipulated that "deeds should be executed . . . to Churches without compensation," but Powell Clayton and his associates undoubtedly felt the need to impose regulations which would insure that such buildings would be of a permanent nature, as well as additions to the overall beauty of the growing City. The foundation for the church was laid in the autumn of that year and since the Crescent Hotel was nearly complete and a quantity of stone was left over it was given to the Presbyterians for their use. An American Gothic structure where 300 may worship in either the sanctuary or the lecture room was completed twelve months later. The corner stone had been laid in 1886 on May 13. A munificent gift of $3,000 by William L. Lee, together with the courtesy of the Eureka Springs Improvement Company in donating the lot is held in grateful rememberance by all who worship in this beautiful church.

St. James Protestant Episcopal Church originated in the 1880's through the efforts of a Reverend Vaulx who came from Fayetteville to conduct a monthly service. This monthly service was continued for some time even after a frame chapel was built on Mountain Street. The church organization was not effected until September, 1883, when thirty members were enumerated. After the W. H. Reid School was built the parish was able to obtain the building that had housed the Comer School and soon began to transform it into a substantial church. Like many other congregations, St. James had its vicissitudes, but it successfully weathered them.

The followers of the Roman Catholic Faith were first organized in 1881 by the Reverend Smythe during a temporary stay in Eureka Springs. He left before an effective organization could be completed and it was several months before further action was taken. In December, 1882, Bishop Edward Fitzgerald of the Diocese of Little Rock purchased a beautiful pine grove in block 41 of Freemans addition to Eureka Springs. (This was in the vicinity of the place where the water tower was later built). A Catholic Church was soon erected in this location; although it was quite far out for those who had to walk, it continued in use for many years.

The Sisters of Mercy had come to the Springs and were operating a hospital on Fairmount Avenue, known as the Hotel Dieu. In order to have the Church closer to the Hospital, Bishop Fitzgerald, in 1902, purchased two lots of the Clayton survey at the corner of Prospect and Fairmount Avenues and moved the Church to that location. Two years later when it was decided a school was needed a two story frame building was constructed adjacent to the church.

The old church was abandoned when Richard C. Kerens built and donated St. Elizabeth's Chapel to the community in 1908. The four pieces of statuary in the vestibule of the chapel are the only reminders left of the original Church. The first mass was held in the new sanctuary on New Years Day, 1908.

The story of the building of St. Elizabeths has been told too often to need retelling here. From time to time additions were made to the grounds but the chapel remained unchanged.

So it was that only six churches were definitely organized by the year 1885, but others were soon to follow.

In 1879 the new religion called Christian Science was in its infancy. The first edition of *Science and Health with Key to the Scriptures* was published in 1875. It did not immediately meet with the overwhelming response that greeted the healing water of the Springs, but its appeal was to outlast their popularity. The early days of the new religion were beset by trials, but sufferers continued to investigate the new faith. A church was organized in Boston, Massachusetts, and a small magazine named the *"Christian Science Journal"* made its appearance and soon grew into a powerful organ for the church. Students began to practice Christian Science healing as far west as Chicago and Denver. A resident of Eureka Springs, Mrs. Laura E. Evans somehow obtained a copy of the *Journal* and became greatly interested in the new movement. When Mrs. Eddy came to Chicago in 1888 to address her western students, Mrs. Evans could not go herself, but she persuaded a friend to make the trip. The new teaching so appealed to the visitor that she soon went to Boston for instruction under Mrs. Eddy. Returning to Eureka Springs her work eventually bore fruit, for in 1896 the card of the Christian Science Society appeared in the *Journal.* Like many other early churches the services of this young organization were first held in a log house. In 1914 a suitable church was built on Mountain Street, which later when free from debt was dedicated.

During the latter part of the 1880's an African Methodist Episcopal Church was established in Eureka Springs, as large numbers of Negroes were living and visiting here at that time. The visitors were for the most part servants of well-to-do summer residents, while those who lived here were employed in the dozens of hotels and rooming houses then in the city. This church was in existence until about 1925 when it was disbanded. By that time the colored population was practically nonexistant. The building used as a colored church was torn down and no records of the organization are left except a few worn hymn books which bear the name of the church.

The first two decades of the history of the town were exciting times with hundreds of people arriving to enjoy the healthful and recreational benefits of the Springs. As they arrived, hundreds left as their beneficial sojourn ended. In the churches of the city the pastors looked from their pulpits upon a constantly changing congregation at Sunday services and could not help but count the extra number of visits to be made while the visitors whiled away the long summer in pursuit of health and recreation. The work of the preachers was not easy, when to call on one of his flock meant a long walk and steep climb with numerous flights of stairs to surmount. Small wonder that at least one of the ministers saw fit to excuse himself for not visiting all of his parishioners more often. The following is part of the annual report of one minister to his local Curch Board:

> "the work devolving upon the pastor has been more than that ordinarily placed upon the pastor of a City charge. In addition to his own membership to whom pastoral visits must be made, there has always been . . . especially during the summer months . . . a large attendance of visitors who become more or less regular attendants upon the Church Services, and to whom the pastor owes the duty of visitation almost equally as much as to his own membership. With such increased duties to be performed in a City like Eureka Springs where pedestrianism to any extent means extensive physical exertion, it can be imagined that members and visitors alike may . . . without thinking of the time and work required . . . sometimes think their pastor is a less frequent visitor than he should be."

Writing for the magazine *Points* in August of 1900, the Reverend P. C. Fletcher calls Eureka Springs the "City of Churches." He goes on to say:

> "In matters of religion she looks after her guests. They are extended a Christian welcome and made to feel at home. At whichever Church the visitor desires to attend, he will receive a most cordial welcome. Special attention is paid to strangers for 'thereby some have entertained angels unawares'."

He went on to stress the deep interest of the churches in the sick and distressed whom the ministry of the city were ready and willing to serve at any time. The Reverend Fletcher closed this glowing account of the churches of Eureka Springs by saying, "Her Churches are broad and liberal, progressive and peaceful."

At the end of her second decade of development nearly all of the leading religious denominations were to be found in Eureka Springs. Visitors, however, were surprised to find her so poorly equipped with church buildings but bore in mind that the city was indeed young and all looked forward to a time when more substantial and attractive architectual efforts would be in evidence. It was the fervent hope of many a church goer that the various denominations would soon "worship in edifices which will grace these hills."

A description of one of the early churches is taken from the magazine *Points,* the April-May, 1901, issue:

> "The new house of worship, upon the beautiful and accessible site gives the church a fresh impetus. The new edifice is modest and graceful, simple and unpretentious in its proportions. The interior arrangement and furnishings are especially happy and pretty. The walls are finished in ingrain, with blue effect while the trimmings are an imitation of frescoed work. A very handsome suite of hand carved furniture adorns the platform and chancel. The floors are carpeted, and the building is lighted by electricity. All told it is a very beautiful house of Worship, and one which the membership has every right to feel proud of because it represents their loyalty, liberality and devotion."

So with only a little imagination one might picture the scene on a summer Sabbath morning with the members of the congregation seated serenely and quietly, each in fresh meeting house clothing and each presenting the best possible appearance. The ladies would undoubtedly be pictures of feminine beauty and charm in ruffled and beribboned muslin dresses with sweeping trains, their picture hats abloom with silken roses and other summer flowers. The gentlemen would be the epitome of masculine grace and dignity in the fashionable suits of the day, topped off with high collars and flowing ties, though each was also adorned with a handsomely groomed beard or flowing moustache.

One might well imagine one of the flowers from the elegant bouquet of charming young ladies rising to add to the worship with an offering of her vocal talents. With gentle look, eyes turned heavenward and hands clasped before her she renders in heartfelt manner "Hark, Hark, My Soul" or some other sacred melody of the day.

Now the minister would arise and with stern countenance and impassioned voice would admonish man to come away from his sinful ways and lead a spotless life.

Who could go out from such an uplifting experience into a community where men received physical healing from pain and disease and not feel that the "City of Healing Waters" was indeed an earthly paradise.

Without doubt the functions of the various churches played an important part in the life of the community, but even more the Church and its collective membership had been a moving force for good through the first turbulent years of the development of the new town.

PART III

CHAPTER X

Slow Fades the Dream: 1900-1929

At the dawn of a new century the people of Eureka Springs looked about them at their city and its accomplishments from two widely divergent points of view. Those of a more romantic nature waxed poetic and rhapsodized about the charms of the place. One of the poets of Eureka Springs, W. J. Moore, wrote

"For Eureka's close to heaven,
    You can see it shining through
With your eyes uplifted to
    the starry blue."

Wilma Jarrett Ellis, the wife of one of the city's most influential men, took pen in hand to pay tribute to "A Fair Little City." Mrs. Ellis wrote

"T'were useless and vain to endeavor
    The charms of this place to name o'er" . . .

This sentiment was no doubt shared, at least in part, by her husband and his business acquaintances. However, men of business and political acumen were beginning to sense a spirit of change in the life of the community.

For twenty years the resort had enjoyed a popularity which brought throngs of visitors to the city. Business was good and many modest fortunes had been made by catering to the needs of these seekers after health. The community was well-established, as a Business Directory for the year 1904 attests. A newspaper editorial notes the population at that time as being 5,000 residents, and a city of such size required many suppliers of goods and services to meet its needs.

Fourteen physicians, as well as six dentists enjoyed a thriving business, and the resort supported a sanitarium for chronic diseases, located in what had previously been the St. Louis Hotel, near the foot of Pine Street. The townspeople had a choice of eighteen grocery stores from which to purchase supplies, as well as a Tea and Coffee Store which proudly offered its patrons "every imaginable grade of tea, coffee, spices, etc." Two bakeries and two candy manufacturing concerns added further to the food supply and provided employment for a number of people.

Six drygoods stores and two milliners saw to the fashion needs of milady, while two tailoring establishments kept the local business man well dressed as befitted his station in life.

Five photographic studios provided lasting remembrances to those desiring such, and nine jewelry stores offered their treasures for those occasions when a gentleman might wish to purchase a small bauble for his lady.

Livery stables, dye works (dry cleaning establishments), laundries, book shops, shoe stores and several undertaking parlors lined the streets. Business was literally booming, and two successful banks, the Citizens and the First National, kept pace with the financial affairs of the community.

Perhaps the future had never looked better, yet there was indeed change afoot. Within the next ten years Eureka Springs was to experience an alarming reversal of its growing trend through a shocking bank failure and the loss of the railroad shops, one of the principal business enterprises, as well as a nationwide change in the public attitude toward medicine and surgery versus natural healing. Even before the community would lose some of its finest young men to the First World War, its citizens were to witness the advent of the horseless carriage. Improved cross-country roads brought the new-fangled contraptions to Eureka Springs, and with them came a new kind of traveler requiring a new kind of resort.

The advent of the first automobile in Eureka Springs is told in an amusing way by Sam A. Leath in his unpublished manuscript giving important events in chronological sequence. One day in 1906 a young man arrived in town driving one of the new contraptions with the intention of demonstrating it to local businessmen. As he motored about the streets of the town the young man unfortunately met with a horseback party at a very sharp corner on Spring Street. The horses promptly decided to leave the field to this noisy tin carriage and stampeded onto sidewalks and into any conveniently open door. It is not recorded exactly what happened to the riders involved, nor how long a time elapsed before the automobile demonstrator sought customers in some other community. It was some two years later, according to Mr. Leath, before an automobile was again seen in Eureka Springs. At that time the vehicle encountered another horseback party near the home of the Butt family on West Mountain with the same disastrous results as before. The ladies in the group reportedly "lost half their hair on the black-jack limbs" when the horses took to the woods nearby.

Such disastrous occurrences notwithstanding, the automobile soon gained acceptance in the community as elsewhere. By 1917 there were some twenty-five of the vehicles in Eureka Springs belonging to local residents, as well as an ever-increasing number passing through town, their drivers bent upon both business and sight-seeing pleasure. It is sadly reported by Leath that the number of gaited saddle horses for hire had dropped to about twenty five.

How quickly the change came about. From that day in 1906 when the horseless carriage frightened the local horses into a wild stampede it was to be only a few short years until auto tourism was to become a principal source of income for the community. In 1929 it was estimated that the automobile brought nearly 500,000 people to the Ozark Mountains area annually and Eureka Springs was deeply involved in the struggle to interest a goodly number of them in visiting this unique resort.

Throughout the years of change from health spa to pleasure resort, Eureka Springs retained the support and encouragement of one of its principal builders. From Mexico City, or from his home in Washington, D. C., General Powell Clayton still watched over the community and expressed his interest and concern through frequent visits. The General still dreamed of great things for the resort, but even he had lost the enthusiasm for and faith in the healing properties of Eureka Springs water. Over the years Mrs. Clayton had developed a severe ear problem and the General searched all over the country and also abroad for a medical specialist or a surgeon who would be able to bring her relief from pain and suffering and cure her malady.

Frequently visiting Eureka Springs, General Clayton continually gave advice and encouragement to local civic leaders as well as keeping informed through his correspondence with them. Finally in 1906 during one of his visits the community paid tribute to the General with an elegant banquet and in speeches honoring him. It was on this day that Clayton spoke at length concerning his continuing dream for Eureka Springs, which had for more than a quarter of a century been an important part of his life.

An early magazine *The Beautiful Ozarks,* Volume 1 Number 1, dated October, 1906, devoted the whole of its first page to a story headed "General Powell Clayton banquetted on his Seventy-third Natal Day." The story begins with the fact that Clayton had spent August 7 quietly at the Crescent Hotel and retired to his room late in the afternoon for a rest. In the early evening a large group of distinguished local business men and civic leaders, with their beautifully gowned ladies, gathered in the Sun Parlor of the Hotel. When all were assembled a committee was dispatched to the General's room. The committee, B. J. Rosewater, S. E. Hays and Dr. R. G. Floyd invited Clayton down to the lobby where he found the aggregation of friends of all political and business leanings. After exchanging greetings, all were ushered into the dining room where "an extraordinary spread, with superb service, was set forth."

After the feast ended, Dr. C. F. Ellis, as the able and sometimes eloquent toast master, reviewed the changes which had taken place in the United States and the developments in Eureka Springs during the life span of the General. This was followed by more toasts and speeches, and then it was time for the General to answer. Always an eloquent speaker, Clayton poured out his deepest feelings for the community which he had helped bring even into existence. This response was considered one of his most masterful speeches, and at the close he expressed his desire to be allowed to help in every way within his power in the improvement of the resort. Surely those present could see through his eyes, if only for a moment, that long-cherished vision as General Powell Clayton spoke of even greater accomplishments for Eureka Springs which, he asserted, "would eventually be surrounded by beautiful drives and country clubs on a scale almost beyond belief."

The General never lost hold of his dream as witnessed by his continuing correspondence with friends through the years. Even after his death at the age of eighty-one, on February 19, 1914, his concern was carried on through the lives of many local people whom he had influenced.

Looking back from this point in time, it is difficult to understand why such devotion and endeavor as displayed by Clayton and dozens of like thinkers was not rewarded by the continuing development of an outstanding resort community. Yet underlying their efforts and failing to provide a strong support for them were the myriad lesser individuals who could not dream so well. Their timidity and apathy, their pettiness and jealous regard for an equal share of the credit and financial gain, was to be the determining factor in the future. Rather than dream and build upon that vision, the majority of citizens seemed content to wait for whatever happened to come along, then try to make something worthwhile from happenstance.

Perhaps another related factor which limited the continuing development of the community was the almost constant turmoil in local political affairs. Over the years a goodly number of worthy men had given of their time and abilities to guide the affairs of the people, yet for every good man in office there always seemed to be a dozen others looking on who felt that they . . . or someone else . . . could do a better job.

From the time of the long townsite litigation the City had been deeply in debt. Restricted by State laws to only a limited taxation insufficient for its needs, and finding it necessary to provide services and facilities for hundreds of visitors besides its own legal residents, the civic leaders faced a constant uphill battle of finances. When such a problem exists in city government, there exists also accusations of mismanagement and worse toward those men currently administering public affairs. As the election of mayor and aldermen approached every two years, issues and personalities assumed increasing importance and the citizens divided sharply into warring factions. The elections of 1901, 1903, and 1907 were particularly stormy events, and in each instance the disputed issue had to do with the financial affairs of the city.

In spite of the constant bickering over local government, some progress was made. *The Daily Times Echo* issued September 11, 1905, includes a lengthy report of the Board of Commissioners of the Water and Sewer Districts, which enumerates accomplishments made in those areas since 1903. The Board, with James T. Pomeroy as chairman, pointed an accusatory finger at the last three administrations for willfully misusing public funds meant for water and sewer improvements and called such malfeasance "so flagrant and unjustifiable a betrayal of public trust as to warrant prosecution both civil and criminal." However, no such prosecution seemed to be forthcoming as the report was written two years after these unidentified individuals had left public office. Pomeroy went on to give a glowing account of work accomplished, with funds to spare, during the two year tenure of service of the Board, including numerous improvements in the water pipe line system. Their proudest accomplishment, and rightfully so, was the construction of a modern septic tank and the installation of aerators for the sewage disposal system. The new system was put in operation before the end of 1903 and according to Pomeroy

"It is not denied by even those who, from sinister motives, predicted and hoped that it would fail—not denied that it did its work to the entire satisfaction of every one who inspected it."

The following two years were relatively calm ones, with eforts being made to somehow effect a more satisfactory water supply and to pave and light the city streets. It was almost a decade later, however, before anything practical was accomplished along these lines.

The year 1907 opened with a bang, although "snarl" would perhaps be a more descriptive word, as the citizens immediately found themselves split down the middle over the forthcoming city election. Personalities were at issue, but of more importance was the rumor going around that the Missouri and North Arkansas Railroad was considering the relocating of their entire maintenance shops in Eureka Springs. At that time the Eureka Springs shops were a fairly small operation, as the company had maintenance work done in Leslie as well. This move would mean the gain of a hundred-thousand dollar annual payroll for the community. The Railroad Company, whose main business offices were located here, put out the word that first it wanted to know the attitude of the people of Eureka Springs and the result of the election to be held in April would indicate to them whether it was one of friendliness, or otherwise.

On February 20th a mass meeting of citizens was called, and both newspapers announced the time and place, the Barnes-Blocksom Building. A fine crowd turned out, and after much discussion of the issues the people chose a committee of twelve men to submit a slate of candidates for mayor, aldermen and other city offices, under the name of the Citizens Ticket. This ticket was duly prepared and presented to the people in a fine spirit of togetherness and good will. Dr. R. G. Floyd was nominated for the office of mayor, with B. F. Putnam, F. W. Maxwell, H. Goudelock and S. F. Pyatt named to be his attendant Council. Immediately *The Daily Times Echo* came out in support of what was called the Independent Ticket made up of three members of the present Council, Aldermen Jim Henson, Oscar Johnson and Frank Willis, with the addition of Claude A. Fuller for Mayor. Both Fuller and the *Times-Echo* editor, Miller, had spoken at the public meeting in favor of the adoption of the Citizens Ticket, so their about-face caused a furor among the townspeople.

Claude Albert Fuller had come to Eureka Springs in 1885 as a small boy and grew up in the very modest home of his parents, Mr. and Mrs. W. P. Fuller. He read law and began his practice as an attorney about 1896. Through the years Fuller was elected two terms as City Clerk for Eureka Springs and in other ways made a place of importance for himself in the community. When the election of 1907 took place, he had only recently returned from four years in the State Legislature where he represented Carroll County. During that time Representative Fuller had introduced a bill in the legislature which became a law requiring the Missouri and North Arkansas Railroad to fence its right-of-way, at a cost to the company of some thirty-five or forty thousand dollars, and at a time when the small struggling railroad could ill afford to do so. According to popular belief there was no demand by the people who lived along the right-of-way for this law, as the company was allowing the farmers to cultivate the land included in the right-of-way up to the very edge of the track. It was a hard blow for the Missouri and North Arkansas, and many of the people of Eureka Springs were of the opinion that the railroad company felt this action had emanated from an unkindly disposition on the part of Fuller toward the railroad.

Small wonder many of the people were afraid that the election of Claude Fuller to the position of Mayor would mean the end of their chance to secure the Missouri and North Arkansas Railroad shops in Eureka Springs.

It was a bitter, but fortunately short campaign, with both sides waging a strong battle of ugly charges and counter charges. Dr. Floyd and the Citizens Ticket received the support of the *Flashlight*, while Fuller's Independent Ticket waged its campaign with the able assistance of *The Daily Times Echo*. According to talk on the street the Citizens Ticket had the strongest public support, for what might be considered obvious reasons, but the Independent Ticket was receiving the backing of some very influential citizens, including William M. Duncan, owner of the various enterprises which had begun operation under Powell Clayton's directorship of the Eureka Springs Improvement Company.

Election Day, April 2, 1907, came and went. The voting was close, but the Independent Ticket won the victory, and a short time later Claude Fuller was sworn in as Mayor. The press, particularly that of the opposition, had very little to say, and the new administration began its work which resulted in a fairly progressive period for the city. The Missouri and North Arkansas retained its small shops in Eureka Springs and announced plans to construct a new depot building. It was never known by the man in the street whether the election of 1907 really was of any importance to the Railroad company as they formulated their plans, but in 1913 the general offices and maintenance shops were moved to Harrison, and that community derived great benefit from them.

Among those who fought so hard for the right to administer public affairs there was a great deal of bitterness. Usually after such events there is a period of time in which tempers may cool and hasty words spoken in anger may be forgotten. Flaming issues dwindle to tiny embers and subsequently die out of mind until some future time when the prospect of another election may set them blazing once more. But such was not to be the case in Eureka Springs in 1907. Before the election faded into memory, the community was shaken to its very roots by a financial catastrophe unequaled in its past or in time to come.

On a hot summer morning, Monday, the first day of July, 1907, the people of Eureka Springs were shocked to hear that the Citizens Bank would not open its doors for business that day. Nine o'clock, the regular hour for opening, came and the doors of the bank remained locked. An hour later Giles E. Miller's *Daily Times-Echo* hit the streets with an extra edition carrying a banner headline, "Citizens Bank Asks For A Receiver." The paper printed a statement from William M. Duncan, president of the bank, which attempted to explain the matter and reassure the people. Duncan stated that owing to circumstances over which he had no control the bank was temporarily closed. There had been "an unprecedented run on the bank," and he wished to see that all local creditors shared the assets of the establishment. Duncan pledged everything he owned outside the bank, if its assets were not sufficient to pay back every dollar of indebtedness.

Surely no one could have asked for a more straight-forward statement of purpose. William Duncan was a successful business man of twenty years standing in the community. In addition to the Citizens Bank, he owned or had a controlling interest in five other companies. The Syndicate Company, his major business endeavor, was the successor to the old Eureka Springs Improvement Company, and owned several hundred thousand dollars worth of valuable city property, most of it located in the business district on Spring Street. The Citizens Electric Company operated the two mile long electric street railway and furnished the municipal electric supply. The Eureka Springs Water Company shipped water to a wide area of the Southwest, and was one of the town's most successful endeavors. The company held a contract with the famous Harvey System and furnished Eureka Springs water (under the patented name of "Ozarka") to all of its eating establishments throughout the Midwest as well as all Harvey-controlled dining cars on the Frisco Railway. There were other offices and warehouses located in Kansas City, St. Louis and Oklahoma City. The "Ozarka" water came from two springs, Bay's and Magnetic, and was being shipped at the rate of about four train carloads per week, plus local sales equivalent to two carloads weekly.

Another Duncan enterprise, the Eureka Stone Company, furnished building stone for every major construction job in the community. The recently completed Basin Park Hotel was the fifth of Duncan's apparently very successful business endeavors.

Duncan arrived in Eureka Springs in the late 1880's and almost immediately began to play a prominent role in the civic and business life of the city. No record of his previous life is available, but newspaper accounts show that he won easy acceptance into the social whirl and was often listed among those present at parties given by the more prominent citizens of the town. Duncan became active in community life also, serving as a member of the Water and Sewer Improvement Boards and the Board of Public Affairs with Powell Clayton, Z. P. Freeman and Dr. C. F. Ellis. No doubt this was a man respected and admired by his fellow businessmen, yet when the *Times-Echo* called him "Eureka Springs greatest benefactor" on the day of the bank failure, there began a controversy which rocked the community for some months to come. While some were content to await with patience the reinstatement of the bank and return of their deposits, still others were not so positive that the outcome would be so favorable. When Malone and Barrows brought out their weekly edition of the *Flashlight* a few days after the bank closure, the editors questioned Miller's description of Duncan as a "benefactor" and wondered quite blatantly whether he might be a "beneficiary" instead. With one newspaper speaking for Duncan and his staunch supporters and one for those who had little faith in the man and his methods the battle was on.

In the regular edition for July 1 the *Times-Echo* reported that Duncan had taken immediate steps to secure the appointment of a receiver for the bank. His good friends Colonel C. D. James, a lawyer by profession, and R. S. Granger, a lumber businessman, had gone to Judge Humphreys of the Chancery Court on the previous night, and the judge had already appointed Digby West, vice president of the Carroll County Bank in Berryville, to act as receiver for the institution. West accepted and made application for the necessary bond on the very same day. The paper also carried statements from twenty-five of the leading citizens of the town, who were also large depositors of the Citizens Bank, expressing their confidence and trust in William Duncan. All were sure they would receive "one hundred cents on the dollar" as soon as the affair was settled, though some admitted that "the misfortune . . . would affect business all over the city."

The paper also quoted Myron D. Jordan, manager of Duncan's Citizens Electric Company and other interests, as saying that "the business of the other concerns will proceed as usual."

The issue of the *Flashlight* for July 5 carried the report which Receiver West submitted to Judge Humphreys listing the liabilities and assets of the bank. According to the *Flashlight,* "a study of that report is enough to send the hopes of the creditors to their sock feet." At first glance, this seemed to be anything but an exaggeration of the facts, as the report showed the liabilities of the bank to be several thousand dollars more than its assets. The paper went on to take note of the "remarkable fact" that out of nearly $260,000 of deposits from the "dear people" that the bank loaned only $45,000 of this amount, with $10,000 being loaned to the Eureka Springs Water Company, one of Duncan's corporations, and another $3,000 to Giles Miller, a close associate of Mr. Duncan and editor of the *Times-Echo.*

The *Flashlight* also took exception to the $39,000 listed as "overdrafts," particularly as this total included $18,700 overdrawn by the Eureka Springs Water Company. The Basin Park Hotel, Duncan's latest venture, was shown to have written checks amounting to $4,000 over the amount in the corporation's account. The Syndicate Company, another Duncan enterprise, had overdrawn $6,000 and the *Times-Echo* nearly $2,000. Another $4,500 in overdrafts was accumulated by several persons connected with Duncan in his business ventures.

The *Flashlight* concluded its report with the news that the Eureka Springs Water Company had also asked for a receiver on the 3rd of July and asked the people to decide for themselves whether Duncan had been a "benefactor" or "beneficiary" of the city. Malone and Barrows, editors of the *Flashlight,* assured the people that the "cause of the bank's failure may be easily seen by looking at the report" and ended the news story with a plea in behalf of those "orphans, widows, sick people who came here to woo back health" and who had deposited their savings in the Citizens Bank.

Through the pages of the *Times-Echo,* William Duncan had promised and continued to promise that he would "pay every valid claim of the Bank, if it takes every dollar I have on earth." Editor Miller lashed out in print at the *Flashlight* for "attempting to discredit Mr. Duncan's business methods," and for totally ignoring that portion of the assets in Receiver West's report which alluded to the first mortgage bonds of the Citizens Electric and the Syndicate Companies amounting to more than a quarter of a million dollars. Duncan claimed that these bonds, being "absolutely first-class and desirable and worth par," along with other extensive real estate holdings, would assure the return of every dollar due the creditors of the bank.

Editor Miller of the *Times-Echo* went on to prove that he could be every bit as insulting as editors Malone and Barrows by printing this story on the editorial page of the *Times-Echo*:

> "A lady came walking down Spring Street this afternoon, and when near the Post Office she gazed up at the magnificent Basin Park Hotel, and it brought to mind the efforts of Mr. Duncan in the up-building of Eureka Springs. She could not withstand her inclination to make comparisons. It happened that just yesterday she was a member of a party that rode by the septic tank, that monument to the memory of James T. Pomeroy, a short distance below the entrance to the city. The grandeur of the Hotel and the odor from the septic tank settled the question of worth with her. And it will for anyone else with a head worth carrying."

James T. Pomeroy was another prominent business man who had served as a member of the City Council a few years earlier. It was largely through the efforts put forth by Pomeroy that the city purchased and installed the septic tank and aerators at the outlet of the sewer system near the north city limits. The work had been accomplished in 1903 and had proved a vast improvement over the old system. The *Flashlight* had supported Pomeroy and the Council in the efforts to effect this improvement in public service.

For the next few days there existed a period of relative calm as the people awaited further developments and the feuding editors retired into their respective corners until the beginning of the next round.

Two weeks later the *Flashlight* announced that a meeting of the creditors of the defunct Citizens Bank would be held on July 22 at the Rosewater-Ellis Building. While openly voicing suspicion as to the source of this call for a public meeting, the *Times-Echo* nevertheless urged everyone interested to be present. When this paper came out the following day it carried a notice of an open meeting of creditors at the Barnes-Blocksom Hall, which also served as the Court House, to be held Monday evening, July 22. It was discovered that these two meetings had come about as the result of a desire in some minds to have a man in the bank with Receiver West to "look after matters, and see that his report was in all things correct." While shaming each other for this reflection on the integrity of West, still the two committees went forward with plans for the meetings. Judge Humphreys had informed all interested parties that it would be satisfactory with him for the creditors of the Citizens Bank to hold a public meeting and select three men from whom Receiver West was to select one, his salary to be paid by the creditors, to go into the bank and work under West.

The two public meetings were duly held with the attendance being somewhat bitterly divided between those who elected to stand behind Duncan and those who were suspicious and anxious about eventually seeing the return of their deposits. William Duncan spoke eloquently of his intentions to 156 cheering creditors at the Barnes-Blocksom Hall while only thirty persons met in a business office in the Rosewater-Ellis Building. Each group selected three persons to represent their interests in the bank, and on the following day submitted the names to Receiver West. On the 25th of July Chancellor Humphreys refused both requests as neither represented a majority of the creditors, and West continued to work without assistance.

On the same day Humphreys appointed a receiver to handle the affairs of Miller's *Times-Echo* Company. It was evidently floundering in heavy financial seas, and nearly a year later the printing plant and equipment was sold to meet the claims of its creditors. It must be noted that Malone and

Barrows of the *Flashlight* evercised gentlemanly restraint in not printing any gloating reference to this eventuality.

Receiver West now had in his possession $95,000 worth of first mortgage bonds of the Syndicate Company, and the Court ordered that creditors might accept these bonds as dollar-for-dollar payment of their claims. They were allowed until November 10 to do so. In the meantime the Court was rejecting any and all preferred claims, allowing payment to creditors on an equal basis.

In August the Citizen's Bank building and fixtures were sold at auction. The First National Bank purchased it for $12,000. This amount added to other cash on hand made possible the payment of 15% of creditors claims after November 10, and the Court also allowed creditors to take City warrants on a dollar-for-dollar basis for their claims or any part thereof.

The new year 1908 began with the Citizen's Bank still owing $198,000 to its creditors, and on January 2 Duncan's Citizen's Electric Company asked for receivership. Later in the year the Fidelity Trust Company of Kansas City foreclosed its mortgage, and all the company property and holdings were sold at auction. At that time Citizen's Electric owned the street railway, the city-wide electric lighting system and power generating plant, the Opera House, the Summer Auditorium, the ice plant and "sundry properties." The ice plant had a capacity of four tons of marketable ice daily plus 6400 cubic feet of cold storage.

In July, 1908, Receiver West was ordered to pay out a 5% dividend on claims, which amounted to only $12,300. The balance of liabilities was still in excess of $150,000. At this time, almost a year after the Citizen's Bank closed its doors, the affair culminated in the sale of the remaining assets of the Bank to the newly incorporated Central Bank, which advertised its authorized capital of $50,000 and solicited the business of local citizens. Among those involved in the new bank were Dr. John Jordan, Captain T. F. Hawley and C. F. Humphreys (not to be confused with Chancellor Humphreys).

A final dividend was paid out by Receiver West to the creditors, leaving a balance of over $18,000 due to those persons not assigning their claims to the new banking institution. A total of $135,000 in claims was assigned to the Central Bank, and there ends the Chancery Court record of the settlement of the confused financial affairs of William Duncan. It is assumed that some creditors received satisfaction for their claims through the new bank plan, while at least some received no more than 25% of their deposits through the Court ordered liquidation of the Citizens Bank.

The financial empire to which William Duncan had gained access and which involved several businesses important to the entire community, no longer existed. Only a part of it remained, and that too had been badly shaken, but Duncan himself remained and he set to work to rebuild what he had lost.

The life of the community had long since dropped back into its normal routine as it would be impossible to sustain a burning interest through all the months while the wheels of justice ground out their ultimate solution. The same newspaper, the *Flashlight* of November 20, 1908, which carried advertisements for the new Central Bank reported a "new era of prosperity never before witnessed at any summer resort in this fair land of ours." This enthusiastic comment was based on the fact that at a recent meeting of the Commercial Club $1500.00 had been subscribed by local individuals for the purpose of "boosting." That is, the money would be spent to advertise Eureka Springs to the traveling public. It seems that hope does indeed spring eternal, for the newspaper reported that there had never been a more harmonious or enthusiastic meeting and,

> "knockers, fault-finders, kickers, hangers-on and calamity howlers are as dead as a door nail, and everyone is doing his level best to boost, boost, boost."

It was beginning to look as though Eureka Springs was set on a course of continuous ups and downs. Gone were the days of full-steam-ahead development such as the town had known a few years previously. The future must have looked black indeed to many citizens, in spite of the new "booster" theme, and how welcome it must have been when in 1910,

Mayor Fuller and Council, reelected in 1909, literally lightened their darkness by contracting with the Eureka Springs Electric Company (now under new ownership) to provide 150 electric street lamps. Half of these lights were 32 candle power, the balance 40 candle power lamps. They were indeed a pleasant sight on the streets of the city and at specific locations such as the City Hall, the fire company hose houses, the fire bell and the band stand. The streets were still unpaved, dusty or muddy by turns, but the citizenry could at last enjoy their well-lighted city by night in perfect comfort and safety.

Even in times of political upsets, financial frustrations and those disappointments that affect the community in general, there are still to be found those persons who keep working on one project after another . . . if it be for the public good. There were many such persons in Eureka Springs in that first decade of the new century, and one of the things for which they saw a great need was a free public library. These forward looking citizens realized that such an endeavor would cost a great deal of money, but they could not see how any city worth its name could continue to exist without the cultural advantage of free access to books. When the desire for something is strong enough, a way can usually be found to achieve it, and more than one of these interested individuals had heard of the generosity of one Andrew Carnegie.

In the early years of 1900 this Pittsburgh philanthropist began to give money with which to build buildings suitable for public libraries to those cities able to meet his very simple qualifications. First, a suitable site was necessary and, secondly, the community must agree to maintain the building as a free public library. Mr. Carnegie did not have his organization seek out communities in which to build a library. The initial request must come from the community which desired to have, or needed, a library, and such a request was made by a Mr. Southerland, who to the best of anyone's recollection was not a citizen but a visitor to Eureka Springs. The date of this request for funds with which to build a library is as obscure as are the details concerning Mr. Southerland but must have been well before 1907. It is a matter of record that on February 17, 1910, a Board of Library Trustees had been organized and on that date plans for a building and photographs of the proposed site were sent for Mr. Carnegie's inspection. The St. Louis architect who designed the Memorial Chapel for R. C. Kerens had drawn plans for a very dignified library building for which Mr. Carnegie agreed to donate the amount of $12,500.

When the idea of a library was first proposed some liked it, some did not. The city went ahead and gave a building lot which proved to be a filled ravine unsuitable for the stone structure such as the architect, George W. Hellmuth, had planned. Approximately fifteen hundred dollars was spent trying to make the site suitable and it began to look as though the library would not materialize, when B. J. Rosewater, who had been elected president of the Library Board of Trustees, turned to his good friend R. C. Kerens for help. Just down the mountain extending from the site of the Memorial Chapel to Spring Street was a solid stone cliff. This Mr. Kerens donated as a site for the library, as it was thought the stone would be suitable either for the building or could be sold for other commercial purposes. By this time nearly three thousand dollars had been spent and the building wasn't even started. In order that their hopes for a library would be realized Mr. Carnegie was appealed to again but at first seemed reluctant to add to the original grant. It was found that the stone in the cliff was not suitable either for the building or for any other purpose, but the foundation was excavated and the building started in spite of the difficulties so far experienced. Now delays caused by bad weather and slow delivery of materials kept the project dragging along. The contractor wanted money and an emergency due to the reluctance on the part of Mr. Carnegie to increase his donation finally made it necessary to raise three thousand dollars from local citizens with the promise to repay them as soon as Mr. Carnegie would increase his donation. Things had dragged along until July of 1912; the citizens wanted their money back and the contractor wanted more of his money, so at last a final sum of three thousand was sent by Mr. Carnegie which cleared the building obligations. While the corner stone bears the date 1910 it was really 1912 before the building was completed.

While this had been taking place the City administration had apparently been blowing hot and cold over the promise to maintain the library, which was one of the stipulations to be met before the money for the building was forthcoming. In 1910 the City administration agreed to furnish a sum of eighteen hundred and fifty dollars yearly, but the next year they repudiated their offer. After much legal wrangling it was found that under the law of the State of Arkansas a city could not sell bonds or impose taxes for library purposes. However, by the time Mr. Carnegie made his final grant the City had again promised to provide twelve hundred and fifty dollars a year for the maintenance of the library. There is no record that this was ever done.

From the beginning of the project, B. J. Rosewater had been in charge of all the arrangements, including the construction, and the Library Board elected him life president.

Some way book stacks, tables and chairs found their way into the building, and by 1914 gifts of books had made it possible to open the doors to the public. Memberships were sold for one dollar each which permitted the member to withdraw books. A librarian was hired and the library was kept open three afternoons a week. A news item in the newspaper of October 26, 1916, stated that the library would be closed for the winter as sufficient money had not been taken in to pay for fuel, janitor, librarian and needed upkeep.

The news story continued, "Do you want a library?" Some did and some frankly acknowledged that they did not believe in a library. Others had the idea that because Mr. Carnegie had provided money for a building he would furnish everything else needed so that there would be a library whether the local citizens helped or not. The story closed with a very pertinent appeal:

> "We need fairs, poultry association, good roads and everything that will help to make a better Eureka Springs, and does that not include our Public Library?"

By every means at their disposal a few dedicated library members raised funds to keep the library open. A news story for February 12, 1920, tells of needed repairs finally paid for, while the president of the Library Association, organized to assist the library, came forth with her appeal:

> "It is not right that an institution like this should suffer for lack of funds, so that the Board should have to beg money from the public for its support. To run and equip it properly we should have five hundred members willing to pay one dollar a year."

Social events were continued to raise funds and during 1920 the library was open six days a week.

Eureka Springs was indeed in the forefront of the struggle to provide books to the people in Arkansas. In 1920 less than 7% of the population had access to free public libraries.

In 1921 at the annual meeting the Board of Trustees became the Board of Managers rather than an executive board. During the summer electricity was installed free of charge with a nominal monthly bill for the service. Since no municipal aid could be forthcoming due to the peculiarity of the Arkansas State Constitution, the library continued to furnish such services as its meager funds would allow. Many people were generous in the matter of donating books and the Carnegie Memorial for Peace made a sizeable donation of books relative to International Peace.

It is interesting to note that only four libraries in the state of Arkansas received funds from the Carnegie Library Grant. Also, while Mr. Carnegie did not ask that his name be used, Eureka Springs is one of the libraries which did so. In 1907 when the offer to finance library buildings was closed, over 2500 buildings had been constructed with funds furnished by Andrew Carnegie and approximately one third of them acknowledged his generosity by using his name.

Eureka Springs finally achieved the objective of providing its citizens with a free public library, but the resort faced other needs of a more pressing nature. Throughout the first dozen years of the new century the city government, continually hampered by a lack of public funds with which to operate, sought desperately to effect improvements to the municipal water supply. The numerous springs in the area poured forth their healing balm in the form of clean, fresh and exceptionally pure water, while the water obtained from the city mains was anything but clean and clear. Indeed, it was described as being undrinkable at times. The citizens were demanding "a better water supply in the reservoir right now."

In the face of increasing dissatisfaction some definite action was needed and B. J. Rosewater, a prominent young business man, stepped into the fray. Rosewater had been a citizen of Eureka Springs since 1882, when he came to the new town from Illinois for the sake of his health. His health improved very quickly and he began to show an active interest in the life of the community, serving on various boards with such men as Powell Clayton, Z. P. Freeman and Dr. C. F. Ellis. Appointed postmaster in 1898, Rosewater was still serving in this capacity when on March 12, 1908, a large group of citizens was called together at the Barnes-Blocksom Hall for the purpose of finding a solution for the water problem. At that meeting the Municipal League was formed and Rosewater, apparently the one more than others who promoted the organization, was elected president. He spoke at length and with eloquence about the purpose of the League. The first great work undertaken was the finding of a plentiful supply of good water for public use.

Dr. R. G. Floyd, a physician who had resided in Eureka Springs a number of years and who had become very prominent, was given earnest attention by the crowd as he reported on the damage being done to the resort by the use of the present water supply. While the water did not in fact produce fevers, he stated plainly that the vegetable matter it contained did ferment, thereby rendering it offensive to the taste.

Captain John DeBois, owner of the popular Chautauqua and Southern Hotels at that time, appealed for concerted action, and with hearty good will the pledge was made to find a way to fulfill the need, in the face of near bankruptcy and the alleged lack of business-like economy in the management of the City finances.

The League authorized a committee to take action on the matter and a plan was devised to seek water through the drilling of a deep well. Almost immediately workmen were employed who began to drill three test holes near the dam at the existing reservoir. Water was reached at a depth of 22 feet in one opening and at 43 feet in the others, but upon testing the amount of flow it was found to be insufficient for prolonged use.

On the streets of the town the argument raged on. Those who favored the idea of an unfailing water supply provided by a well were often called foolish by their neighbors who said it was impossible to find an abundance of water in the deep rock strata of the surrounding area. *The Weekly Eureka Springs Times* cited examples of fifteen wells, none deeper than 120 feet which had proved by continued use to be unfailing. The well at the Eureka Stone Company quarry north of town was only 40 feet in depth, yet furnished 12,000 gallons of water every 24 hours and had not failed in five years.

All agreed on one point, regardless of their opinion regarding the wells. The resort could not afford to enter another summer season using water from the reservoir in its present condition. The resort did, however, endure a number of summer seasons before the problem reached a final solution. Mayor F. O. Butt and his council, elected in 1911, strove mightily to find a way to finance a water improvement project but were unsuccessful. At one time some local promoters raised the possibility of selling the municipal waterworks to a group of New York capitalists. Publicity and talk on the streets concerning the idea raised expectations, but the transaction was never completed. The water supply continued to remain a problem for the civic leaders to work out.

It was not until 1913 when the General Assembly of Arkansas took a good hard look at municipal affairs that a way was opened for the people of Eureka Springs to effect an improvement to their water supply costing over $200,000.

The Council and Mayor, T. J. Gordon, upon petition of the people, established an Improvement District encompassing the entire city for the purpose of improving the present water supply. Late in 1914 the city let a contract for a modern and efficient filtering system at the waterworks plant, the best quality and most effective system to be had at that time.

The work of the numerous individuals and civic organizations toward securing an adequate water supply for Eureka Springs was finally accomplished in 1916 by the building of a larger dam and power plant at the site of the waterworks.

The Joplin (Missouri) *Globe* reported the completion of the dam in a newsstory of September 14, 1916, under the headline "Eureka Springs gets Ozarks' Highest Dam." A Joplin engineer, Albert Moore, was in charge of the construction which had covered a period of nearly two years time and cost the citizens of Eureka Springs $130,000. The paper also stated that the dam, being 56 feet high and 450 feet long, was two feet higher than the one at Powersite, Missouri, which had previously been considered the highest such structure in the Ozarks.

When the contract was awarded to Moore he had determined that the best way to build the new dam was to place it directly over the existing one. In this manner the construction could be completed while keeping the usual water supply on hand. This engineering achievement won the construction the name of "Moore's sliding dam," the name being adopted by the townspeople because it appeared to the average person that while the dam was under construction it kept sliding downstream.

The reservoir now had a capacity of 116,000,000 gallons of water, being continually replenished by a total of 19 springs. The city had also installed two new pumps, costing $35,000, a short time later, which along with the new filters could provide the city with over a million and a half gallons of pure and healthful water every day.

Eureka Springs financed the long awaited new water system by issuing revenue bonds. This action was made possible by the recent enactment of Act 13 by the Arkansas

General Assembly in 1913. The new law allowed cities of the first and second class to issue revenue bonds for public improvements. It was the first time Arkansas municipalities were allowed to enter into this type of financial arrangement and proved to be a boon to cities both large and small.

Within the next few years the community was able to bring about the installation of other facilities which added to the overall comfort and convenience of life in Eureka Springs. In 1920 work began toward the installation of electric lights on all of the streets in the city at a total cost of approximately $30,000. The streets themselves were as yet unimproved and remained so for another five years, until this project, also financed through the issuance of revenue bonds, was completed in 1928. By that time the traffic on the streets was almost entirely motor vehicles with a few horse-drawn wagons. The electric street cars had disappeared from the scene and most of the tracks had been removed from the streets. The street railway began to run into difficulties about 1911 and finally had to suspend operation when the time came that the line collected only seventy cents in fares in an entire day.

Although the streets remained unpaved for many years, visitors could safely walk about the town on the well made sidewalks. The sidewalks of the town were a unique feature of the scenery, as various attractive and durable materials were used in their construction. An ordinance passed in 1904 instructed property owners to build walks and gutters under the direction of the Street and Alley Committee of the Council, but allowing them a choice of any materials so long as they were of a permanent nature. Some builders chose to use concrete, sometimes inlaid with pieces of glass or stone for decorative purposes, while others used large slabs of smooth native stone in varying colors; and as a whole the sidewalks were both durable and presented an attractive appearance.

During all the years of change and striving in the face of adversity to effect needed improvements, the community benefitted greatly from the leadership of several able men, particularly those elected to the office of mayor. Some have been mentioned in connection with various events, but there were others like Wade H. James, Fred C. Cook and J. H. DeLano who rendered fine, if unsung, service to their community. They and their attendant councils of aldermen faced numerous set-backs in attempting to administer public affairs, but their occasional successes undoubtedly blotted out the failures and some progress was made.

Perhaps the most colorful public figure in Eureka Springs during the first half century was Festus Orestes Butt. A native of the nearby community of Green Forest and to a great extent self-educated, Butt read law and set up a practice in Eureka Springs about 1894. This took place shortly after a bill was introduced in the Arkansas General Assembly to remove his disability of minority and permit him to be licensed to practice law before he was twenty-one years of age. Within a few years time Butt ran for and was elected to a seat in the General Assembly where he served for four years, then returned home to his law practice and to the office of County Examiner of Schools. In 1902 and 1904 he was elected to two successive terms in the State Senate and in the ensuing years served the public as local school director, Chairman of the Carroll County Board of Education, member of the State Constitutional Convention and also mayor of Eureka Springs for a total of ten years.

First elected Mayor of Eureka Springs in 1911, Butt served for two years, after which he again sought and won a seat in the General Assembly. During his term as Mayor the city was in a particularly bad fiscal condition and because of this faced many almost insurmountable problems.

Ever since 1882 Eureka Springs had been a City of the First Class because of its population and operated under the Mayor-Alderman form of government. By 1910, however, the population had dropped to the point where there was danger of losing this classification and its various attendant privileges. If possible, F. O. Butt and others wished to avert this eventuality, and Representative Butt brought before the Assembly a special bill which would allow the small city of Eureka Springs to retain its first-class status under the Commission form of Government. The act was passed, and this city joined just two others, Little Rock and Fort Smith, in the entire state, by adopting an optional charter embodying a commission form of municipal government.

The City of Eureka Springs enjoyed this distinction among its sister communities for many years. No other cities followed suit, and a few years later the General Assembly outlawed the practice of passing local or special acts such as the one submitted by Representative Butt. In 1916 the city reorganized under the new form of government after electing a commission of three men . . . William Kappen, H. Goudelock and, very fittingly, F. O. Butt, who became Chairman of the Commission, a position equivalent to that of Mayor.

Butt promised the people that if elected he "would turn the municipality upside down" and that he intended to see they never elected him again. He did not seek the position but carried every ward in the city by an overwhelming majority. The next four years were stormy ones in many ways and Butt, Kappen and Goudelock are generally credited with having purified the moral atmosphere of the community and also with having put the City on a sound financial basis for the first time in many years.

As he had promised, Butt and his associates did turn over the community in many ways, but surprisingly his popularity was not seriously damaged. Four years later F. O. Butt was again drafted by his fellow townsmen to serve on the Commission and won an easy victory.

Through the years F. O. Butt was very closely involved with the changes which shook his adopted community and was always to be found in the foreground where any controversy raged, for his life was firmly bound to the political, economic and moral life of Eureka Springs. Through the years he witnessed many changes in the community, participated wholeheartedly in effecting improvements, and felt keenly the many losses it suffered. One of the most crippling losses was the decline and final suspension of the Missouri and North Arkansas Railroad which began life at Eureka Springs when General Powell Clayton and his associates conceived the vision of a railroad to connect this health resort with the outside world.

On April 2, 1908, the *Eureka Springs Times* indicated in a brief editorial comment that Eureka Springs was in danger of losing the Missouri and North Arkansas Railroad shops and general offices unless local businessmen would awake to action. The writer insisted that a way must be found to organize an effort to remove any obstacles to the retention of this valuable source of income to the community.

In spite of such effort on the part of the citizenry the Missouri and North Arkansas line made plans to locate the shops elsewhere but went forward with the construction of a beautiful new stone depot building and other structures. By 1914, however, traffic on the line had fallen off to such an extent that it was necessary to reschedule the trains to Eureka Springs. This resulted in great difficulty and inconvenience for people traveling to or from the resort and was the source of many complaints.

The railroad, although still in operation in 1920, was not making a profit and there was a great deal of speculation as to what was to become of the Missouri and North Arkansas. In the issue for February 12 of that year the *Flashlight* commented:

> "The Missouri and North Arkansas road has always been a money loser instead of a money maker. It has been in the hands of a receiver for ten years or more with no prospects seemingly of ever getting out"
>
> "There is one thing certain and that is the public will have to assume a more sympathetic attitude toward the road, rates will have to be increased and more favorable consideration in the matter of legislation will have to come or else the road cannot operate. It would be a blow of immeasurable misfortune to this county if the M. and N. A. road is not held on its feet . . . "

Within less than a year's time the ill-fated railroad company was deeply involved in a crippling strike with its employees, and before the trouble had been settled several persons were to lose their lives.

Early in March of 1921, two striking employees of the company were arrested for burning the railroad bridge at Alpena. All up and down the line citizens of the various communities through which the Missouri and North Arkansas line passed were organizing themselves to protect their interest while the strike was in progress. In Eureka Springs some sixty people from all over Carroll County gathered to pledge their support to the railroad company and its practices. This body deplored the actions of reckless men who resorted to incendiarism and other violations of the law, and recommended the railroad receive the full protection of the law in the legitimate operation of its business.

What had started as an attempt by the employees to bargain for and to determine the rate of compensation for their labor had quickly gotten out of hand. A goodly number of the M. and N. A. employees were on strike, resulting in a suspension of the railroad service, and one lawless act followed another until tempers reached a flaming pitch. Harrison became an armed camp in which men actually lost their lives in the battle over the rights of labor and capital.

The depot and office at Eureka Springs remained open; only one employee had gone on strike. There were a number of passenger and freight trains arriving at this point on a fairly regular schedule through the early summer of 1921. The full effect of the strike was centered further down the line in Boone, Newton and Searcy counties, and the citizens of Eureka Springs could only pledge their support to the people much more deeply involved in the controversy.

The strike dragged on for nearly two years, and though a settlement was finally reached between the Missouri and North Arkansas and its employees, by then the company had given up all hope of saving the railroad from ultimate abandonment.

Although Eureka Springs was not so intimately concerned in the tragic occurrences related to the strike, still the eventual loss of railroad service dealt a keen blow to the community. There were many who were without doubt glad that those men who had invested so willingly and with such high hopes in the development of the Eureka Springs Railroad, and later the entire Missouri and North Arkansas line, were no longer living to witness its sad decline.

While constantly beset by financial difficulties and later by the demands of labor, the Missouri and North Arkansas might yet have succeeded had it not been partially a victim of the changing times. People who for years had been accustomed to travel to the health resort by rail, were now in the early 1920's arriving by private automobile or passenger buses. In 1915 the forward-thinking businessmen of Eureka Springs were organizing to finance the building of a toll bridge across the White River on the new Jefferson Highway connecting this city with Seligman, Missouri. The traffic on this road increased steadily, and it was kept in good repair by volunteers in each town who organized "Shovel Clubs" for that purpose. By June, 1920, motor bus service had been established between Eureka Springs and Seligman and to points north and west in Missouri, and more roads were being built in every direction from the resort.

Eureka Springs, which had suffered many set-backs and known numerous changes in its history, was rapidly entering a new era in which motor tourism would play a prominent part. In bygone days visitors to the resort arrived by train to be met at the station by a handsome horse-drawn tally-ho. They were carried through the streets to one or the other of the elegant hotels which would provide them with both comfort and pleasure during their stay. This pleasant and convenient mode of travel had now given way to the noisy touring car, driven for many miles over dusty and bumpy roads, until finally the passengers would alight at their destination in Eureka Springs. Many times this destination proved to be one or the other of two rustic and rather primitive accommodations called "tourist camps." The first of many to be built in the years to come, Camp Leath and Camp Joy were enjoying a thriving business by the time the resort reached its half-century mark.

One factor which was for many years of paramount importance to the early success of the Missouri and North Arkansas Railroad was the mining of lead and zinc in north central Arkansas. Just before the turn of the century the Eureka Springs railway was lengthened to Harrison, about fifty miles to the East, and a great deal of ore was shipped from the Boone and Newton County area from that time until about 1917 when the mines shut down. This loss of paying freight was just one of the many reasons why the Missouri and North Arkansas finally faded from the scene.

For many years local residents, too, heard persistent rumors about the treasures to be found within the surrounding hills. Lead and zinc had been found in Carroll County and some prospecting and a small amount of mining was carried on particularly in the Winona Community on the Kings River. The June 6, 1901, issue of the *Flashlight* reports that C. S. Craigen recently struck a three foot vein of zinc at a depth of thirty feet on his property at Winona. Others were reportedly doing the same, but the metal was never found in sufficient quantities to warrant any real development of the mining industry in that area. There were also a number of individuals who believed that a fortune in silver waited to be taken from the nearby hills. Many tried to seek their fortunes in this manner and failed, losing their investments in the process. but the rumors persisted for many years.

About 1920 a rumor that the people of northwest Arkansas were literally sitting on top of one of the richest oil fields of this continent began to make the rounds and gained wide acceptance. Who or what touched off the resulting furor to drill for the "black gold" will perhaps never be known, but drilling operations were set up in various places, including Capps, a community just west of Harrison, Centerton, in nearby Benton County, and at Huntsville, thirty miles south of Eureka Springs in Madison County. Evidence of some oil had been located, and the people had it on the "best geological authority" that the composition of the land across a wide area of the Ozark Mountains was perfectly suited to contain rich pools of oil and that one need only dig for it in order to become extremely wealthy in return for a small investment of capital and effort.

When the rumor reached Eureka Springs and began to take hold of the imagination of the townspeople cannot be determined with any degree of accuracy, although as early as December of 1916 the *Eureka Springs Flashlight* reported that a visitor to Eureka Springs from the oil fields of West Virginia and Southern Ohio

> "After having carefully inspected several places near Eureka Springs where oil was said to be in evidence, informs this office, that beyond doubt, oil of fine quality has in several places forced its way through the rocks in sufficient quantity to warrant the drilling of one or more test wells, which alone can determine the volume of oil underlying the dome foundations."

Neither the identity of the informant nor his qualifications were revealed to the reader, but the news was sufficiently exciting as to create more than a passing interest among individuals more than willing to become involved in an adventure of the "get-rich-quick" variety.

In 1919 one F. Prudom, described as a one-time owner of the Seidel House in Eureka Springs, added fuel to the fire with his statement to the *Times Echo* that he was positive there was oil in the vicinity of the town. Said Prudom

> "I don't think, I know there is oil here. Do you think I would come here and invest $20,000 in property if I didn't know this to be a fact?"

The interest in drilling for oil reached its peak by May of 1921 when H. C. Harrison, purportedly representing great Texas oil interests, arrived in Eureka Springs to promote the drilling of an oil well. By July sufficient capital, amounting to about $10,000, had been raised from local businessmen to secure a tract of land, and Harrison sent for a crew, drill and other tools. These were to come from Texas as soon as possible. Harrison's company was called The Sure Pop Oil Company, and practically every businessman in the community was wielding whatever influence he might have to encourage others to invest in shares of company stock.

Sure Pop purchased a large tract of farm land from Claude A. Fuller located west of the town where the new Eureka Springs-Seligman highway (called by many the Jefferson Highway) crossed the White River. It was at this spot that Hugh A. Tucker, a geologist from Dallas, Texas, said to be connected with some of the biggest oil concerns in the country, had inspected and reported the spot to be one of the best indications for oil that he had ever seen.

The company foreman and chief driller, F. B. Crane, let contracts locally for erection of the derrick and work began immediately. By the end of July the drill was ready to go into operation.

Sure Pop leases were selling rapidly to people all around the Eureka Springs area as they rushed to snap them up before "outside interests" could do so. The company assured the public that a well would be drilled "in the best workmanship manner" to a depth of 2500 to 3500 feet, unless gas or oil in paying quantities was found before that. The public was further assured through a barrage of newspaper advertising that oil or gas would be produced in tremendous quantities and that the price of oil leases as blocked out around the well would greatly increase in value.

As summer turned into early autumn the Sure Pop rig drilled on, day and night, with the local press giving progress reports as to the depth reached. The rush to purchase oil leases continued as H. C. Harrison had published in *The Daily Times Echo* a letter to him from Col. George Thompson, one of the biggest "wild-catters" for oil in Texas, the man who, according to this paper, "brought in the big Bowers gusher and opened up the Electra field."

According to the letter, Thompson could scarcely contain his enthusiasm and interest in the oil well at Eureka Springs after having visited the site two weeks previously. He had reportedly purchased quite a large block of acreage nearby and assured Harrison that he was holding in readiness for shipping one of the best standard drilling rigs in Texas. He awaited only a wire from Harrison telling him that Sure Pop had struck oil, and the equipment would be shipped immediately to begin drilling more wells in the vicinity.

If there was one person left in the community in doubt about investing his hard-earned money in Sure Pop oil leases, this type of publicity soon made up his mind for him.

On October 4 the people of Eureka Springs closed their doors and went out to see "their oil well." Sure Pop invited one and all to a tremendous barbecue dinner and it was reported that 2,500 people turned out for the occasion. They inspected the equipment, took a squint down the oil well, expressed the opinion that they would be lucky and strike oil, then sauntered off a short distance to eat their fill of fine barbecued beef and other plentiful dishes. One and all returned home full of enthusiasm, beef, and hope such as only those who dream of sudden wealth can know.

Local photographers captured the scene for posterity and the *Eureka Springs Flashlight* of November 3, 1921 carried a picture of the great crowd thronging about the derrick. The Sure Pop ad for that day took up half a page, including the picture, and announced that the well was now down to 530 feet. Said Sure Pop

> "The hole is perfect . . . and the indications are wonderful . . . come out and smell the gas yourself."

The ad also informed the public that as of that day there would be a very substantial increase in the prices of all oil leases, and urged them to buy before the prices got beyond their limited means.

From time to time, through newspaper accounts, the oil company threw out small tidbits of exciting information, such as:

> "the drillers passed through what was apparently the largest and strongest strata of gas so far encountered," and, "Thursday morning the day force passed at 540 feet into fossil rock and sand with 'oil rainbows' being distinctly seen on the water brought out by the bailer from this depth."

In early November Sure Pop withdrew from sale further oil leases at any price, and a few days later announced that they had closed a "big lease deal" with the Associated Bankers Investment Corporation of New York and Chicago which had purchased every oil lease that the Sure Pop Oil Company would sell. The *Flashlight* of December 1, 1921, reported that a Mr. Thompson, identified only as Mr. Harrison's personal assistant, had made a trip to Chicago to close the deal, and he, Thompson, would be in full charge of the affairs of the Associated Bankers Corporation in Eureka Springs while continuing to aid Harrison with Sure Pop business.

The newspaper reported

> "one significant fact which ought to impress us here at home," and went on to say, "if the men of the North and East who have money will put their money into 4,500 acres of oil leases around our well at an average of $10.00 per acre, even to resell again, they must think very strongly that we are going to get a big one."

However, they failed to point out that no one actually representing the Associated Bankers Corporation had arrived on the scene, except Thompson . . . who had been and continued to be associated entirely with the Sure Pop Company.

In the "big lease deal" Harrison and his company retained the 360 acres immediately surrounding the well and a large number of 40 acre tracts checkerboarded throughout the entire original tract of 10,000 acres. This, according to the *Flashlight,* was sufficient, in the event of a big strike, to make Sure Pop one of the wealthiest companies to be found. The rumor was becoming wide-spread in Eureka Springs that Harrison's organization had paid dividends of 150 per cent before coming to this area, and to say that this news raised the hopes of the local citizenry is to speak mildly, indeed.

Associated Bankers Corporation advertisements of half- and full-page size began appearing in the local papers, offering investors an opportunity to reap returns of as much as $5,000 for every hundred dollars invested . . . when the gusher came in.

On December 17, Associated Bankers announced the permanent and immediate withdrawal from sale of all Sure Pop oil leases, the deadline being 9:00 P.M. on that day. Doubtless many took advantage of the opportunity to invest before the deadline, as they were assured leases sold after the well was in production would go at prices of 100 to 1000 per cent above those which had previously prevailed.

There then followed such a dearth of news about the oil well endeavor as to cause wonder at the patience of the investors. One small news note early in January, 1922, said that H. C. Harrison had arrived in the city after spending the holidays in Texas. Another reported that the Commercial Club, with president A. G. Ingalls presiding, agreed to write a letter to Governor McRae,

> "petitioning him to call an extra session of the State Legislature for the purpose of enacting legislation to put a severance tax on all oil products produced on Arkansas soil."
>
> "Revenue from such a tax would be divided equally between roads and schools."

On January 26 the *Flashlight* reported that a depth of 780 feet had been reached and more gas pockets encountered.

In the early morning hours of July 31, 1922 . . . a year after the Sure Pop Company began drilling . . . the hopes of its investors literally went up in smoke. Sometime between two and four o'clock the derrick, buildings and a new 2,500 foot drilling line, just being prepared for use, were totally destroyed by a fire of unknown origin. The loss was estimated at $20,000 and the company had no insurance whatsoever. That same day H. C. Harrison left for Dallas, Texas, to secure another drilling rig. The Sure Pop office was to remain open and business transacted as though there had been no fire until his return, surely a matter of only a few days time.

Nearly two months passed with no word from Harrison. Finally S. A. Diehl, editor of the *Flashlight,* pointed out in print that a word of encouragement from Mr. Harrison would be most welcome as the citizens had shown a great deal of confidence in the man and his organization and certainly deserved a show of good faith on his part. On September 21, Diehl's paper printed a statement from the local office of Sure Pop saying that the company's other wells in Texas were again in production and proceeds from that source would be forthcoming to get the Eureka Springs endeavor going again.

Thus ended the newspaper coverage of one of the most exciting . . . and disappointing . . . adventures which ever involved the community of Eureka Springs. Throughout all the months of high hopes no one spoke out publicly to advise prudence or caution on the part of the citizenry, and it is impossible to tell how much the people turned over for shares in what came to be only a dream of wealth. Within a short time the Sure Pop Oil Company closed its doors and its local employees found themselves without a job. If H. C. Harrison appeared upon the scene again there seems to be no record of the visit, nor can it be shown where any of the townsmen ever received his money back.

Another dream had ended short of fulfillment, but before the townspeople could settle back into their usual quiet routine an event occurred which shook the entire community and which perhaps would not have happened except for the widespread publicity concerning Eureka Springs and its wealthy potential of "black gold."

In the early days the town often resounded with the roar of gunfire as reckless men, inspired by the strong drink too readily available, shot off their pistols and dashed through the streets on rearing horses . . . all in the best tradition of the pioneer West. But thirty years later, two decades into the civilized twentieth century, the last thing any one expected in the course of an ordinary day was to hear gunfire in the downtown business district of Eureka Springs and to find men lying dead or dying of serious wounds. All in a matter of a few moments time the peaceful law abiding citizens of this quiet small community had of necessity taken the law into their own hands and ended the career of a bandit gang from nearby Oklahoma, caught in the act of robbing the First National Bank.

It was almost eleven on a quiet autumn morning, September 22, 1922, when five strangers drove into downtown Eureka Springs in an open Model T. Ford touring car. The men had spent the previous night camped out on Leatherwood Creek just west of town and made their final plans as to how they would go about holding up one of the banks in Eureka Springs.

Of the men, Charles and George Price were brothers from Salisaw, Oklahoma. The two of them, along with Si Wilson of the town of Cookson in that state, were a part of the Henry Starr gang which had broken up a short time after Starr's death in a robbery attempt in Harrison. These three were wanted by the Oklahoma authorities for robbing the Muldrow Bank and were also suspected of a robbery at Everton, Arkansas. The Prices and Wilson looked up two old friends, Mark Hendricks of Parkhill and John Cowan of Tahlequah, persuaded them to come along and set out for Arkansas to keep out of the way of Oklahoma police.

Apparently John Cowan was driving the car and would later act as a lookout while the holdup took place. Cowan parked the vehicle on Spring Street, headed downhill, and just a few doors below the First National Bank building. The other four stepped out and went quickly into the bank, leaving one man, Wilson, near the door to cover them.

It had been a busy morning for the five employees of the bank and when the bandits arrived they were seeing to the wants of four customers. According to the statement given by the cashier, E. T. Smith, later in the day, the men were not masked and at first displayed no weapons. Smith had the presence of mind to step on the burglar alarm button concealed in the floor near his desk as the four men pulled their guns and herded all of the nine patrons and employees into a back room of the building. An assistant cashier, F. M. Sawyer, also stepped on an alarm button near him without being noticed by any of the bandits. The men worked quickly and efficiently, talking little, as they gathered up $60,000 in Liberty Bonds and $10,000 in cash, stuffing it into sacks.

Suddenly the man at the door noticed their car start down the street and realized that something had gone wrong. None of the bandits had heard the alarm bells activated by Smith and Sawyer which sounded in four nearby business houses, the Basin Park Hotel and the Bank of Eureka Springs. As men from these places began to run out into the street Cowan had seen them and evidently fearing only for his own safety tried to flee in the getaway car.

The cashier, G. E. Burson, at the Bank of Eureka Springs, less than a block away, stepped out the door, gun in hand. Seeing the car pulling away in a hurry, Burson fired at the driver, wounding him in the arm. Cowan managed to drive as far as the Basin Spring before two shots fired by citizens Jesse Littrell and Sam Harmon caused him to lose control of the car, smashing into a power pole on the east side of Spring Street.

Ernie Jordan was working at the repair bench in his jewelry store when the disturbance began. He also kept a pistol close at hand and grabbing it he ran out into the street in time to see Wilson, with a drawn gun, step away from the doorway of the bank. Jordan immediately fired at Wilson, who fell dead in the street. An attorney, Joe McKinney, also shot Wilson from an upstairs window over the bank where he had his office. In the confusion it was never determined who had actually fired the shot that killed Wilson.

Inside the bank the Prices and Hendricks had the loot in hand and were preparing to take Smith and Sawyer with them as hostages to assure their safe getaway. At that moment Robert Bowman, the desk clerk from the Basin Park Hotel and Claude Arbuckle, who had been chatting with him when the alarm sounded, dashed into the bank building, Bowman carrying a .45 pistol. The three bandits immediately forced them to put up their hands, then rushed out of the door with Sawyer and Smith between two of them. Jordan, not realizing what was happening inside the building, ran to Wilson to examine him and was met by the three bandits and their hostages. One of the armed men shot point blank at Jordan as they ran across the street toward a stairway between two buildings which would take them down to Center Street. Jordan, despite powder burns to his eyes, fired several more times, as did other men coming from both directions as well as those leaning out of upstairs office windows.

Seeing the confusion of the bandits, Smith and Sawyer jerked free and fell to the street where they stayed unharmed until the shooting ended.

Constable Homer Brittain arrived upon the scene just in time to find himself caught between Charles Price and Mark Hendricks, who had reached the bottom of the steps, and George Price, still on the upper street level. Brittain crouched low, firing in both directions. As the shooting continued George Price slumped over the railing at the top of the steps, fatally wounded. His brother Charles also fell to the ground having sustained near fatal wounds, and Hendricks, also seriously wounded, gave up the battle. Throwing away his gun he slumped down on the steps and waited to be captured. The five men were carried a short distance to Huntington Hospital, at the foot of Pine Street, where they were attended by Doctors Pace, Bolton, and Albert Tatman.

Si Wilson was dead with eight bullets in his body. George Price had sustained only one wound, in the chest, but the bullet had taken his life. His brother, Charles Price, was seen to be dying of stomach wounds though he lived four more days. Mark Hendricks received two wounds, both from a shotgun, but neither was serious enough to end his life, and John Cowan, who had tried to flee from the scene, was wounded twice in the arm and leg.

Within a few days, three women, sisters of the Price brothers, arrived from Oklahoma to claim the body of George Price. Two of them returned the body to Salisaw for burial while the third remained by the bedside of their brother, Charles, until he died the following Sunday without ever regaining consciousness. The body of Si Wilson, whom no one seemed to know, remained unclaimed until Sunday when at six o'clock in the evening he was buried in a lonely corner of the community cemetery.

Cowan and Hendricks survived the ill-fated robbery attempt and were lodged in jail until the following February when they were tried and convicted for bank robbery. Just twenty-one years old, Hendricks was sentenced to three years in prison, but Cowan, because of his past record, received a sentence of ten years imprisonment.

So ended what proved to be the bloodiest and most disastrous criminal act in the history of Eureka Springs . . . except for an aftermath of publicity which was picked up by newspapers all over the United States and reached ridiculous heights of praise and honor bestowed upon the community and its citizens.

Six young men were given the credit for having "killed one and assisted in mortally wounding two others." They were Ernest Jordan, Constable Homer Brittain, Joe McKinney, Jesse Littrell, Robert Bowman and Sam Harmon. Though all six owned and kept at hand in their places of business either hand pistols or shotguns, not one of them had ever seriously considered an eventuality which would necessitate their use against another human being. After having reacted courageously to the necessity of stopping a criminal act and protecting themselves from the actions of desperate men, they found themselves subjected to an embarrassing barrage of publicity. Newspaper reports on the local scene used words like "honor," and "glory" and begged to be forgiven if each man were not allowed sufficient "credit" for the deaths of the robbers in their news coverage of the event.

The Daily Times Echo of October 2, 1922, in an article entitled "Our Heroes" enumerated each of the six men in turn, pointing out qualities of their character and past life which had enabled them to make such a fine showing against evil men. Said the writer of this editorial:

> "To be unpopular in Eureka Springs is to express sympathy for the robbers who were killed or wounded last week, when they attempted to loot the First National Bank. Man or woman who express themselves in this vein are looked upon by the loyal citizens and friends of our heroes as the German sympathizers were during the Great World War." The reporter concluded, "We imagine it will be difficult to tell just who fired the fatal shots. Nevertheless honor is due to all who participated in the shooting."

Newspapers far and near received the story of the attempted bank robbery at Eureka Springs, and apparently every paper from the *Grand Rapids* (Michigan) *Herald* to the *Salt Lake City Tribune* made the story even bigger and better than the original occurrence. The *Grand Rapids Herald* reported:

"Yesterdays news report from Eureka Springs, Arkansas, read like a leaf out of the yellow-back Atlas of the Old West; but in the news was a lesson for every American community large or small."

The *Arkansas Gazette* noted:

"Eureka Springs deserves the prominence it won in the news, for its handling of this desperate emergency was remarkable. It is doubtful whether there is a case in the history of outlawry in the United States to equal it."

The *Tulsa,* (Oklahoma) *World* said:

"Law makers have for years attempted to prescribe a cure for banditry. They have been uniformly ineffective or only partially effective. There is but one really successful cure for the atrocious practice some worthless citizens have of forcibly taking from other citizens the means of subsistence. That cure was administered in the orthodox fashion to a band of worthless citizens by the citizens of Eureka Springs Wednesday . . . whenever a citizen has the opportunity to kill a highwayman, a housebreaker or other specie of the criminal element, in the act of his unlawful practice, he should do so."

The six heroes of the day began to receive letters of congratulation from near and far, and were even lauded from the pulpit by ministers who commended them for "their act to humanity." However, the whole affair reflected an element of farce in an article printed in the *Wichita* (Kansas) *Eagle,* which bore small resemblance to the truth of the matter.

"Five bandits robbed the bank the other day and thought things were going about as usual. But just as they headed for their car at the curb, in the customary manner, they suddenly realized that they had made a mistake. They were in Arkansas! No helpless crowd of hopeless citizens stood agape while the dashing bandits sailed right out of their ken like a meteor on a starry night. That's not the way they do in Arkansas. Two pedestrians on the way to visit a sick friend, saw what was going on and stepped inside the bank door in time to open the battle with a few well-directed bullets toward the bandits vital organs. A lawyer in an office overhead said to his earnest client, "excuse me a moment please," stepped to a front window and put a half dozen bullets where they would do the most good. A dentist asked his patient to keep open wide please just one moment, and rested his rifle on the window sill long enough to make sure that at least one of the bandits would fail to leave town that day. A school boy hustling home to lunch whipped out his automatic and joined the attack."

"Now the merchants began issuing from the lunch counters and the housewives from their kitchens. Each individual had his pistol spitting fire and steel as soon as he came within range. And not an innocent bystander was scratched. No wild shooting down at Eureka Springs. Needless to add, not one of the five bandits got away, and all the money, $70,000, was carried back into the bank.

"The Congress of the United States should vote a medal to the town of Eureka Springs, and a diploma to Arkansas, where every citizen is a peace officer, always on the job, never missing fire, never hitting the target far from the bulls-eye."

The citizens of Eureka Springs may or may not have enjoyed the rash of publicity which had been thrust upon them, but as is the case with most sensationalism it soon passed and the town was once again restored to peace, quiet and order. Perhaps the days following such an exciting happening were dull ones by comparison, yet the normal routine of small town living was soon re-established and was welcomed by many, particularly the six young business men most intimately involved, who may have entertained second thoughts as to what might have happened . . . tragedy for the townspeople rather than a measure of triumphant publicity.

The years following the events which brought Eureka Springs to the end of its first half century as a town were probably the most uneventful in its history. The political scene locally was decidedly cool with very little controversy involving either candidates or issues. A great deal of effort was expended toward promoting auto tourism, as thinking minds began to see this as the next potential boom for the economy of Eureka Springs.

In the spring of 1927 Claude A Fuller was again elected mayor. Fuller had served in this capacity numerous times in past years and easily won the office with a handsome majority. One of the most obvious needs at that time was a system of good streets, particularly in view of the fact that much was being done to encourage visits by tourists traveling in motor vehicles. Mayor Fuller proposed and saw to its conclusion the paving of the town's major streets with concrete. The project cost $214,000 which was financed through a bond issue. It was during this time that the City built the Municipal Auditorium, a large and beautiful building of natural stone, which seated 1500 people and provided facilities for most any type of stage show. The building, also financed by a bond issue and costing $75,000, was one of Fuller's fondest dreams and he saw it completed before leaving the office of mayor. In 1928 Fuller was elected to the Congress of the United States and served ten years in that august body.

In 1929, one Albert G. Ingalls succeeded Claude Fuller as mayor. A native of northwest Arkansas, Ingalls had lived most of his life in the western United States, coming to Eureka Springs about 1920. One early historian says of him:

> "He is not at all embarassed to tell that he was broke when he came here and also heavily in debt."

Nevertheless, Ingalls and his wife were soon involved in the social and civic life of the community. By 1922 he was elected president of the Commercial Club and was rapidly becoming one of the most influential and respected citizens of the town. When elected to the office of mayor he owned a goodly portion of Eureka Springs real estate, including the Crescent Hotel and Girls Preparatory College, the Basin Park Hotel, the Palace Bath House and a floral business, and had leased the local newspapers, *The Times Echo* and the *Flashlight.*

Mayor Ingalls ran what might be called a "clean-up, fix-up, paint-up" administration and undoubtedly left the town much more presentable for townspeople as well as for visitors at the end of his tenure of office.

Eureka Springs had come a long way in fifty years. What had started out to be the greatest health resort in America had evolved into a well organized, attractive, but typical American small town. While supporting a large number of substantial businesses which provided every service required by the citizens, still Eureka Springs was no longer what it set out to be. Nine physicians were in residence to attend the sick and a fine well equipped Municipal Hospital had been completed in 1929, but the throngs no longer came to seek the healing waters and beneficent climate.

While still a resort catering to the needs of people seeking relaxation and quiet, Eureka Springs could no longer claim the title "Siloam of the Afflicted."

CHAPTER XI

NEWSPAPERS

Weeks of research make it apparent that a clear day-by-day story of the early newspaper business cannot be written. Changes in ownership and/or editors, format and political leanings occurred with astonishing rapidity at Eureka Springs.

Writing to the Carroll County Historical Society, D. Elmer Jones could remember when several newspapers were published in the city, two of them dailies. He says: "A printer would work for awhile on a paper, and if it seemed to be making money, quit that paper and get another printer to go in with him, order type from Chicago or St. Louis with a small down payment and start his own paper." Thus many different papers were launched at different times. Even that authority, Fred W. Allsopp, in his *History of the Arkansas Press for 100 Years or More,* does not clarify the scene in Eureka Springs. Neither does Goodspeed's, *History of Carroll County,* though both agree that T. J. Hadley moved his printing press from Olathe, Kansas, and issued Vol. I, No. 1 of *The Echo* on February 21, 1880. It would seem this to be the first newspaper published in Eureka Springs were it not for the mention of a paper published in 1878 by A. H. and H. E. Jones, also a paper called the *Herald* was printed in 1879 with a Mr. Hinman as owner. No specific authority could be found to verify the supposed publication in 1878 and while the *History of The Arkansas Press* would seem to give it credence the early settlers did not arrive until 1879. It seems some one wrote a bit of news before it happened.

Be that as it may, during the period from 1879 to 1899 at least eleven different owners and/or editors made their appearance, made changes in the newspapers and most faded from the Eureka Springs scene. Unfortunately the many disastrous fires, particularly those in 1883, 1888 and 1890, burned those copies of papers which would be of value to a newspaper history.

Before starting a trip in time through such papers as are now available a table of the owners of one paper that survived most of the changes of ownership will be attempted. The present *Times-Echo* dates its beginning to 1880, so a brief table of the past history of this paper follows:

Date	Name under which it appears	Owner
1880	Echo	T. J. Hadley
1881-1882	Echo	H. A. Nickell
1883	Echo	S. B. Lowe, A. B. Adams
1885	Daily Echoing Nemesis	A. B. Adams & Co.
1886	suspended, later published as Daily Echo	D. P. Cloud
1891	Daily Echo	White & Pulliam
1893	Daily Times Echo	W. E. Moore
1898	Daily Times Echo	E. L. Eastman
1899-1904	Daily Times Echo	Clark Hudson
1904-1909	Daily Times Echo	Giles E. Miller
1910-1925	Daily Times Echo	S. A. Diehl
1925-	Daily Times Echo	W. E. Diehl

The dates for this paper are approximate, and during S. A. Diehl's ownership he had several partners beginning with W. E. Moore, also Mrs. W. E. Moore. In addition he was joined for brief periods of time by Overstreet, Davenport and Pulliam. It seemed that running a newspaper in Eureka Springs was no sinecure and while Diehl would work alone for short times soon he would again be in partnership. Most of the time it was with a different man though a few times his old partners would return for short periods.

In tracing the changes that went on through the years with *The Daily Times Echo* the other papers are not forgotten nor is the fact that the *Echo* was sometimes a weekly as well as a daily. Another paper had made the scene in 1879. It was called the *Herald* and the owners were Hinman and Company. It didn't spend many years heralding the glad tidings of the "Water that Healed."

In 1881 a paper named the *Eureka Springs Register* was started by Butler Bros., who were not satisfied with the name and changed it to the *Eureka Springs Republican.* That didn't last long and both ownership and name changed in 1883. Perry and Spears were the new owners and the new name was *The Eureka Springs Times.* As owner Spears couldn't have lasted long either, for an advertisement published in *Cutter's Guide* in 1884 proudly credits Don Perry with ownership. Late in 1884 the ownership changed to W. E. Reece though the name of the paper remained the same until Giles E. Miller took it over in 1891. However, by 1893 W. E. Moore was owner of both the *Times* and the *Daily Echo* and began publishing *The Daily Times Echo.*

During 1890 *The Eureka Springs Star* rose for Miller and Sams but set in 1891. The year 1891 was quite active for those whose business was publishing the news of Eureka Springs.

A paper called the *Rainbow,* and having John A. Betton as owner, was added to the newspaper collection. It must have been a fairly colorful rainbow as it stayed on the scene until 1903 when it too faded from view.

It was also the year 1891 that Giles E. Miller and his *Republican* joined the newspaper complexity. Mr. Miller continued to be counted as a force in the publishing business for years. Apparently in 1904 he merged his *Republican* with *The Daily Times Echo* and dropped the name *Republican.* He was associated with both *The Daily and Weekly Times Echo.*

During 1897 what was to be another major newspaper for Eureka Springs was started by Moore and Overstreet. Each of these men had at one time or another associated themselves with other Eureka Springs papers and brought their past experiences to a paper of their own. Evidently their combined experience couldn't keep the newspaper, the *Flashlight,* flashing and Overstreet bowed out and Mrs. W. E. Moore, a most able newspaper woman, took over. This combination didn't continue long when the *Flashlight* changed hands again and Washburn and Ferguson replaced the Moores. But the *Flashlight* wasn't quite done with changes as Malone and Barrows took it over in 1906 and continued it as a weekly until all of the Eureka Springs papers were gathered into one fold under S. A. Diehl in 1910.

While a few other publications may have made brief appearances, copies of most do not exist though a record remains of two of them. The *Expositor,* edited by L. E. Smith, appeared in 1899, and in 1900 the *Tribune* was published by H. S. Holden. How long they lasted or why they couldn't make it is not known.

The Carnegie Public Library opened its doors in 1914 and soon became the repository for a few newspapers presented to the Library by citizens who had been able to keep them from being destroyed by fire.

1883 . . . Good fortune preserved a copy of the April 12, 1883, edition of the *Eureka Springs Times.* It is a four page, six column paper with a half page of advertising. It bore the name of Don J. Perry and Thomas F. Spear on the masthead and was published on Thursday. Most of the paper was devoted to a City Council meeting where a motion to reimburse Isaac Chidester for the sum of $937.50 was passed. That sum had been advanced by him to defray the expenses of the townsite case held earlier in Washington, D. C. Later we find a news item telling of a visit Chidester was making in Eureka Springs from Green Forest, so one wonders if he found that locality more to his taste. At the same meeting a vote of thanks was tendered Mayor Carroll and the members of the Council for their services during the year just passed.

If papers were saved for the next several years they were not kept where they are available for research as the next paper in the file at the Library is:

1891 . . . *The Daily Echo* for December, 1891, carried the names of White and Pulliam on the mast head. During 1882

Powell Clayton had arrived in Eureka Springs to guide the destiny of the town. His ideas had not met with universal approval and now were met with vigorous protest, at least by the *Daily Echo*. The front page is given over entirely to the constitution of the Mohawks. The Mohawks were organized to resist Powell Clayton and all of his ideas. General Clayton, having the most money and influence on his part, continued to wheel and deal and the Mohawk braves were never able to take his scalp . . . Inside the paper were columns devoted to National events together with a large number of ads by local merchants. The back page ran a three column letter from the Editors on the advantages of Eureka Springs as to location, accommodations and other useful knowledge. Such as

> "The population cannot be excelled in this world for honesty. There are no sneak theives, house pilferers or robbers in the City. Fakers and sure-thing men are not permitted to abide within her gates. Bawdy houses and places of assignation are not allowed and there are only three places where ardent spirits are sold and these are under heavy license, bond and strict surveillance by the law."

Six months later a sheriff's posse had to clean out the teamsters lot and arrest fourteen men and four notorious women who had caused trouble for a long time. It would seem the good editors bragged a bit too soon.

1893 . . . the publishing business continued on its changing ways and the next paper saved is a *Fountain* for December 14, 1893. It was published by Clayton and Edwards and the news was mostly local with quite a lot of local advertising.

1894 . . . Once again an issue of *The Daily Times Echo* made the scene. It had changed in format and was now a small size two page sheet of six columns devoted to personal news of local celebrities together with a fair amount of advertising. The editor was W. E. Moore and he devoted one of the inside pages to "Eureka Springs, The Gem of the Ozarks." The content is similar to an earlier open letter on the advantages of the city, but with later embellishments added. The back page was devoted to advertising while one column was given over to a letter from a "Father to His Dissipated Wayward Son."

1896 . . . The August 27 issue of *The Fountain* makes its first appearance. *The Fountain* had started to play back in 1893 with Clayton (no relation to Powell) and Edwards as publishers. It had been Democratic and now switched to being Republican and this issue was devoted to the county candidates of this party, as well as editorial comment concerning the Republican aims for the city of Eureka Springs. Carroll County in company with other counties in Arkansas was in debt $30,000 . . . It was urged that William McKinley be voted into office as President . . . Mr. Clayton continued to keep the *Fountain* flowing through 1897. This year was not one of the best years for Eureka Springs. A severe drought threatened the flow of even the most gushing springs. This situation all but shut down the electric light plant, which in turn affected the street cars. Under such circumstances the town wasn't especially gay though steps were soon taken to remedy the water shortage.

1898 . . . The July 7 issue of *The Daily Times Echo* comes next. It had changed owners and editors several times since 1894. The copy saved shows the policy of the paper was to continue to boost Eureka Springs and Carroll County, as a full page advertisement listed the real estate available to home seekers. Eureka Springs had now been a city for nineteen years but the paper made no special achnowledgement of this achievement.

1900 . . . By July 6, *The Daily Times Echo* had grown considerably. It was now a large size, seven column paper. The name of the editor was omitted from the masthead. Life seemed to be getting real and earnest as the front page was largely devoted to the third meeting of the Economic League "to discuss living ideas and closely investigate the problems of the day" . . . A year earlier in 1899 the *Weekly Flashlight* had begun to shed light on the local scene under the direction of Moore and Overstreet. It was a large eight column paper with large amounts of both news and advertising from all over Carroll County.

1902 . . . By January 30 *The Daily Times Echo* was edited by Clark Hudson, and the format had been changed to a small five column paper. Memory of the disastrous fire of 1892 was still fresh in the minds of all citizens so the report of a fire which destroyed the upper floor of a building between the Opera House and the Basin Bath House on Main Street and seriously threatened both buildings was worthy of a long news story, for in the past fires had usually burned over large areas.

1904 . . . The May 4 edition of *The Daily Times Echo* was a very special issue paying tribute to the Public School System. Much praise was given to Principal Barnett, and his photograph, together with those of the teaching staff, covered half a page. The Graduation exercises were reported in detail and the address given by F. O. Butt in behalf of increased salaries for teachers was printed in full . . . A brief writeup on the most prominent business men in Eureka Springs filled the balance of the paper.

By the time the July 18, 1904, edition of *The Daily Times Echo* went to print Giles E. Miller had taken over as editor and the size of the paper had been reduced to a small six column sheet . . . Two news items were of some interest, one that the Citizens Bank was opening a Savings Department . . . the other noted that Eugene V. Debs was to be the speaker at Chautauqua. Apparently it was assumed that the great socialist was well known as not a great amount of publicity concerning him was provided . . . A larger space was given to the fact that a contract had been let for the stone retaining wall up the mountain behind Sweet Spring.

During the next several months the makeup of *The Daily Times Echo* remained unchanged. It reported among other news a Temperance Lecture as the idea of temperance had become a most active National issue . . . Also reported was a story on the visit of George W. Hellmuth, the architect from St. Louis in charge of building the Kerens Memorial Chapel. Mr. Hellmuth was spending a few days at the Crescent while inspecting the excavation work and approving the start being made on the foundation of the Chapel . . . During the summer the new lighted trolley made its appearance and was most popular . . . Concerts by Stewarts Band were a regular nightly and Sunday afternoon feature at the Basin Park during the summer . . . A bowling alley had been added to the attractions for visitors and was doing a rushing business . . . the candy factory advertised for a woman to dip chocolates . . . the Citizens Bank continued its large advertisements.

Occasionally a member of the rougher element got upset to the extent of cutting up a friend, so a few cutting scrapes were reported but none of really major importance.

A printing of the new city ordinance pertaining to streets, sidewalks, curbing and gutters along Spring Street from Main to Hillside caused a flurry of "letters to the editor" as citizens expressed themselves pro and con. The need for good sidewalks came in for a lot of comment . . . As the holiday season approached, advertising began to feature gift items for Christmas giving. What one paper in 1891 had referred to as "ardent spirits" now was openly called whiskey in a large size advertisement . . . Entertainment was not neglected and the Byran Miller Dramatic Company was coming to the Opera House . . . Street car tickets sold for three cents and three and three fourths cents each "by subscription" and with this low fare everyone could afford to ride the street cars.

1904 . . . December 8 *The Weekly Times Echo* became *The Eureka Springs Times.* It continued to be edited by Giles E. Miller who also continued to publish *The Daily Times Echo.* This issue advanced the idea that the Honorable R. C. Kerens, donor of the Kerens Memorial Chapel, might run for the United States Senate . . . The well known St. Louis naturalist, James Gurney, was planning to put a show garden on East Mountain and had purchased land for that purpose.

1905 . . . On February 23 the beams from the *Flashlight* once again illumine the scene. A large weekly of eight columns with the names of both Mr. and Mrs. W. E. Moore on the masthead, it is notable as being the first paper to devote several columns of the front page to a continued story . . . It also had a column of news from Carroll County. Soon Mr. and Mrs. Moore were succeeded by Washburn and Ferguson but the continued story was not interrupted. For many years all papers printed a listing of the daily arrivals at the principal hotels and this practice was continued . . . The proposed ordinance on streets was kept in the public eye by Democratic opposition . . . The paper carried a quantity of advertising for the Magnetic Sanitarium. Where once the accounts of the cures affected by the healing waters were given prominent space it was now mostly taken over by ads for patent medicines and doctors who were trying to capitalize on the local conditions by helping the effects of the healing waters.

1905 . . . The March 5 issue of the *Flashlight* chronicled one of the most important events which had taken place up to that time. The Arkansas State Legislature paid a surprise visit to Eureka Springs. That august body had been on a junket to inspect the University at Fayetteville and having a couple of days left after their inspection they yielded to the persuasive invitation of State Representative Butt and arrived in Eureka Springs without advance fanfare. They arrived at 9:00 P. M. and were rushed to the Crescent Hotel where a gala evening of dancing to the music of a hastily assembled orchestra was enjoyed. The next morning the lawmakers marched down to the Opera House on Main Street to the music of the Fayetteville Cadet Band. Many addresses of welcome and as many responses were made before the meeting was adjourned to return to the Crescent for a luncheon. This was followed by a tour of the city on the new trolley cars. All good things have a way of ending and the gentlemen now returned to Little Rock by way of Seligman. They expressed much pleasure concerning the trip and were greatly impressed with Eureka Springs and especially the Basin Park Hotel just being readied for guests. This copy of the *Flashlight* had more than the usual quota of advertising as well as many admonitions scattered through its pages urging each citizen to appoint himself a committee of one to boost Eureka Springs . . . To add to the excitement Col. C. D. James warmed up the city political scene with a lengthy speech, reported in full. It was over two months before another paper was saved. Then *The Daily Times Echo* of May 29 was preserved. The paper was still edited by Giles E. Miller who used the front page to congratulate the Public Schools.

1905 . . . The issue of September 11, printed a lengthy report on the Sewer and Water District and devoted the rest of the paper to local news and advertising.

Whoever had the foresight to save such copies of the local papers as are now in the Carnegie Public Library managed to save sufficient numbers of each to permit later readers to sample not only the type of newspaper and what it stood for, but the current events in the still growing city.

1906 . . . The September 20 issue of *The Eureka Springs Times* which was published by Giles E. Miller and was a rewrite of the items which had appeared in his *Daily Times Echo* notes that the new Court House will be built on South Main Street at a cost of approximately $15,000.

1907 . . . The paper issued on March 25 gives space to the coming election. Both the mayor and city council were to be elected. The differences of opinion reached a point where a "now and then" publication calling itself *The Daily Searchlight* made an appearance. Only three issues of this paper have been preserved. It was put out by Malone and Barrows who published the *Flashlight* and had as its aim the countering of claims made by *The Daily Times Echo.* It shows to what lengths a disgruntled citizenry will go when aroused. It seems a nonpartisan citizen's committee had been organized to prepare a ticket for the city offices, including that of mayor. These twelve leading citizens had selected their candidates and the ticket was made public in the seemingly perfect harmony of all concerned. At the last minute, aided and abetted by *The Daily Times Echo,* an independent candidate for the office of mayor was advanced. The local political scene was at a good bubbling boil and how many *Searchlights* it took before the bubbling ceased and calm was restored is unknown. Unfortunately copies of *The Daily Times Echo* detailing their manuevers to get their "independent" candidate elected were not saved to record his victory.

The city scarcely had time to recover from the excitement caused by the election when . . .

1907 . . . the July 1 issue of *The Daily Times Echo* (Giles E. Miller, editor) broke out an EXTRA with the headline

"Citizen's Bank Asks for Receiver, Eureka Springs greatest Benefactor Meets Misfortune." This was followed by W. M. Duncan's statement on the closing of the bank. Since the newspaper was one of the smaller debtors involved, it remained staunchly on the side of Duncan.

It is not until a July 19 issue of the *Flashlight* (Malone and Borrows, editors), that an account of the other side of the story appears. The *Flashlight* was always eager to shed light on the local scene and headlines this paper "Report of Receiver for Defunct Citizens Bank"; then follows an account of the receivership under Digby West. According to the *Flashlight* large overdrafts by the many other enterprises headed by Duncan were responsible for the failure. The bank failure took with it the Citizen's Electric Company, the water shipping company, and the new Basin Park Hotel. It is intimated that Duncan might have been playing the role of beneficiary rather than benefactor.

A *Daily Times Echo* of the same date defends Duncan and his "empire" and hopes that in the future he will make a comeback and head up a larger bank. The paper used the headline "Mr. Duncan's Statement" and a secondary headline, "Eureka Springs Great Benefactor Shows a Sense of Honor Unknown to His Traducers." After giving a brief account of the financial situation Duncan "regrets . . . that placing the Citizens Bank in the hands of a receiver has embarrassed many of his friends," and so on and on.

It took several weeks for this event to get off the front pages of both newspapers. Both debtors and creditors held meetings to see what could be saved or recovered from the tangled financial affairs of the bank. While confidence in the Receiver, and the ability of the bank to pay off even included an ovation for Duncan, many took a less optimistic view and both newspapers continued to agitate the public mind for several months. It was not until October of that year that *The Daily Times Echo* was able to print an issue that did not mention the affairs of the bank. All along that paper had urged the citizens to stand behind Duncan and his financial ability. Their urging had a practical aspect as the paper was in debt to the now defunct bank. Many months were to pass before the snarled finances of the many enterprises controlled by W. M. Duncan were to be straightened out.

1908 . . . A January issue of *The Weekly Times Echo* shows a change of ownership. The retiring Postmaster, Clio Miller (no relation to Giles) now takes a whirl at the newspaper business. He changed the name to the *Eureka Springs Times,* and published a small five column paper of no great distinction. Meanwhile Giles E. Miller continued to get out *The Daily Times Echo* in a somewhat subdued form. He also published a small tabloid, *The Daily Grist.* How long this ground along is unknown. Both newspapers took cognizance of the impending city election, but relied on the end of the school year and similar events for news.

The March 19 issue of the *Eureka Springs Times* took notice of a bill in Congress to provide Eureka Springs with a new Federal Building to house the Post Office. Aside from that local political news occupied each newspaper. The *Times* brought up the water question and also urged a Republican victory for "A More Beautiful Eureka Springs." They also editoralized on what they considered a lapse in the moral attitude at both the National and local levels.

1908 . . . May 28, a single copy of the *Carroll County Record* was saved probably for the announcement of a donation by R. C. Kerens of the site for the proposed Carnegie Public Library. This plot was given to the city and was just down the mountain below the Kerens Memorial Chapel.

1908 . . . The August 18 edition of the *Flashlight* is a large eight page edition featuring the men who were prominent in the development of Carroll County and Eureka Springs . . . A large ad for the new Crescent College also an ad for the Kelly Granger Lumber Company, are prominent features. The next paper saved is a *Daily Times Echo* now published by Phillips and Block. The big story concerning the local scene is the desirability of changing the location of the highway up past the railroad station and the septic tanks.

1908 . . . The October 15 issue of *The Daily Times Echo* with Clio Miller still in command, fills up the front page with what will continue to be a feature of that paper. Mr. Miller evidently was fond of poetry and encouraged the local poets . . . the same issue attacks the saloons for what he refers to as "the pall of indebtedness" still hanging over Eureka Springs . . . difficulty at the water works had resulted in the resignation of the superintendent . . . later in a November issue Miller hailed Taft and Sherman on the National political scene and a column headed "Man About Town" again appeared to needle those who held office at the local level . . . Carrie Nation was welcomed to Arkansas and regret expressed that she did not settle here . . . the front page gave equal prominence to a poem and the account of the yearly banquet of the Commercial Club . . . General Clayton had made one of his infrequent visits, during which he announced the possible extension of the railroad as far as Helena . . . another featured article was on a crusade for sanitary dairy products.

1908 . . . After November 20, the name of S. A. Diehl appeared as owner of the *Flashlight*. He had acquired ownership sometime between August 7 and that date. He immediately improved the format of the *Flashlight*.

1909 . . . Early in the year the *Eureka Springs Times* was transferred to L. E. Baird by Clio Miller who fades out of the newspaper picture. Baird continued with this paper until March of 1910 when it, like the owner, also faded away.

1909 . . . The March 18 issue of the *Flashlight* carried photographs of all the candidates for city office . . . it also carried a report of the city finances made up by the County Clerk . . . a very brief mention that oil might underlie certain nearby areas appeared for the first time. During 1909 Diehl continued to guide the *Flashlight* and since several copies have been preserved we have a sketchy idea of what went on during that time . . . the Governor proclaimed Arkansas the Diamond State . . . a statewide campaign to fight hookworm was proposed . . . on the local scene the clubs held their regular programs . . . a clean-up program was urged . . . spring water under the trade name OZARKA had been shipped for years but now certain citizens agitated against such a practice. The agitation was brief.

1910 . . . February to be exact, the *Flashlight* rejoiced that the long litigation with the Massman heirs had been settled by arbitration. During the early years the Massman's had moved saw mills to different sites and logged timber, claiming the land by squatter's rights. Later when the land claims were settled these heirs refused to accept the settlement until it was finally worked out in 1910 . . . a rather large gap occurs in newspapers saved and it is July 5 before an issue of *The Daily Times Echo* was preserved. Apparently S. A. Diehl had just taken over the paper and also taken W. E. Moore as partner, as both names appear as publishers. The majority of the news concerns the recent celebration on July 4 . . . and an account of how the County Farm is run . . . Carry Nation had returned to Eureka Springs; she gave a large dinner at Thach Cottage and announced her proposal to give the city a home for indigent old ladies, also a school to teach temperance . . . the Home Electric Light and Power Co., was granted a franchise, according to this paper.

1911 . . . During this year several copies of the *Flashlight* with Diehl as sole editor were saved. The street cars were not running, nevertheless the paper hopes for a new era in local affairs. Early in February Diehl added the name of Mrs. W. E. Moore to the masthead of *The Daily Times Echo.* Only one copy was saved and the next paper saved is the *Flashlight.* The ownership of the Magnetic Spring had never been decided and on May 4 of that year Powell Clayton deeded it to the city . . . to the *Flashlight* was left the sorrowful task of headlining the death of Carry Nation, and her burial during June in her native state of Kansas . . . on the local scene water meters were advocated to help the financial status . . . a long letter to the editor set forth the beauties and advantages of Eureka Springs in the most flowery terms.

1912 . . . a *Daily Times Echo* is the first paper saved for posterity in the new year . . . most notable quote was the Sunday dinner at the recently reopened Allred Hotel priced at 50 cents. For the balance of the year the issues available alternate between the *Flashlight* and *The Daily Times Echo.* During the summer they announce the usual weekly band concerts in Basin Park . . . meetings of the various clubs including the Tourist Club are given much space . . . so is the ever present plea to clean up Eureka Springs and keep it clean . . . also trade at home and help the local merchants.

1913 . . . The March 27 issue of the *Flashlight* is the first issue of a paper saved. Apparently Diehl had replaced Mrs. Moore with Overstreet, as Diehl and Overstreet are listed as owners. This partnership continued throughout 1913. In March of that year the *Flashlight* advocated a new auditorium park . . . the summer band concerts continued to be given as usual in Basin Park . . . plans for a larger water supply were proposed . . . otherwise the local affairs were about as usual . . . lyrical advertisements on the advantages of Eureka Springs continued . . . the only excitement was the occasional item on the possibility of oil almost at the door.

1914 . . . The January 1 issue shows the Diehl and Overstreet partnership continuing and the *Flashlight* begs everyone to "work to build up the City into a year around resort" . . . the Carnegie Public Library was about to open and herald a new cultural era in the life of the city . . . there were 600 pupils enrolled in the Public Schools. The issue of the *Flashlight* for July 30 had a big headline "Austria Deliberately Brings On War," (this is the first mention of war in the local press.) A single copy of *The Daily Times Echo* shows Diehl and Overstreet as editors and uses three columns to advocate the superior advantages of Eureka Springs. From there on to the end of 1914 while the war news takes a large share of the front pages of both the *Flashlight* and *The Daily Times Echo,* the local news and the poetry is not slighted.

1915 . . . The February 9 issue of *The Daily Times Echo* shows Diehl and Overstreet still in partnership and continues to extol the beauties of the city. No special mention is made on the thirty-first anniversary of the beginning of the community with the exception of letters of reminiscence from former residents . . . during July a Society from New York City brought a dozen or more babies to Harrison for adoption . . . summer in Eureka Springs featured the usual band concerts in the Basin Park . . . the local flower show had a summer revival . . . everyone was urged to plant sweet peas as a city beautification measure . . . a restroom for the downtown area is advocated . . . agitation for good roads continues. The copies saved were *The Daily Times Echo* and the *Flashlight* but the news was not spectacular.

1916 . . . the January 4 issue of the *Flashlight* has Diehl alone on the masthead, but the February 7 copy of *The Daily Times Echo* continues to use Diehl and Overstreet in the announcement of ownership . . . the street cars were starting to run again, but the seventy cents in fares collected the first day wasn't encouraging, so how long they would continue to run was doubtful . . . a Mr. Clark, the architect for the Sweet Spring steps came up from Rogers to oversee the start of their construction. He was also the architect for the Penn Memorial Chapel. Several copies of the *Flashlight* were saved during the balance of the year. One copy reported the death of Vernon Castle, a partner of the popular dance team of Vernon and Irene Castle.

1916 . . . War news was not greatly stressed although the local charitable organizations were urged to unite . . . the difficulty on the Missouri and North Arkansas railroad was a jarring note on the local scene . . . the death of R. C. Kerens, recent donor of St. Elizabeth's Chapel, added a sad note, as he was greatly admired. He had also been the donor of the site of the new Carnegie Public Library. The last paper saved that year was the December 28, issue of the *Flashlight* which announced that the contract had been let for the new Post Office building.

1917 . . . The issue for January 25 is full of accounts of the many good things in store for Eureka Springs . . . oil seems to be one of them . . . the new broom factory is making a clean sweep having sold four hundred brooms in two months . . . later in the month the question of water as a cure for cancer receives much publicity . . . in February, on the world stage, President Wilson asks the world to join in action against Germany . . . in Eureka Springs a Boy Scout troop is organized . . . the United Charities makes an appeal for funds . . . just outside Eureka Springs a ranch where elk are to be raised to relieve the meat shortage, is started.

1917 . . . The next papers are for the month of April and Congress calls the Nation to war . . . to help get Eureka Springs into the spirit of the times a patriotic parade is organized . . . women plan to do more knitting . . . a new auto highway from Seligman, Missouri, gives promise of many tourists and plans are being made to accommodate them . . . oil is still a prospect as a major boost for the financial status of the town . . . the railroad picture is brighter as the striking section hands have returned to work.

1918 . . . An early issue of *The Daily Times Echo* calls for a three day general clean-up for the city . . . the Food Administration rules are listed . . . and a full page is devoted to the Third Liberty Loan . . . several issues of the same paper for the month of June give space to the German U-Boat activity on the high seas . . . space is also given to a warning of poison ivy around the Harding Spring . . . also to an urgent request that all weeds be cut . . . Red Cross activity is reported . . . In a December issue it is proposed to erect a monument for the Carroll County boys who were lost in the war . . . the list of food prices fixed by the County Board also has a prominent place.

1919 . . . Beginning with the issue of the *Flashlight* for January 8 many copies of that paper for the months of April, May, June and July were saved as were many of *The Daily Times Echo.* A few items which indicate the most pressing problems of the times have been selected . . . the local monument fund was started . . . on the National scene the Prohibition amendment was ratified . . . appeals for funds to build the soldiers monument, help the Carnegie Public Library and keep the rest room open appeared and reappeared. As in other years a general city wide clean-up was urged . . . in May the Missouri and North Arkansas railroad moved its traffic department to Harrison . . . during May the Modern Priscillas were sufficiently recovered from their war time programs to entertain in the lavish pre-war manner . . . on the education front the schools continued to make progress, though as yet sufficient funds were not available to add a Domestic Science course to the curriculum . . . the usual long rhapsodies used to advertise Eureka Springs were continued . . . in June the

Peace Pact was signed and in the wake of that good news on the National scene came an announcement that economically and otherwise Arkansas was not keeping up with her sister states . . . in July the Equal Sufferage Amendment was ratified . . . in Chicago grievances reached an explosive point and resulted in a race riot . . . in Eureka Springs all was serene; clubs met as usual, though lack of interest in the Red Cross was regretted . . . citizens were warned to watch for promoters of fake stock. From other news in the papers the city kept on its usual routine, while the usual clean-up continued to be urged, not in politics but of private premises and public places.

1920 . . . The *Flashlight* for February 5 reports the usual club meetings . . . also a story that five roads were soon to converge at Eureka Springs . . . the usual three column reprint of the delights to be found there is used once again . . . the issue for March 18 is largely devoted to editorial bouquets and brickbats for the homes and places of business in Eureka Springs and calls for an increase in civic pride . . . paving from Main Street to the Harding Spring area is urged . . . to better sanitary conditions closed garbage cans are advocated . . . a face lifting for Basin Park is called for . . . also electric lights for residential areas . . . and the oft-reiterated appeal for a clean city . . . a city ordinance forbids foot washing or bathing in any of the springs . . . an appeal was made for clean sidewalks, as a man slipped on a banana peel and fell and broke his back . . . politics occupied many newspaper columns as 1920 was an election year . . . the oil promoters came on the scene and hope soared anew . . . Eureka Springs had been a member of the Ozark Playgrounds Association for some time, but lately it had been increasingly hard to pay the fee so agitation to withdraw was argued pro and con.

1921 . . . Again the first paper saved in the new year is a *Flashlight* for February 3 . . . the feature story is a strong plea to remain in the Ozark Playgrounds Association . . . in March the Commercial Club started a Civic Improvement fund . . . and the League of Women Voters (local branch) was organized . . . strikers on the Missouri and North Arkansas railroad returned to work, but management warns that any lawlessness will cause service to be discontinued . . . in May a Citizens Committee decides that drilling for oil is favorable and later in the year a site is selected and a barbecue held at the site . . . during the summer, in line with the usual clean-up campaign it was announced that arrest and fines await those who throw trash on vacant lots . . . in October a movement to induce manufacturing in Eureka Springs was started with "MADE IN EUREKA SPRINGS" as a slogan . . . a new ad "Arkansas, Nation's Wonder State" began frequent appearances, and together with the three column writeup about Eureka Springs that had been used for many years extolled both state and city . . . all through the year appeals were made for funds to assist the Library, also to keep the rest room open, appeals which yielded barely enough to keep them from closing . . . ads for the "Sure Pop Oil Company" began to appear and stock was offered for sale by a company organized for that purpose . . . a Christian Science lecture took up over a page of the paper, it was the first time a local paper had printed such a lecture in full . . . agitation for a Community Camp Ground was started . . . also to have a community nurse on duty . . . prohibition began to reap the toll of lawlessness and a moonshine still near the Blue Spring was raided . . . late in December the Stock Company announced that oil leases would not be available until the well began producing . . . somewhere in the timber near Eureka Springs four wolves were shot . . . reprints of "Arkansas, Nation's Wonder State" continued.

1922 . . . The January 5 issue of the *Flashlight* continued to publicize the manufacture of "white mule" and the other unlawful activities associated with it . . . the Sure Pop Oil Company announced it had a years work planned . . . the sale of the Missouri and North Arkansas railroad was advocated . . . Ozarka Water was now being sold by W. M. Duncan, once of local banking circles . . . for some time the Agricultural Agent for Carroll County had put forth various ideas to help the county economy and now he tried to work up enthusiasm for poultry raising as a money maker . . . in March the grounds of the old auditorium were procured for a city park . . . that same month a long letter from R. R. Thompson roundly scolded Eureka Springs for its lack of cultural consciousness . . . a big still was raided and it was hoped that now an end would be put to the moonshine business . . . all during April, May and June the usual campaign to clean-up Eureka Springs and keep it clean continued . . . the regular summer concerts began in Basin Park . . . the time of year apparently getting to him, a man ran an ad for a wife.

In August the Sure Pop Oil Company derrick went up in smoke, and with it the hopes of many investors (Pop goes the weasel). In September an appeal was made to "pull together for Sure Pop" as other wells owned by the company in Texas were producing. This appeal didn't stay on the front page very long as The First National Bank was held up and robbed of $70,000 on September 27. The five bandits attempting the robbery were from Oklahoma, two of them were shot dead as they left the bank, a third died shortly after and the remaining two were quickly captured. Prompt action by the workers in the bank and by citizens in adjoining business houses was given full credit for the almost instant return of the money.

1922 . . . During the latter part of this year quite a lot of space was devoted to letters from early settlers.

1923 . . . The first issue of the *Flashlight* saved called for a meeting of the citizens of Eureka Springs to pledge their support to both the city and the railroad. It requested an early settlement of the strike and also threatened that those citizens who differed in their views would have a committee call on them as they were no longer welcome in Eureka Springs. In all the years this was the most drastic action ever advocated in a local newspaper by a local group. To lose the railroad would be to lose one of the things the city depended on . . . the railroad question was not settled, nor was it helped by the lynching in Harrison. Sometime in March the train service to Eureka Springs was cut off although the train schedule continued to appear in the papers until March 29. Trouble along the right of way continued and in April it was necessary to place a guard along the tracks between Eureka Springs and Seligman, Missouri.

Now the papers turned attention to brighter things and brought out the fact once again that Eureka Springs was a health resort, and late in September a bumper crop of summer tourists was reported . . . Fire Prevention Week was observed with two disastrous fires which pointed up the obsolescence of the local fire fighting equipment. One of the early landmarks, Christian Cottage, would have gone up in smoke but for the prompt efficient action of a near neighbor who organized a bucket brigade to keep the roof of the cottage wet . . . the first Rotary Club was organized . . . the IOOF held an election of officers . . . Federal Aid to highways was not very popular and the paper hoped it had been blocked, though earlier it had advocated and agitated for five highways into Eureka Springs . . . a local resident, Claude Fuller announced his candidacy for Congress . . . and the long suffering County Agent opined that Eureka Springs was not living up to its potential . . . during September the various items on moonshiners belied the hope that the illicit manufacture of that product had been wiped out.

1924 . . . The issues of the early papers in January began on a hopeful note . . . the Commercial Club got down to business according to the lead story in the *Flashlight* for January 10 . . . a cure for cancer being one of the chief claims made for the water from the Springs, a sanitarium for its cure was to be established in Kimberly Cottage on Hillside . . . funds to continue the golf course were being sought as its financial affairs placed it in jeopardy . . . on January 17 a letter concerning Crescent College was published which sounded a very sour note. The College was being forced to close as lack of interest, lack of funds and lack of backing by the citizens made the closing necessary . . . issues of papers for the month of May were full of reports of the public school year and many letters from alumni written in a nostalgic vein were published . . . in July the State Fire Chief inspected Eureka Springs and pointed out the many fire hazards. Not very many papers were saved in 1924 and the next issue is for October 23, in which the *Times Echo* complains of the depression . . . the Commercial Club had been attempting to promote a Business College in the Waco Hotel but the attempts had come to nought.

1925 . . . an issue of the *Flashlight* for February 5 has a prominent front page ad on starting vineyards in the hope that extensive grape culture would raise the economic level of the county . . . citizens held a meeting to discuss the question of garbage disposal and other civic improvements . . . advertising, together with the vineyards, was advocated as the key to prosperity . . . during the months of February and March local news stories stressed the fact that civic improvement can not longer be delayed . . . the March 12 issue of the *Flashlight* printed the final news on the selection of Berryville as the county seat of Carroll County, although the Courts of the Western District remained in Eureka Springs . . . the Crescent Hotel building was being refurnished as a hotel in anticipation of a spring opening . . . the next issue saved in October reports the steps up the mountain from the Sweet Spring completed; their cost of $700 had been raised by the Woman's Club . . . also during October *The Daily Times Echo,* the *Flashlight* and the job printing plant were transferred to the editor's son, W. E. Diehl, and so another change took place in the newspaper situation in Eureka Springs. There was no change in either the policy or the format of either paper. Letters to the editor from the Woman's Club declared the city water smelled bad while letters from the sick were again praising the water from the springs. Paving for Spring Street was being considered.

1926 . . . Early in the year the railroad had resumed operations and pullman service to Eureka Springs was a possibility . . . in March the local High School was given an "A" rating by the North Central Teachers Association . . . during this same month the usual committee was appointed to clean up the city . . . more columns of advertising seemed to promise renewed prosperity . . . the State Health Officer made a visit and gave the Eureka Springs hotels a good rating . . . later the usual summer band concerts were being given in Basin Park and financial assistance for the band was requested . . . pleas for help to keep both the Library and the rest room open continued as neither of these necessary civic endeavors had been placed on a permanent financial footing . . . during the month of August the railroad reported an increase in freight traffic, a hopeful sign . . . the public school enrollment was reported as the largest in local school history . . . after years of efforts to attract visitors the autumn coloring was finally extolled, but in November when the season was nearly over . . . the usual three column ads on the beauty of the region were continued word-for-word as they had been for over thirty years . . . the December 9 issue added a listing of points of interest in the Ozarks . . . during the year the usual reports of club meetings and social events continued to be published.

1927 . . . The January 30 issue of the *Flashlight* started the year with an appeal for a better Eureka Springs . . . the Commercial Club came out in opposition to the Commission form of city government and for a return to the Mayor-Alderman form . . . one of the active leaders in local affairs, A. G. Ingalls took up his pen and in a long letter to the paper severely criticized local conditions, and in turn was met by a storm of criticism, It is not recorded what, if any, improvement took place . . . during May the Commercial Club dismissed the promotion of the usual summer concerts in Basin Park . . . on July 4 the issue of the *Times Echo* was devoted to an account of the celebration on that day . . . July 7, the resignation of Professor C. S. Barnett from the Public School System saddened all concerned, for thirty eight years he had guided the Eureka Springs Schools to their present state of excellence; health was given as the reason for his leaving . . . the announcement that four State Normal Schools were to be located in Arkansas was accompanied by the announcement of the Commercial Club that they were determined to have one located in Eureka Springs. Their efforts were in vain as they did not get one . . . during the summer the Crescent Hotel was open and dances were again gala affairs, but without the brilliance of earlier years . . . in November a building boom began on Main Street . . . news of the drives for funds being made by the various charitable organizations occupied much space. According to the newspaper the year ended on a more hopeful note as *The Daily Times Echo* declared that 1927 had been its most prosperous year.

1928 . . . The January 5 issue of the *Flashlight* began the year by urging everyone to pull together for Eureka Springs during 1928 . . . the Commercial Club had given place to the more modern Chamber of Commerce and its civic committee was planning to make Eureka Springs a model city.

Here a gap of several years occurs in the copies of newspapers saved. Disastrous fires had earlier wiped out newspaper files and in spite of pleas to do so, no one took the time to ransack attics or old closets for the early copies so badly needed to tell the story of Eureka Springs during the Depression.

A brief summary of the way in which the local news was handled seems a fitting way to end the chapter.

A comparison between the journalistic styles of the newspapers of Eureka Springs and other Arkansas localities has never been attempted. Such a comparison might prove both entertaining and enlightening as well as a clue to the economic rise and fall of the community. Newspapers in Eureka Springs reached a kind of mediocrity, neither too good nor too bad, and seemed to stay in that particular spot for many years.

Local political celebrities either didn't care or else could not control the papers for any prolonged period of time. Their comings and goings were chronicled among the items of daily news without headlines. Any major efforts at either the national, state or local level which they made or success they achieved were seldom, if ever, given major headlines. Perhaps the papers didn't own that kind of type; if they did they used it sparingly. Bank failures, bank robberies and the hope of striking oil were about the only subjects which called forth headlines.

Once every two years the local political scene warmed up and both state and local politics would be given space for a few issues, but an interested citizen would have to be either clairvoyant or read an out of town paper to really learn anything about what was going on in politics. As a result of the heritage left by Powell Clayton and his friends Eureka Springs always had a group of "never-say-die" Republicans in the state where the Democratic Party was the only political party recognized as being such. Although surprising to outsiders and casual visitors, this was no surprise to serious politicians trying to make sense at the local level. Even the "Constant Reader" had trouble keeping the local politics straight.

For over the thirty years included in this survey, the newspapers carried two "set pieces" advertising Eureka Springs. They extolled the healthful climate, beautiful mountain scenery, blue Italian skies and other aspects of Eureka Springs, ending with an analysis of the water. Day after day, week after week, year after year the same words occupied from three to four columns of space. Fifty years later the lyrical style of writing soon becomes boring to the reader and with constant repetition even funny. Read once they were undoubtedly passed over from then on. Circulation figures are not available for these newspapers of long ago, but were they sufficiently large and did they reach a wide enough area so that the panygerics would attract visitors, patients, tourists? Looking through the pamphlets, circulars and other advertising, it is apparent that the "set pieces" used in the newspapers were copied for that variety of advertising or vice versa. It seemed that once said, adjectives were exhausted, as well as inventive genius and that only repetition was left. It is said that constant dropping of water wears away stone; did constant repetition of the same advertising have the same effect on visitors, for during the years a steady decline set in.

The first newspapers devoted much space to the testimonials of healing and many of the prominent citizens who gave the city its early stability had come in search of health, and finding it, stayed on to establish homes and businesses. Unfortunately it wasn't too many years before advertisments for patent medicines and cure-alls began to fill an ever growing number of advertising columns. They were paid for, while the testimonials were free, so naturally Doan's Kidney Pills and other quick remedies were an easy financial assist to the subscription list.

News had never been far reaching and other than items about the immediate locality and a few from Carroll County, few stories carried a date line from as far away as Little Rock. The exception was those acts passed by the State Legislature which had an application to local affairs. Instead, filling space with one, and sometimes two, continued stories became the custom.

Early in the 1890's poetry began to appear as a feature of each paper. Local poets were especially encouraged and they were most vocal, once given the chance to "speak their piece." Frequently three or four long poems would be printed in a single issue, a tribute perhaps to the culture of the age. When visitors left Eureka Springs for other localities they often took pen in hand to voice, in verse, their longing to return, and the paper printed it.

After County Agriculture Agencies were established the agents took many columns of newsprint to promote the aids to a good life, both economically and domestically. Gradually the continued stories gave place to this good advice, which had it been acted upon would have made both Carroll County and Eureka Springs blossom as the rose.

Editors themselves used very little space to voice their political policies. They endeavored to steer a neutral course, for the early history of the newspaper business was frought with danger. Numerous instances have been told of disgruntled readers gunning for the editors, and down in the Central and Southern counties one or two duels were fought by editors called on to protect their honor, although such an occurrence never took place in Eureka Springs.

After scanning fifty years of the newspapers published in Eureka Springs only two instances were found where the editor was sufficiently outspoken as to label him partisan. Mostly they begged for good streets, sidewalks, a city wide clean-up and tin can disposal. On the whole, not a very exciting editorial policy.

EPILOGUE

A child is often said to be born with a golden spoon in its mouth, meaning that its future outlook is golden. That could also be said of the infant Eureka Springs. The first few hectic years of the land settlement were soon forgotten in the flow of the many promises for an illustrious future, a future which would undoubtedly last as long as the healing water flowed from the Springs. The water continued to flow but as years passed the promises began to tarnish and the outlook for the future had lost its golden hue.

The early years of the twentieth century saw the first herald of these changes. The men who dreamed the dream and saw the vision were called to larger responsibilities and while affairs were left in capable hands, the dreamers and their vision were gone. No new dreams of grandeur were presently forthcoming and nothing appeared in the same golden light which colored the early years. The water flowed on and continued to embody the qualities which had once found such eager acceptance, but life in the outside world was changing. People were being caught up in a quickening rhythm, as if those who danced the waltz and two-step now heard music of a different beat and hurried to keep step. Only the music sounded too faintly in Eureka Springs for any large number to try to follow.

World War I soon involved the entire United States in a conflict which eventually took many of the most promising young men to other scenes and distant shores. Those who returned had glimpsed wider vistas and to many of them the home town now seemed small and isolated. Though some stayed and continued to have faith in the future of the community, many left and others did not come to take their places. The whole country was restless and when, immediately after the war, a few homeseekers looking for land on which to settle moved into the area it might have provided a boost, but the number was not sufficient to greatly help the prosperity of the town.

Visitors seeking the therapeutics of the water began to give place to those seeking rest and recreation. Efforts to attract additional visitors began to extol the recreational aspects of the area rather than the healing qualities of the water. Springs had been discovered in other parts of the state and large sums of money were being spent to develop them. They were located in an area convenient to the state capitol and could depend on political help to attract visitors. Many seekers for relief from physical ills preferred to go to a place with more spectacular surroundings and one which offered more worldly pleasures.

The bright shining vision for Eureka Springs began to dim and even before the Depression efforts were made to destroy and remove many of the earlier ventures, now fallen into disuse. The Chautauqua Auditorium and the Opera House were torn down and the street car tracks were torn up. Limitless vision had given place to immediate expediency.

Houses had once crowded the hillsides and occupied every available lot. Many were abandoned as people moved to greener economic pastures and the vines and squirrels moved in. When the Depression seemed at its worst many of these houses were torn down, the lumber was sold and much of it was shipped to Kansas. Now the vacant lots soon grew up with brush which gave the community a rustic appearance and changed the character of the town completely. Houses which belonged to absentee owners often presented a rundown appearance and different sections of the town began to show a difference in the financial responsibility of the property owners. The area adjacent to the Crescent Hotel was least affected, while among the smaller householders and businesses on Main Street the change in fortunes was more apparent.

A news story in the *Carroll County Courier* for December, 1932, states that Eureka Springs was probably suffering less from the Depression than many other towns and that actual suffering was unknown as most people were faring better than those in other areas of the United States.

The next month in fact, an issue of the *Courier* for January 5, 1933, tells the facts concerning relief in Eureka Springs. The story came from Red Cross headquarters which was apparently carrying out the official relief work. The story stated that over 800 unemployed had been provided with work through this agency, though over how long a period of time was omitted. Only 38 hours of work a month could be allocated to those qualifying. Road work also provided funds for those able to engage in this type of labor. The Red Cross had distributed 1900 pounds of flour and 6000 yards of material from which garments could be made. Other clothing such as jumpers, overalls, bloomers and stockings were being distributed free.

Another news item in the same issue tells of the entertainments being given by the Alumni Association, the proceeds to be used to help keep the schools open. Hungry school children were being fed by the Red Cross and the P.T.A. Relief rules were stringent as only unemployed industrial or farm workers were eligible. Any one owning property could not get on the relief rolls.

Through all of the adversity people continued to come, although in greatly diminished numbers. Business went on and a "Buy Eureka Springs" campaign was tried in order to stimulate business. The town kept neat and clean though visitors found little of the early glamour, but the aura still clung, as in the words of the old poem, "You may break, you may shatter the vase if you will, but the scent of the roses will cling to it still."

To the south of Eureka Springs the Tulsa Colony of approximately 500 members had dwindled down to eight families. Started in 1931, a group of unemployed persons from Tulsa had each chipped in one dollar with which to purchase cut-over timber land to be cleared for farming. Unrest, discontent and impractical leaders had dogged the effort from the start. Hardship proved to be the most notable ingredient of the endeavor in spite of help from sympathetic manufacturers who provided donations of food. The Red Cross also helped and local business men who headed up the organization continued to hope for improved conditions. These were not forthcoming and eventually as a colony it was forgotten.

While the character of the town had already undergone a great change other changes were to come. By the middle 1930's a revival was in the making which would add still another dimension to Eureka Springs. All over the United States people looked back to what they began to believe were those happier days and ways which characterized the turn of the century. Artists painted, authors wrote, composers began to use more country themes and theaters began to show what now seemed the unsophisticated past as one which was not only wholesome but which had a certain kind of glamour. Word got around that Eureka Springs was a combination of all these qualities now so popular. It was possible to live on a less expensive and more simple scale, and so began the first steps which changed Eureka Springs into a mecca for artists. The artistic-minded now flocked to the town that water built to paint its scenes of former grandeur and write stories about the unique characters they found there. Once again reechoed the cry "We have found it" as the colony grew.

When the first writers arrived they found a local writer already setting down the pioneer tales and folklore of the region. Born in Eureka Springs, and in spite of a physical handicap which finally yielded to the curative properties of the water, Cora Pinkley Call had written from early childhood and her writing was beginning to gain acceptance in regional publications. She was to continue to write for many years and to be one of those who organized the Ozark Writers Guild where those who came later would gladly find welcome.

The age of the automobile had caught northern Arkansas with its bridges down and its roads little more than wagon tracks, with an occasional puddle where hogs enjoyed their cooling mud packs. As late as 1932 what is now U. S. Highway 62 was mostly dirt or gravel with good stretches for a short distance on either side of Harrison. Now the prosperity of every community began to depend on whether or not it could be easily reached by automobile. State funds for roads were more often spent closer to Little Rock so it was several years before U. S. Highway 62 was greatly improved.

When improvement did come, so did those new-fangled places to spend the night, and tourist cabins and motels sprang up like toadstools along Route 62 quite a distance away from the town proper. Tourists could stop and spend the night and their money without going into the Eureka Springs business section.

With increased activity local taxes still barely kept abreast of the services necessary to encourage people to come and stay. Population continued to dwindle and so did the revenues for civic improvement.

To encourage artists to come and work a most unusual structure was built and dedicated with great fanfare in 1931. A local citizen, Sam Leath, was usually in the forefront of any scheme to bring added prosperity to Eureka Springs. He owned a tourist cabin camp near the water tower where there was sufficient acreage to erect a bridge across a near ravine. This bridge was approximately 125 feet long and wide enough to allow five small studios to be incorporated in the structure. These small places of quiet and repose were to be used by working artists for painting or writing. The venture got off to a most auspicious start with a former governor of the state, Governor Blough, dedicating the structure. It was christened with water from the two springs, Iron and Johnson, which bubbled up in the ravine. The studio did not fulfill its purpose for too many years as Mr. Leath heard a call from greener pastures and like so many others, answered, and left Eureka Springs and the studio to its fate. This was only one of the ventures which Mr. Leath promoted. Later he returned to the Springs and busied himself with promoting tourism.

About this time Robert Ripley, a popular newspaper columnist, discovered the unique Eureka Springs and publicised the Crescent Hotel, the Basin Park Hotel, St. Elizabeth's Church and Miss Annie House. She was the little woman who had chronicled the events of the town for over 65 years. Annie wasn't available for visitors, but this publicity brought many tourists to the other sites. Usually these visitors did not stay long enough to add greatly to the economy of the town.

By the early 1930's Crescent College had finally closed its doors forever. The outlook for the community seemed to depend largely on the artists who were being attracted in ever growing numbers, plus the greatly diminished number of short-term visitors. Gone were the days when whole families brought their servants and came to spend the summer months.

A writer whose enthusiasm for the Ozark Hills was contagious moved to Eureka Springs in 1945. With her husband, referred to as "the Judge," Marge Lyon had first settled in the Missouri Ozarks, but once having seen Eureka Springs she fell in love with it and decided to make it her home. Mrs. Lyon was well known to readers of the *Chicago Tribune* as "Marge of Sunrise Farm." Her articles appealed to people who wished to return to the simple pleasures afforded by mountains, streams and Nature's bounty. Soon many visitors came to investigate the retirement possibilities of the community and the trend continued.

Mrs. Lyon assisted Cora Pinkley Call with the Ozarks Writers Guild and they soon gathered a notable colony of writers in residence, including Vance Randolph, Constance Waggner and Otto E. Rayburn. Rayburn began to publish the *Ozark Guide* which was busily promoting the Ozarks as well as Eureka Springs. Local writers joined the group, Bonnie Lela Crump, among others.

Rayburn worked hard at trying to analyze and correct the decline of Eureka Springs. In his column called "Reflections" in the *Times Echo* for September 1, 1949, he once again pointed out that "Eureka Springs owes its existence to water." He went on to say that the decline in the fortunes of the town had been helped downward by "completion of other spas and health resorts, also by good roads and tourist travel, and of course the Depression." He speaks of the "shot in the arm" which began after World War II and which was fostered by the awakening desire of large numbers of people to "get into the country and into small towns." He also generously gave credit to the group of writers who helped with the promotion of Eureka Springs. If all of the millions of words recounting the charms of Eureka Springs had yielded a crop of silver dollars it would have eclipsed the early golden era, but they only attracted enough interest to keep the town alive.

In the late 1940's a fellow Arkansan went on the radio to exploit the backwoods charm of the entire state. His broadcasts were followed by increased interest in country music and dancing. Festivals celebrating this kind of entertainment soon became popular and Eureka Springs joined the fun and games. Soon the elegance which had characterized the town for the first fifty years of its existence was forgotten by all but a few, in the effort to attract visitors. In October of 1946 a "Pioneer Week" was staged. This was to be the first of the annual Fall Festivals. These festivals have survived for 21 years and have become well known musical events, nationally advertised. Directly related to the popularity of the folk music and dancing were the shops selling gifts fashioned in homes by local craftsmen. Dolls, sunbonnets, aprons and articles made from the native walnut all made their appearance and added income to the townspeople. Eventually they were joined by shop keepers who added numerous other gift items, and gift shops began to be one of the chief sources of what interest the town had to offer. The year 1946 also marked the beginning of the annual Summer Musical Colony at Inspiration Point. This continues to attract serious students of both voice and instrument with its excellent teaching staff.

In the early 1950's the Crescent Hotel finally acquired a firm financial basis when a group of Chicago and local business men organized and began a series of "package" vacation tours to the big stone hotel. These continued to bring numbers of Northern people to the town, some of whom returned to buy retirement homes and become permanent residents.

The dream of a future for Eureka Springs which would rival or surpass its early grandeur has never quite died, though many have been the promises. Through the years the dream has been pursued in many ways by many men, but none have ever posessed the combination of qualities, the vision, perspicacity and access to unlimited financial backing to make the dream come true. Many have lived comfortable and even somewhat notable lives on the crusts left from the once sumptuous table set for the citizens of the early town. Yet none have ever achieved the stature of the men who could be called the "founding fathers." No busts or public monuments commemorate them, but they left more lasting monuments in the orderly beauty of the entire community.

Many have been those who held forth promises which were mostly expedients being used in the hope of reaping a quick return. None of them ever planned well enough to build upon the solid foundation which would, like the stone walls, survive the vicissitudes of time.

The years have brought more promises than fulfillment to the town that water built. The dream of greatness has never been completely achieved.

Will there yet come a time when those who have a larger vision and qualities of leadership like the men who laid such splendid foundations discover the potential and fulfill the original promises in a more lasting manner?

Eureka Springs

She sits, complacent, on the porch of Time
Surrounded by her petticoats of hills,
Like an old belle, in her green finery,
Dreaming of her past triumphs,
Of her many suitors
Who promised many things.
For some were giants of their time
And for a time fulfilled their promises.
Her youthful beauty was too fresh,
Too innocent, to hold them
And they went their way;
And with them went their promises.
Others soon took their place.
They, too, tired of her simple charms
And went to more sophisticated arms.
This happened many times
Until at last
She took refuge in arrogance.
She had known a fame, not easily forgotten,
Been courted by the great.
Now suitors ceased to come;
At last she sat alone
Waiting on the porch of Time,
Too lost in dreams of grandeur past
To think of any change
Til now . . . .
A shadow falls across her petticoats of hills,
Across the porch of Time itself;
It seems a portent of new things to come, new promises.
Has she been too long complacent
Or will she wake and listen once again . . .
To promises?

A FAME NOT EASILY FORGOTTEN

Source Material

PROLOGUE

Nevins, Allan, *"The Emergence of Modern America"* 1865-1878, published by Macmillan Co., 1927.

Cutter, Charles, *"Cutter's Guide to the Eureka Springs of Arkansas"* 1884, published in Eureka Springs.

Kalklosch, Prof. L. J., *"The Healing Fountain"* 1881, published in Eureka Springs.

The *Arkansas Gazette,* 1878, 1879, 1880, 1881, microfilm, Gazette office, Little Rock, Arkansas.

Copies of newspapers in Carnegie Public Library, Eureka Springs, Arkansas.

CHAPTER I

"In the Beginning"

Kalklosch, Prof. L. J., *"The Healing Fountain"* 1881, published in Eureka Springs.

Carroll County Historical Society Quarterly, Sept. 1961, report of an interview with Annie House.

Carroll County Historical Society Quarterly, Oct., 1956.

Ibid., June 1964.

Ibid., March 1965.

The *Arkansas Gazette,* microfilm, Gazette office, Little Rock, Arkansas.

Stereoscope views, Carnegie Public Library files.

CHAPTER II

"A Firm Abiding Place"

Kalklosch, Prof. L. J., *"The Healing Fountain"* 1881, published in Eureka Springs.

The *Arkansas Gazette,* Dec., 1879, microfilm, Gazette office, Little Rock, Arkansas.

St. Louis Republican, Sept. 15, 1879.

Goodspeed, *"History of Carroll County"* 1889, arranged by Klute Braswell, Braswell Printing Co., Berryville, Ark.

Call, Cora Pinkley, *"Pioneer Tales of Eureka Springs and Carroll County"* Eureka Springs, 1930.

The Echo for Nov., 1881, pub. in Eureka Springs.

Carroll County Historical Society Quarterly, Dec., 1960.

Ibid., Dec., 1966.

CHAPTER III

"The Dream Begins"

Clayton, Powell, *"The Aftermath of the Civil War in Arkansas"* pub. by Neale Publishing Co., New York, 1915.

Hempsted, Fay, *"A History of Arkansas 1541-1930"* pub. by Lewis Publishing Co., Chicago, 1931.

Thomas, David Y., *"Arkansas and Its People"* pub. by American Historical Society, New York, 1930.

Fair, James R., *"The North Arkansas Line"* pub. by Howell-North, Berkeley, California, 1969.

CHAPTER IV

"The Years of Grandeur"

Eureka Springs, Minutes of Meetings of the City Council 1885-1895 (yearly).

Eureka Springs, Minutes of Meetings of the Board of Public Affairs, 1887-1895.

Eureka Springs, Record of Official Ordinances, City of Eureka Springs 1882-1900.

Eureka Springs, Minutes of Meetings of the Board of Commissioners for Improvement Districts, 1887-1895.

Various maps, charts and architectual drawings in Archives, Eureka Springs Courthouse.

Arkansas Gazette, May 1886, microfilm Gazette Office, Little Rock, Arkansas.

Notebooks of City Engineers, Archives, Eureka Springs Courthouse.

Rosewater, B. J., Speech to Eureka Springs Board of Trade, 1900.

Rayburn, Otto Ernest, *"The Eureka Springs Story"* pub. in Eureka Springs, 1954.

Daily Times Echo, pub. in Eureka Springs, copies in Carnegie Public Library.

CHAPTER V

"The Dream Falters"

Russell, J. L., *"Behind These Ozark Hills"* pub. by Hobson Book Press, New York, 1947.

Call, Cora Pinkley, *"Pioneer Tales of Eureka Springs and Carroll County"* pub. in Eureka Springs, 1930.

Daily Times Echo, July 30, 1891, Eureka Springs.

Clayton, Powell, Letters to B. J. Rosewater. Courtesy of Jeannette Rosewater Bullock.

CHAPTER VI

"People - Hopeful and Confident"

Goodspeed, *"History of Carroll County"* 1889 arranged by Klute Braswell pub. Braswell Printing Co., Berryville, Arkansas.

Lee Tucker Carroll, unpublished speech made in 1941 on the occasion of a birthday party for Annie House, in Carnegie Public Library.

Daily Times Echo, Eureka Springs, July 6, 1890, in Carnegie Public Library.

Ibid., 1904, advertisement.

CHAPTER VII

"Education for Everyone"

Ferguson and Atkinson, *"History of Arkansas"* 1966, pub. by Arkansas Historical Commission, Little Rock.

Mills, Nellie, *"Other Days in Eureka Springs"* 1950, pub. by Freewill Baptist Gem, Monett, Missouri.

Crescent College Yearbooks, 1908-1918.

Times Echo, May 20, 1890. Eureka Springs Newspaper.

Ibid., Dec., 1890.

Ibid., Jan. 5, 1891.

Ibid., Oct. 3, 1897.

Flashlight, August 7, 1897, Eureka Springs Newspaper.

Arkansas Gazette, Nov. 12, 1888, microfilm, Gazette office, Little Rock, Arkansas.

Carroll County Historical Society Quarterly, Sept. 1961, June 1962 and Dec., 1965.

"Interstate Summer Normal Educational Assembly" program for July-August, 1891.

Miller, Giles E., *"The Beautiful Ozarks"* issue for Feb., 1907.

CHAPTER VIII

"Society - Fashionable and Benevolent"

Stereoscope views in Carnegie Public Library.

Cutter, Charles, *"Cutter's Guide to the Eureka Springs of Arkansas"* 1884, pub., in Eureka Springs.

Carroll County Historical Society Quarterly, Dec., 1960.

A magazine, *"Points"* issue for April and May 1901.

Russell, J. L., *"Behind These Ozark Hills,* pub. by Hobson Book Press, New York, 1947.

St. Louis Globe Democrat, May 21, 1886.

Tourist Club, Record of Secretary, 1919.

Modern Priscillas, Recording Secretary's book, Jan. 1908-19.

Annie House, her scrapbook (clippings not dated).

Mills, Nellie, *"Early Days at Eureka Springs 1880-1892"* pub. by Freewill Baptist Gem, Monett, Missouri.

Crescent College, Prospectus, 1908.

Winston, Alvin, *"Doctors, Dynamiters and Gunmen"* (about Norman Baker) pub. by TNT Press, Muscatine, Iowa, 1936.

Times Echo, 25th Anniversary Edition, pub. at Eureka Springs, April 24, 1905.

Eureka Springs Newspaper, *"The Register"* 1881.

Correspondence relative to Carnegie Public Library between B. J. Rosewater and secretary to Andrew Carnegie (courtesy Jeannette Rosewater Bullock).

Newspapers in Carnegie Public Library.

CHAPTER IX

"Sin . . . and Salvation"

Kalklosch, Prof. L. J., *"The Healing Fountain"* pub. in Eureka Springs, 1881.

Goodspeed, *"History of Carroll County"* arranged by Klute Braswell.

Carroll County Courier, letter from D. Elmer Jones, 1930.

Times Echo, Dec., 1891.

Young Women's Christian Temperance Union, Secretary's notebook, 1886-

Nevins, Allan, *"The Emergence of Modern America"* 1865-1878.

Nation, Carry A., *"My Life and Work"* 1909.

Carroll County Historical Association Quarterly, June 1964.

Marie Dobbins, letter on origins of Catholic Church in Eureka Springs, May, 1969.

CHAPTER X

"Slow Fades the Dream"

Sam A. Leath, unpublished manuscript in Carnegie Public Library.

Powell Clayton, private correspondence with B. J. Rosewater. (courtesy of Jeannette Rosewater Bullock).

Western District of Carroll County, Arkansas, Records of Chancery Court, 1907 and 1908.

Carnegie Foundation, correspondence with B. J. Rosewater, president of the Carnegie Public Library Board. (courtesy of Jeannette Rosewater Bullock).

Eureka Springs, Minutes of meetings, City Council 1910-1916.

Eureka Springs, Minutes of meetings, City Commission, 1916-1920.

Call, Cora Pinkley, *"Pioneer Tales of Eureka Springs and Carroll County"* pub. in Eureka Springs, 1930.

Alexander, Henry M., *"Government in Arkansas, Organization and Function at State, County and Municipal Levels"* pub. by University of Arkansas, Fayetteville, Ark., 1957.

CHAPTER XI

"Newspapers"

Carnegie Public Library files of old papers.

Allsopp, Fred W., *"History of the Arkansas Press for a Hundred Years or More"* published by Parke-Harper Publishing Company, Little Rock, Arkansas, 1922.

EPILOGUE

Carroll County Courier, January 5, 1933.

Times Echo, September 1, 1949.

ABOUT THE AUTHORS

June Westphal was born three miles from Eureka Springs, and Catharine Osterhage was born three hundred and sixty four miles away, in Clinton, Illinois. But the two women met in the City That Water Built in 1966, and spent the next four years poring over old newspapers, hand-written accounts, historical documents and unpublished manuscripts. They compiled pieces of a puzzle that became an original and authentic account of early Eureka Springs.

June has spent her life as a crackerjack researcher, writing numerous articles for the Carroll County Historical Society; radio vignettes; *The Eureka Chronicles: Ten Decades of History, 1880s to 1980s*; *Centennial Postcard History* (co-authored with Bob Rennels, 1979); and *For All the Saints: A History of Methodism in Eureka Springs, Arkansas*. For more than thirty years, she has put together the Annual Historical Pictorial Calendars distributed by Cornerstone Bank (formerly the Bank of Eureka Springs).

She raised her family in Eureka Springs and is still discovering previously unpublished nuggets of life in her peculiar hometown.

Catharine Osterhage was a draftsman for the Crane Company in Chicago from 1918 to 1963, when she retired to Eureka Springs. She became librarian at the Carnegie Public Library and collaborator on the first definitive history of the town. Catharine died in 1970, shortly before the First Edition of *A Fame Not Easily Forgotten* was off the press.